Reviewers love Alan Bradley's New York Times
bestselling Flavia de Luce series!

WHAT TIME
the SEXTON'S SPADE doth RUST

"I *love* the Flavia de Luce novels! I identify, though I unfortunately didn't have an Uncle Tarquin and was forced to make do with a Christmas chemistry set from the Sears catalog. Flavia is the best female detective I've ever read, full of realism, self-confidence, and emotion (in roughly equal parts), and her tales are hilarious, engaging, and occasionally heartbreaking."
—DIANA GABALDON, #1 *New York Times* bestselling
author of the Outlander series

"To say I am overjoyed by the return of the magnificent Flavia is a massive understatement. It is a great day when we have her back in our lives with a new, and riveting, crime to solve. Brava, Flavia. Bravo, Alan!"
—LOUISE PENNY, #1 *New York Times* bestselling
author of the Inspector Gamache series

"Cozy mystery fans will love this latest delightful installment featuring Flavia de Luce, Alan Bradley's plucky and spirited protagonist."
—NITA PROSE, #1 *New York Times*
bestselling author of *The Maid*

The GOLDEN TRESSES *of the* DEAD

The GRAVE'S
a FINE *and* PRIVATE PLACE

New York Times bestseller
Publishers Weekly bestseller
Indie bestseller

"Outstanding . . . As usual, Bradley makes his improbable series conceit work and relieves the plot's inherent darkness with clever humor."
—*Publishers Weekly* (starred review)

"As those of us with Flavia-mania know from previous books, the plucky adolescent is terrifically entertaining—the world's foremost brainiac/chemist/sleuth/busybody/smarty-pants. Nobody can touch her in that category."
—*The Seattle Times*

"[Bradley] lets Flavia be her hilarious, inimical best, and perfectly captures village life in 1950s Britain. Historical fiction and mystery readers alike are sure to rejoice at getting to spend another afternoon in Flavia's agreeable world."
—*Shelf Awareness*

THRICE *the* BRINDED CAT HATH MEW'D

"Bradley's heroine is one of the most delightful, and one of the sharpest, sleuths to come along in a long, long time."

—*Alfred Hitchcock Mystery Magazine*

"The preteen version of Miss Marple . . . In addition to the meticulous investigations, what makes these novels, including this eighth in the series, so enjoyable is the personality of the primary character who, while being a murder investigator savant, is also an emotionally vulnerable little girl. It is a very unusual combination . . . and it works."

—*Mystery Scene*

As **CHIMNEY SWEEPERS COME** *to* **DUST**

"Eleven-year-old Flavia de Luce, perhaps contemporary crime fiction's most original character—to say she is Pippi Longstocking with a Ph.D. in chemistry (speciality: poisons) barely begins to describe her—is finally coming home."

—*Maclean's*

"Even after all these years, Flavia de Luce is still the world's greatest adolescent British chemist/busybody/sleuth."

—*The Seattle Times*

The DEAD in THEIR VAULTED ARCHES

#1 *Library Journal* pick
New York Times bestseller
Indie bestseller

"Bradley's latest Flavia de Luce novel reaches a new level of perfection. . . . These are astounding, magical books not to be missed."

—*RT Book Reviews* (Top Pick)

"Young chemist and aspiring detective Flavia de Luce [uses] her knowledge of poisons, and her indefatigable spirit, to solve a dastardly crime in the English countryside while learning new clues about her mother's disappearance."

—National Public Radio

SPEAKING *from* AMONG *the* BONES

"The precocious and irrepressible Flavia continues to delight. Portraying an eleven-year-old as a plausible sleuth and expert in poisons is no mean feat, but Bradley makes it look easy."

—*Publishers Weekly* (starred review)

"Bradley's Flavia cozies, set in the English countryside, have been a hit from the start, and this fifth in the series continues to charm and entertain."

—*Booklist*

I AM HALF-SICK *of* SHADOWS

"Every Flavia de Luce novel is a reason to celebrate, but Christmas with Flavia is a holiday wish come true for her fans."

—*USA Today* (four stars)

"A delightful read through and through."
—*Library Journal* (starred review)

A RED HERRING *without* MUSTARD

"Think preteen Nancy Drew, only savvier and a lot richer, and you have Flavia de Luce."
—*Entertainment Weekly*

"Delightful . . . The book's forthright and eerily mature narrator is a treasure."
—*The Seattle Times*

"Bradley's characters, wonderful dialogue and plot twists are a most winning combination."
—*USA Today*

The WEED *that* STRINGS *the* HANGMAN'S BAG

"Flavia is incisive, cutting and hilarious . . . one of the most remarkable creations in recent literature."
—*USA Today*

"The real delight here is her droll voice and the eccentric cast. . . . Utterly beguiling."
—*People* (four stars)

The SWEETNESS *at the* BOTTOM *of the* PIE

THE MOST AWARD-WINNING BOOK OF ANY YEAR!

WINNER:
Macavity Award for Best First Mystery Novel
Barry Award for Best First Novel
Agatha Award for Best First Novel
Dilys Award
Arthur Ellis Award for Best Novel
Spotted Owl Award for Best Novel
CWA Debut Dagger Award

"Impressive as a sleuth and enchanting as a mad scientist . . . Flavia is most endearing as a little girl who has learned how to amuse herself in a big lonely house."
—Marilyn Stasio, *The New York Times Book Review*

"Sophisticated, series-launching . . . It's a rare pleasure to follow Flavia as she investigates her limited but boundless-feeling world."
—*Entertainment Weekly* (A-)

"A delightful new sleuth. A combination of Eloise and Sherlock Holmes . . . fearless, cheeky, wildly precocious."
—*The Boston Globe*

By Alan Bradley

Flavia de Luce Novels

The Sweetness at the Bottom of the Pie

The Weed That Strings the Hangman's Bag

A Red Herring Without Mustard

I Am Half-Sick of Shadows

Speaking from Among the Bones

The Dead in Their Vaulted Arches

As Chimney Sweepers Come to Dust

Thrice the Brinded Cat Hath Mew'd

The Grave's a Fine and Private Place

The Golden Tresses of the Dead

What Time the Sexton's Spade Doth Rust

Flavia de Luce Stories

The Curious Case of the Copper Corpse

WHAT TIME
the SEXTON'S
SPADE *doth* RUST

BANTAM BOOKS

NEW YORK

WHAT TIME *the*

SEXTON'S

SPADE *doth* RUST

A Flavia de Luce Novel

ALAN BRADLEY

◆ ◆ ◆

Published in the United States by Bantam Books,
an imprint of Random House, a division
of Penguin Random House LLC, New York.

BANTAM & B colophon is a registered trademark
of Penguin Random House LLC.

Library of Congress Cataloging-in-Publication Data
Names: Bradley, Alan, author.
Title: What time the Sexton's spade doth rust / Alan Bradley.
Description: New York : Bantam Dell, 2024. |
Series: A Flavia de Luce novel
Identifiers: LCCN 2024006568 (print) | LCCN 2024006569
(ebook) | ISBN 9780593724514 (Hardback) |
ISBN 9780593724521 (Ebook)
Subjects: LCSH: De Luce, Flavia (Fictitious character)—
Fiction. | Murder—Investigation—Fiction. |
LCGFT: Cozy mysteries. | Novels.
Classification: LCC PR9199.4.B7324 W47 2024 (print) |
LCC PR9199.4.B7324 (ebook) | DDC 813/.6—dc23/eng/20240222
LC record available at https://lccn.loc.gov/2024006568
LC ebook record available at https://lccn.loc.gov/2024006569

Printed in the United States of America on acid-free paper

randomhousebooks.com

2 4 6 8 9 7 5 3 1

First Edition

For Shirley

What time the sexton's spade doth rust,
And he must drink his ale on trust.

—"At the End" by Andrew Dodds

WHAT TIME
the SEXTON'S
SPADE *doth* RUST

· O N E ·

THE GREATEST MINDS IN the world are often cranky when they first awaken in the morning, and mine is no exception. If I am to ascend above the ordinary, I require solitude the way a balloon needs helium.

Which is why, barely a quarter of an hour after a hasty and solitary breakfast at Buckshaw, I am hunched under a black umbrella in the ancient churchyard of St. Tancred's: the only place I can be certain of being left alone and in peace.

There is a particular kind of graveyard soil that bubbles when it rains. I have my own theory about the cause of this phenomenon but have come here for further study before committing my thoughts to paper.

In my experience, nothing is more deeply refreshing than to huddle under a bumbershoot in the rain and the raw fog of a country graveyard. Bare inches above your head, the downpour drums a military tattoo on the taut black silk as your nose greedily drinks in the invigorating pong of tombstones, wet grass, and ancient moss: a smell that opens doors in your mind you didn't even know you had.

Churchyard moss is soft to sit on—but wet. Mrs. Mullet says I'll get rheumatism and need to have my bones replaced.

It may sound cold and clammy, but there is a special warmth in knowing that you are utterly alone—except for the dead.

With the dead, there are no sudden rages; no fits of hissing savagery; no flung plates or cutlery; no petulant sulks or towering rages. Just beneath your feet the deceased are being devoured by fat black beetles, in a vast and grand banquet, while merry mushrooms digest the welcome leftovers of coffin wood. It is a world of harmony and dark contentment, a world of quiet grace and beauty. It is a happy dance of death.

I thought about the year I had sent up an armful of skyrockets from a remote corner of this same churchyard on All Souls' Night, each labeled by hand with the name of one of the nearby but almost forgotten dead:

Blam!

That was Nettie Savage (1792–1810).

Kaboosh!

Samuel Pole (1715–1722).

Blassh! Arden Glassfield (1892–1914).

Boom! Poom! Poom! A triple salvo for Annie Starling, Spinster of this Parish (1744–1775).

Unfortunately, one of Annie's fuses had come down in the gutters of the church, igniting a stupid cluster of accumulated moss and debris and thus setting on fire the House of God. The Bishop's Lacey Fire Brigade had to be called to extinguish the small but fierce blaze. Father had expressed his displeasure by requiring me to make a monthly donation to the Fireman's Fund, which, since it was ultimately his money, was no hardship at all. The tough thing was that I had to deliver each donation in person, which at first was excruciating and made me feel like a worm, but in the end I got to know a lot of firemen and learn the chemistry of quenching blazes.

Oh, those days of glory! And oh, to have them back again!

These days, my only friends are fungi.

Sometimes, when I can't sleep, I pretend that I myself am a fungus, creeping silently and unobserved along some slimy moonlit surface, greedily feeding on unsuspecting bits of bark, smacking my fungus lips as only a fungus can smack them.

Smack! A nice bit of pine needle. *Smack!* A taste of bitter willow. *Smack!* An unexpected splinter of coffin lid, with its faint bouquet of formaldehyde. Encouraged, I move on, hoping for something more meaty.

And so on and so forth . . . until I fall into a gray and groggy sleep.

Which brings us back to St. Tancred's churchyard in the rain.

I needed time alone.

"Flavia!"

Oh, jellied curses! It was Undine, my pestilent little cousin: the Bane of Buckshaw. How had she found me? I had tucked my trusty bicycle, Gladys, away in the church porch, both to keep her dry (Gladys loves running in the rain, but hates standing in it) and to keep her from unwelcome eyes.

I squatted even more deeply, scrunching my body slowly, as much as I was able, as if doing so would make me smaller, or maybe even invisible. Perhaps the pest would mistake my wet umbrella for part of a black marble tomb.

"Flavia!"

I held my breath and gritted my teeth. In her mackintosh and waterproof hat, she looked like an apprentice ghoul.

But she had spotted me.

"What is it, oh precious one?" I finally managed, brushing a raindrop from my eyelid.

She was looking at me, mouth agape, as if I had just climbed down from the sky on a golden rope.

"Why do you insist on following me everywhere?" I asked.

" 'Cause I'm your crocodile," she hissed, snapping her jaws and making a ghastly clicking noise with her throat. "Tick-tock. Tick-tock."

"Kiss my crumpet," I said.

"You're nuts," she said. "Do you know that? You're nuts."

My gorge, as they say, was rising. I bit my tongue.

"I want us—you and I—to take an oath, right here and now," I told her, "on the sacred tomb of Saint Tancred, so to speak, to be kinder and more gentle with each other. We're both orphans, remember, and orphans ought to stick together. Do you know what I mean?"

"Yowza!" she said enthusiastically.

"Don't say 'yowza,'" I said. "It makes you sound like a ventriloquist's dummy. You're spending too much time with Carl Pendracka."

Carl was one of my sister Ophelia's former suitors: an American serviceman from St. Louis, Missouri, by way of Cincinnati, Ohio. Carl's childhood had been, in his own words "seasonally migratory." Although Carl's ardor had been dampened somewhat by Feely's marrying one of his rivals, he nevertheless had taken to hanging round Buckshaw again after the wedding, perhaps, as my other sister, Daffy, suggested: "in search of smaller game."

"Carl is a swell guy," Undine said. "He's teaching me to fart 'Hail to the Chief.'"

"Undine! Don't be coarse."

"I wanted him to teach me 'Rule Britannia' but Carl said that's a concert piece, and too risky for a beginner. You have to work up to it, like the Triple Splutterblast. So far, I've only mastered the Baby Duck. Carl says I need to learn to release the contralto and avoid squizzlers. So, I come here to practice sometimes. In case of an accident, you know. Say, Flavia, here's a riddle for you: What's white, has a handle, and flies?"

"I don't know, and I don't want to know," I said.

"A chamber pot!" she shouted, doubling over with laughter and slapping her knee.

"You're disgusting," I said, trying not to smile. I didn't want to encourage her.

"I'm not disgusting. I'm enterprising. Do you know that a Frenchman named Joseph Pujol became filthy rich breaking wind onstage in front of enormous audiences? And not just musical selections—he could also do animal impressions!"

"I don't want to hear it."

"Carl says I should begin by increasing my cabbage intake—plus plenty of beans. Carl says that will have even the angels begging for mercy."

"I'm not interested."

"You're a prude."

"I'm not a prude. I'm a decent human being."

Undine squinted one eye and sized me up as if I were for sale in an oriental market.

"You're a Buckshaw de Luce. You're all the same. Hoity-toity. Nothing but starch and sauce. Lah-de-dah. Sniff my hem. Ibu used to poke fun at you lot, you know."

Ibu was the name she called her late mother, Lena, who had come to a horrible and spectacular end in a shower of stained-glass shards, some of them dating to the thirteenth century.

Undine peered at me peevishly through a pair of imaginary pince-nez and sang in a haughty and disapproving voice:

"*Hush, hush, whisper who dares*
"*Christopher Wren is designing our stairs.*"

"Hardly original" was the best I could manage.

"She heard it at a show in Oxford or somewhere," Undine said. "But she said it fit all you Buckshaw de Luces to a T."

"She was probably right," I said, snatching at sainthood, even if only for a few moments, but the effort was like grasping jelly, and I suddenly felt oddly soiled.

Was that the best I could do to mend a fractured family? What would Father have thought of me?

Father's sudden death had hit me hard. It all seemed so senseless. At first, I had tried to insulate myself and to pretend he was still alive and merely unavailable, as usual: still toying somewhere with his bloody stamp collection. But as the days and the weeks and then the months crept awkwardly on, I found myself more and more often awakening in the night, weeping. There was a secret shame in finding a tear-soaked pillow that I could not—or would not—explain, even to myself.

The vicar's wife had taken me aside for what she called "a nice little chat." She said she understood what it was to be lonely, and that I mustn't feel bad about it; that loneliness wasn't a sin.

It's always embarrassing when someone steps over that invisible line and into your private life. Even though they mean well, the line has been broken, and can never again be the impenetrable defense that it once was.

I thanked her for her concern but didn't tell her that I wasn't being eaten by loneliness. It was lack of love, and that's no sin either.

Besides, there was more to it than that.

I would be the first to admit that I'm not what you would call a conventional girl, but something else—something strangely disturbing—had begun to take shape in my life.

It was as if a glass wall, nearly transparent, were being imperceptibly formed between me and the real world: a dim haze that was isolating me. I needed to take action before it was too late: before I was trapped and couldn't get myself back to the other side.

Personal nourishment was what I required.

But I needed to begin with practicalities. Spades and chisels come first—cathedrals afterward.

Undine was bending over a nearby tombstone, picking her nose, pretending to read the inscription.

"What are you doing here, anyway?" I asked.

"Dogger asked me to come and fetch you home," she said. "At once."

"Any particular reason?"

"I only know what I can hear through doors," Undine replied. "But it's about Mrs. Mullet. I think she's killed someone."

· T W O ·

GLADYS'S TIRES SANG IN the rain as we tore along the tarmac. In front of me, Undine perched on the basket and handlebars like a broken stork, bellowing some pagan chant with a chorus of "ooga-bunga"s at the top of her lungs. I was too preoccupied to stop her.

Kill someone? Mrs. Mullet? It was scarcely believable. But who?

Dogger was obviously all right: He had sent Undine to fetch me. And the only other person in the house was Daffy. My sister Daffy . . .

I pedaled even harder.

Let her be . . . let her be . . .

We swept through the Mulford Gates and into the long avenue of chestnuts. Ahead I could already see Inspector Hewitt's blue Vauxhall parked ominously at the front door of Buckshaw. Someone was sitting in the driver's seat: a blank-faced young constable who stared out at us as we approached. He was no one I knew. Obviously stationed here on the lookout for criminals trying to flee the house.

I skidded to a sudden stop, sending Undine stumbling across the gravel sweep on unsteady, storkish legs.

"Careful," I called out. I didn't want to actually hurt her.

She shot me a look from beneath her rain hat, but I hadn't time to analyze it.

I twiddled my fingers at the police constable as we passed the car, but his large white face remained as unmoving in the window as an unbaked loaf.

Through the front door and across the foyer, I made straight for the kitchen. Mrs. Mullet, I knew, would not allow herself to be questioned anywhere but in her own domain.

She was seated at the kitchen table, her face a marble mask, but as soon as she saw me, the mask cracked, and she burst into tears.

"Oh, Miss Flavia," she sobbed. "You 'ave to tell 'im . . . I didn't kill nobody . . . I didn't . . . I *couldn't*!"

Inspector Hewitt was standing across the table from her, notebook in hand, motionless.

"Miss de Luce." The inspector nodded.

So that was how it was going to be, was it? Formal to the fingertips. I'd had encounters with him before, each one different, each one starting all over again, as if we had never before laid eyes on each other.

"Inspector," I said. "Can you explain what's going on here?"

Best to establish authority right at the outset, I thought. It was, after all, *my* house. Buckshaw had been left to me in my mother's will via a complicated kind of trust, which was explained to me again and again by a series of dusty gray men with oversized hands.

Inspector Hewitt seemed slightly taken aback. Perhaps he had read my expression.

The inspector and I had a checkered history: He never knew quite what to make of me, whereas I could read him like a telephone directory. I had assisted him with various cases in the past, but as with all those in authority over us (for whom Saint Peter had advised Timothy to pray, "For kings and for all that are in authority; that we may lead a quiet and peaceable life in all goodness and honesty"), it meant nothing. I had tried and it hadn't worked.

It was at this point that Dogger appeared in that sudden, quiet, uncanny way he has. One moment he wasn't there and the next he was, standing half in and half out of the kitchen door. He did not speak, and I knew at once that he wished to be ignored.

Dogger was our mainstay: our handyman, adviser, gardener, protector, and friend. He had been a prisoner of war with Father, and still bore the weeping scars in his mind. He could be at one moment a pillar of strength and the next a frail and trembling leaf. I shot him a quick smile.

"A party is dead," the inspector said at last. "Perhaps Mrs. Mullet can explain."

Very clever of him. I knew that regulations kept him from handing out information to the general public like sowing wheat, and at the same time, Mrs. Mullet might well let slip something she had withheld previously. *Well played, Inspector,* I thought.

"Inspector says it's that Major Greyleigh," Mrs. Mullet said, wiping her eyes with her apron. "'E's dead. You know I've been cookin' and cleanin' for 'im on and off at Moonflower Cottage since your dear dad—Colonel de Luce, I mean. I'm sorry, Miss Flavia. I didn't mean—"

I squeezed her shoulder.

"'E's dead," she said.

But which of them was she referring to?

Major Greyleigh, I knew, had retired to that small dwelling on the edge of Bishop's Lacey a couple of years ago. I hadn't met the man but had the impression that he kept pretty much to himself. A minor civil servant, he had described himself to the vicar. Why would anyone want to kill someone like that?

"I knew 'e fancied mushrooms for 'is breakfast now and then," Mrs. Mullet went on. "So I picked some myself on the way to 'is cottage. They grow behind the stile at Granger's Field. You know the place. An' I cooked 'em myself and served 'em to 'im on toast. And all of a sudden—*bang!*—'e's dead. They was poison, and it's all my fault, nobody else's."

Mushrooms! I could hardly believe my ears. I have to admit that I'd been praying for ages to God, the Virgin

Mary, and all the saints for a jolly good old-fashioned mushroom poisoning. Not that I wanted anyone to die, but why give a girl a gift of science—of chemistry, to be precise—such as mine without giving her the opportunity to use it?

Besides, Mrs. Mullet had been picking and cooking mushrooms for donkey's years and was as sharp about identifying the various varieties as any countrywoman. It was she, in fact, who had taught me the basics of the edible fungi, long before I branched off into studying the more rarefied of the toxic chemicals.

Mrs. Mullet had meanwhile begun quietly weeping. The inspector gave her a look of—what was it? Skepticism?

"Has anyone thought to send for Mrs. Mullet's husband?" I asked, not quite letting my eyes come to rest on Inspector Hewitt. I felt a strange taste at the back of my throat. My brain labeled it tentatively as a new kind of anger.

"We have," the inspector said. "He's not as yet been located."

"'E's went fishin'," Mrs. Mullet whispered. "I told 'im to take 'is waders, but 'e forgot 'em."

I put my hand on her shoulder.

"It's all right, Mrs. M," I said. "I'm sure there's been some mistake. We'll get it sorted out."

She raised her right hand to cover mine, and I knew my words had gotten through.

Inspector Hewitt shot me a wry, bittersweet smile. There was no law against comforting the accused, and he knew it as well as I did.

"I shan't say another word until Alf gets 'ere," Mrs. Mullet said, wiping her face with her apron.

She was handing me time on a plate, and I offered up a silent prayer of thanks.

Undine, meanwhile, was peering warily round Dogger, who still stood motionless in the kitchen doorway. Heaven only knew what she was thinking.

"Just a few more questions, Mrs. Mullet," Inspector Hewitt said, "and we'll take you home."

Mrs. Mullet crossed her arms and glared at the ceiling.

"Very well, then," Inspector Hewitt said, elaborately tucking his Biro away into the cunning little pocket of his notebook and snapping it shut. "Just one thing further. Was Major Greyleigh in good health before his breakfast yesterday? Did you notice anything unusual about him?"

"Well, 'e was quiet. 'E'd been over to Leathcote the night before, to the Officers' Club. 'E knew people there. 'E was like a celebrity to 'em. 'Is brothers-in-arms liked to 'ave a pint and a yarn with 'im, 'e said. They give 'im little gifts, like meat and butter. Coca-Cola, the odd cigar. Things that are rationed. It's ridiculous what them Yanks can get their 'ands on, and us still 'alf starvin' eight years after the end of the war."

"I see," said the inspector. "Was he as quiet before you served him the mushrooms as he was afterward?"

This seemed a little callous to me, but perhaps the inspector hadn't meant it that way.

"They'll take me and 'ang me by the neck," Mrs.

Mullet wailed after taking a deep, sobbing breath. "They'll put my 'ands in shackles behind my back, strap my ankles, put my 'ead in a canvas bag, then stand me on the drop. That's what they do to killers. I've seen it in the papers."

What had come over Mrs. Mullet? Had she gone into sudden shock? Why else would such a practical, imperturbable woman be in such a tizzy?

"But you're *not* a killer, Mrs. M," I said.

"I cooked 'em and served 'em to 'im myself, didn't I? You think they was poisoned, don't you? You think it's all my fault and nobody else's."

She was going round in circles. There was no point in this.

"Inspector," I asked, "may I take her to lie down for a while? Just until her husband gets here?"

"I suppose," he said, wrinkling his brow. "It's not regularly done, but I can see no harm in it."

I could tell from his voice that he was disappointed. He had been hoping for an outpouring of titbits from Mrs. Mullet but had come up with an empty bucket.

Dogger stepped forward and took one of Mrs. M's arms, and I took the other. We walked her slowly toward the foyer and up the stairs. At the top, I steered her toward the west wing.

"We'll put her in Feely's room," I said.

Ophelia was still somewhere in Europe on the Grand Tour, mooing at monuments to Mozart with her husband, Dieter. And I must admit that I missed her terribly: even her cruelty. Feely could make you laugh while cutting you in half. Living with her was sweet torture, and I couldn't help wondering how Dieter was getting along.

With Feely gone, her room had taken on a sad emptiness. I almost missed being physically flung out. It was a strange kind of reverse haunting.

As Mrs. Mullet hung between us like a sack of wet flour, Dogger and I eased her tenderly into the room and onto the bed. Dogger closed the door.

There was a moment of silence.

Mrs. Mullet snuffled loudly and opened one eye.

"Right then," she said, suddenly sitting bolt upright. "That man gets my goat and I don't mind sayin' so. I 'ate bein' pumped like an old 'urdy-gurdy. I knew we needed to procrustinate. I 'ope you don't mind my layin' on a bit of the old theatrics."

Dogger and I looked at each other.

"You were acting!" I said.

"And very professionally, if I may say so," Dogger said.

"Well, I took the part of Ophelia when I was a girl, didn't I?" Mrs. Mullet said proudly, "'Amlet, it was. The Drama League put it on. Twice. A Friday night and a Saturday afternoon."

She leaned back on the bed, resting all her weight on one stiff arm, the other wrist crooked sharply against her forehead. After a brief pause, she said: "O, woe is me, to have seen what I have seen, see what I see!"

The voice was not Mrs. Mullet's, but a voice so rich

and deep, so resonant, so full of pain and tragedy that a cold shiver shook me from head to toe. The words had seemed to issue from a golden trumpet lined with violet velvet. Was there a stranger living inside our cook?

I realized that my mouth had fallen open.

"Crikey!" I said.

"Wonderful, Mrs. Mullet," Dogger said. "The most admirable Ophelia, I dare say, that has graced a stage—or a bedchamber." He smiled.

"Oh, get away with you," Mrs. Mullet said, her neck flushing a pretty pink as she poked at her hair with a forefinger.

But there was no time to lose. The police, after all, were waiting.

"Tell us about Major Greyleigh as quickly as you can," I said. "We may have only a few minutes."

"Yesterday, it was," Mrs. Mullet said. "Like I told that inspector, the major sometimes fancied mushrooms for 'is breakfast. So I fetched some on the way to 'is cottage. Molly's buttons, we call 'em. You've eaten them yourself. Safe as 'ouses. Fried 'em in butter like it says in Eliza Acton's cookbook, just like I always do, with salt, mace, an' cayenne. Fancied 'em like that, 'e did. Just like 'is old mam used to make. Wouldn't 'ave 'em any other way. I set 'em in front of 'im an' watched 'im tuck in. Put on my 'at, come directly 'ere to Buckshaw. Made your breakfasts. 'Eard no more about it till this morning, when that Inspector 'Ewitt shows up at the door.

" ''Oo do you want?' I asks 'im.

"'You,' he says.

"'Me?' I says. You could 'ave knocked me down with a feather!"

"The inspector told you the major was dead?" I asked.

"Not at first," Mrs. Mullet said. "'E asked me when I'd last seen 'im, and what 'e looked like, and 'ow 'e behaved, and all that. Same as 'e did just now. Whether I'd noticed anything odd about 'im . . . whether I'd seen anyone else 'angin' about. And 'oo cooked the mushrooms, and all that. I told 'im what I just told you."

"Did he tell you who discovered the body?"

"No," she said after a moment's thought. "You know what the police are like. Close as clams in a kettle."

"Indeed I do," Dogger said.

"Did you tell the inspector you saw anyone else at the cottage?" I asked. I had just thought of something: Had anyone else been in the house?

Was it my imagination or had Mrs. M's eyes begun to glaze over? I could see her fishing for an answer.

"I went through the churchyard," she said. "An' you know as well as I do what you see in churchyards.

"When I came back with 'em I thought I 'eard a motor drivin' away in Bramblin' Lane, but I was on the wrong side of the cottage to see it."

"Did you see *anything*?" I asked.

I could see her jaw setting like plaster of paris.

"I 'ad a dizzy spell," she said. "Must have been a egg I et."

This was going to take time, I realized. Mrs. Mullet was not to be rushed nor taken for granted.

"We ought to go back downstairs," I said. "Mustn't keep the inspector waiting. You stay here and rest, Mrs. Mullet."

"Oh, I'm all right," she said fiercely, struggling to her feet. "I've things to do."

"Best wait a while," Dogger said. "We wouldn't want the inspector to get the wrong idea. Would we?"

"S'pose not," Mrs. Mullet said, letting her shoes fall to the floor and stretching out full length with a sigh of luxury.

"O, woe is me, to have seen what I have seen, see what I see!" she said again, and the back of my neck curdled.

She crossed her arms and closed her eyes to signal the end of the conversation.

What was going on in the woman's mind? I wondered. Was she hiding something? Was she simply being dramatic? Had the pressure driven the poor creature to the edge of madness?

Or was it me?

I was beginning to learn that when you're bereaved, as I have been, you live in a shattered looking-glass world. Nothing is as it seems. I needed to focus: to pull myself back together into that single, intense, burning intelligence I once had been. And I needed to do it quickly.

I'd start with the inspector.

I put on my Miss Prim armor and started down the stairs.

He was sitting across the kitchen table from Undine, who was happily dealing a hand of Drive Jack Out of Town. Although Undine referred to the game as Beggar My Neighbor, at Buckshaw it was, and always had been, Drive Jack Out of Town.

"Now you'll have to answer *my* questions," she said to the inspector.

"What's Inspector Hewitt been asking you?" I asked pleasantly, barreling into the room somewhat faster than I meant to.

"Nothing," Undine said. "He hasn't beaten me yet."

"Nor will I, in all likelihood," Inspector Hewitt said, squaring the deck and handing it to Undine. "Why don't you go rouse Constable Bunce outside? He's rather a mournful soul. Beg him to show you his handcuffs. That always cheers him up."

"The dreaded manacles, eh?" Undine said. "I'll bet I can give 'em the slip. I have very slender wrists for my age, you know."

And she skipped off to haunt Constable Bunce.

"Now then," Inspector Hewitt said, as soon as she was gone, "I want to make one thing perfectly clear."

I knew what it was before he spoke. And I was right.

"I want no interference from you," he said. "None whatsoever. Is that clear?"

"Yes, sir," I said, leaning forward and sticking out my right hand for him to shake, my left hand behind my back so that he wouldn't see the fingers crossed. "Perfectly."

"Very well," he said. "Now, what do you know about all this?"

"Nothing," I said. "You were already here when I heard about it."

"Well, then, keep it like that," he said, tucking away his everlasting notebook and getting to his official feet.

Ha! The dreaded parting shot. How well I knew it, as does anyone with older sisters. My immediate instinct was to throw him a half dozen salaams, sprinkle invisible rose petals at his feet, then fall to my knees and smother his black door-kicking boots in kisses. But I restrained myself.

"Yes, sir," I said, giving him the old pleasant but serious smile: the one I catalogued S22—for saucy.

He gave me a long look, a microscopic nod of the head, and walked out.

After he'd gone, I got down off my high horse and made myself a jam sandwich.

I was licking between my fingers when my sister Daffy strolled into the room.

"Missed all the excitement, did you?" she asked.

I shrugged.

"Death of a minor civil servant. Sounds like a Ngaio Marsh novel, doesn't it? Or an Agatha Christie. Something green and slim from Smith's to read on the train."

"How did you know that? The minor civil servant?"

Those had been the very words with which the major had described himself to the vicar.

"Stovepipe," Daffy said, pointing upward.

When we were younger, my sisters and I often used to lie on our bellies on the floors upstairs, listening in for hours on a sort of hot-air telegraph that brought news bulletins and tittle-tattle from a remarkable number of rooms in the house. By knowing which dampers to open and which to close, we could even bring in remarkably distant conversations from the guest bedrooms and so forth.

"Which tells us that the inspector must already have informed the vicar," I said, fully aware that this was the first step in a new investigation. Without seeing the body, or viewing the scene of the crime, I would have to work backward, as in a looking glass. The Labors of Hercules on a trick bicycle.

Still, if nothing else, I was going to clear Mrs. Mullet's name. Anything beyond that would be pure gravy.

I needed to consult Dogger, of course. The two of us had formed a special partnership: Arthur W. Dogger & Associates, Discreet Investigations. It has a nice ring, doesn't it? We might have chosen the name Snoops in Kid Gloves, but that would have defeated our purpose. Those people who required our services could read between the lines.

But first I would finish up with Daffy. Mrs. Mullet was still upstairs in another world of one kind or another. Dogger would keep an eye on her.

"So, what do you know about him? Major Greyleigh, I mean."

Daffy shrugged. "No more than you do, I suppose. I've seen him at church. Bulging underwater eyes. Old-fashioned suit, too tight. Sits at the back crunching cough drops during the sermon. Except for the NHS spectacles, he puts me in mind of Mr. Pickwick. Generally beloved by the children of the parish and their doting parents."

"Why?"

Daffy shrugged once more. "Well, he fixed their toys and so forth. He mended Nettie Tuck's skipping rope when she left it in the field and got it mangled under a plow. Braided it up a treat, the vicar said. As good as new. Must have been a sailor. And he carried little Georgie Monday on his back for the sack race at the fête."

Sounds too good to be true, I thought. But maybe I was just becoming cynical.

"Who would want to kill a man like that?" I asked.

"It's really quite extraordinary, isn't it?" Daffy said.

Daffy was always saying things like "It's really quite extraordinary," when I would have said, "Well, I'll be bumfuddled!"

It's a matter of taste, I suppose.

"But to answer your question," Daffy said, "no one would want to kill him—no one in Bishop's Lacey, at least. You know the rigamarole, Holmes. Look to the portents of the past!"

And with that, she rubbed her hands together in a ghastly gesture, picked up the last morsel of my jam sandwich, stuck it into her mouth, and strolled out of the room.

As if on cue, the door to the garden opened and Alf Mullet stepped in, wiping his feet on the doorstep.

"Where's my missus?" he asked. "I've got some fish for her." He stood with his shoulders back and his spine as straight and stiff as a ramrod. Alf, the eternal soldier.

"She's upstairs napping," I said. "I'm afraid there's been a bit of a to-do. Inspector Hewitt thinks she's murdered someone. Haven't you seen him?"

"I came through the garden," Alf said. "As I always do. Who's she gone and murdered now, then?"

"No, I mean it. Major Greyleigh has been poisoned with mushrooms. Mrs. Mullet picked them and served them to him. The inspector's at the front door with his car. You can go out that way if you like."

Alf spat out a word I mustn't repeat on fear of eternal damnation, then wheeled and marched out the kitchen door. He wouldn't dream of taking a shortcut through the house. He would make his way properly round to the front, as a man who knew his place.

But when he arrived, I wouldn't want to be in the inspector's shoes. Not for all the tea in China.

I had learned to flit at a very young age, and I flitted now: from the kitchen into the short, dark passageway that led to the foyer, and across the foyer to the front door, to which I applied my ear. The ancient wood acted as a massive sounding board, and I could hear as clearly as if I were seated cozily inside the inspector's mouth.

"You are Mr. Mullet, I take it?" the inspector was saying.

Drat! I had missed the opening shot.

"Take what you like. It's a free country," Alf said.

"I believe we've met before?" Inspector Hewitt said.

"Most likely here at Buckshaw," Alf said. "A couple of years ago, when they were making that film. Everybody and his dog was here."

Oof! Careful, Alf, I thought. *Don't want to end up in handcuffs yourself!*

"Now then, what's all this rubbish about my wife murdering someone?"

"No one has said any such thing," the inspector said. "I simply need to ask her a few questions. She's very upset, and I would appreciate your assistance."

"You can ask me the questions," Alf said, "and save her the trouble."

"I'm afraid that's not possible," the inspector said.

"Why not?" Alf demanded.

"We believe she may have information about a certain matter. That's all I can tell you at the moment."

Alf's voice rumbled a reply that I couldn't quite make out, and then I heard footsteps coming closer on the gravel.

I mustn't get caught eavesdropping. I turned and crossed the foyer in just a few long strides.

The doorbell rang. The inspector was on his best behavior.

There is a point at which a stranger, having been once admitted to a house, may go outside and come back in without ringing, but it is very brief.

I made a quick about-face, counted to fifteen, and opened the door. The inspector was on the doorstep and Alf was on his way round to the kitchen door.

"Ah!" I said. "Ah" is often enough.

"If you'd be so good as to bring Mrs. Mullet down," the inspector said. "I'm sure we can make short work of this."

I opened the door wide and stepped back.

"Ah! Mrs. Mullet," the inspector said, looking over my shoulder.

I turned and saw Mrs. Mullet, supported by Dogger, at the top of the stairs. Her face was ashen as they began their slow descent. Had she powdered it?

I shook my head to snap my eyes into proper focus.

Down the grand staircase they came. They might as well have been the king and queen of the fairies for all the reality of it. One moment Mrs. Mullet was basking in the warm footlights of memory, the next she looked like Death's breakfast warmed over.

She was hiding something. Of course! Why hadn't I realized it before?

Oh, Mrs. M, I thought. *What have you got yourself into?*

As they approached the bottom, Inspector Hewitt reached out and took Mrs. Mullet's hand.

Isn't that kind? I thought. And then it dawned on me: *No. Wait. He's checking her pulse.*

I know how suspicious minds work because that's how *my* mind works. It is not always easy being blessed with a superior brain.

"Come and I'll put the kettle on," I said, making a magnificent but humble sweep of my hand toward the kitchen.

As one of my late father's dearest friends, the vicar, when speaking privately, could be refreshingly direct. "Tea and faith," he had once said, "conquer all things."

I hadn't missed the fact that he put the tea in first place.

So right now, I needed to open my eyes and ears and shut my mouth. Be Polly-put-the-kettle-on de Luce. I needed to keep my feelings to myself.

"Inspector Hewitt, you and Mrs. Mullet sit at the table. I'll put the tea on, and Dogger will turn out the cups and saucers."

Dogger raised his hand as if to touch his forelock, but diverted it to brush away an imaginary hair on his sleeve. I gave him one of the invisible grins we shared, and he gave it back. A mere glance that spoke volumes.

I busied myself with the tea leaves: a perfect excuse to loiter and listen.

"Now then, Mrs. Mullet," Inspector Hewitt said, opening his notebook. "Shall we resume where we left off?"

"I've told you all there is to tell," Mrs. Mullet said.

"Well, tell it to me again," the inspector said.

Mrs. M pulled a handkerchief from somewhere in the bosom of her dress and touched it to one eye, although she didn't dab, I noticed.

She nodded.

"Going back to yesterday, you stated that you picked mushrooms on the way to Moonflower Cottage in the morning, that you cooked some for Major Greyleigh's breakfast, that you served them to him and then left, and that you have not since returned to his house."

"Yes," Mrs. Mullet said.

"Will you please explain, then, why you were observed, by two independent witnesses, leaving Moonflower Cottage several hours after serving him his breakfast?"

"They must've mistooken someone else for me," Mrs. Mullet said. "It 'appens all the time."

Alf, I noticed, was watching his wife as attentively as the inspector was—perhaps even more so. And she was watching him.

What on earth is happening here? I wondered as I poured their tea. If I were able to get Mrs. Mullet alone, I'd have the truth out of her in a greased minute, but Inspector Hewitt had somehow rubbed her the wrong way. What was it she had said? *That man gets my goat.*

When had he gotten her goat?—and where—and how—and why?

The getting of one's goat is often overlooked as a source of murder—not that Mrs. M was a killer, but in general terms. Even the mildest irritation, sheltered, guarded, and fed, can grow into an immense and sometimes sudden rage.

Dogger once remarked to me, apparently offhandedly, that rage is akin to compound interest, which seemed to me an odd comment from a man who had no use for money. Nevertheless, I remembered it, and it seemed to explain how, even if I didn't yet know why, Inspector Hewitt got Mrs. Mullet's goat.

My head was spinning. Why couldn't I get the upper hand in this supposed case of murder, as I had been so easily able to do in the past? Was I breathing some kind of invisible fog? Was I losing my touch?

Inspector Hewitt and Mrs. Mullet sat across the table from each other, motionless, like figures in some village waxworks.

"Stalemate." That was the word I was looking for.

Without warning, the kitchen door was flung open and Undine shot into the room with a clatter. *Just what I need*, I thought.

"Flavia! Flavia!" she shouted in that piercing drill-hall voice of hers, too loud for human ears. "Guess what? That Major Greyleigh?—the dead man?—he used to be the public hangman! Constable Bunce told me."

There was a crash as Inspector Hewitt's chair toppled backward onto the slate floor. In an instant he mastered the contorted muscles in his face and strode across the foyer, and the front door slammed like uncomfortably close thunder.

"That's done it," Alf said, almost under his breath. He shot me a glance.

"You haven't touched your tea, love," he said to his wife.

She raised her head and looked slowly and mournfully up at me as she spoke: "O, woe is me, to have seen what I have seen, see what I see!"

There are times when you could simply spit sawdust, and this was one of them. I had been beaten to the punch by a brat with a face like a failed pudding. What a fool I must have looked in front of Inspector Hewitt.

Much as I hate saying "Hisst!" and dragging someone out in the hall by the arm, that's precisely what I did with Undine.

"What the devil do you think you're playing at?" I whispered wetly into her ear. I could feel my own hot breath bouncing back at me off the side of her neck. I had an almost uncontrollable urge to bite her, like Dracula.

"Lay off, Flavia," she said, pulling away. "You're just jealous because I scooped you. Think of the headlines: *Young Cousin Gets the Dirt While Girl Sleuth Piddles with Teapot.*"

"I ought to tear your tongue out and give it to the cat," I said.

But she was right: I *was* jealous. I had become used to having the upper hand where murder was involved.

"How did you do it?" I asked. "Get the information from Constable Bunce, I mean."

"I pumped him," Undine said proudly. "Ibu used to tell me, 'A man in uniform is a man with a bull's-eye on his heart. You must learn to aim for it.' So, I started by admiring his police whistle. From there on, it was a piece of cake."

What else had her mother taught this child? I wondered—but only for an instant. I didn't really want to know.

"You know, sometimes you're almost human," I admitted, and she puffed out her breastbone like a harp in a concert hall.

"Get out of my sight," I said, but I said it with a smile, and Undine skipped off to do whatever it is that balls of slime do when they're dismissed.

I needed to get a grip on the situation: to come at it on my own terms, rather than having it handed to me like a plate of leftovers.

As I returned to the kitchen, Dogger caught my eye

and moved casually—almost invisibly—toward the pantry, and I followed.

He turned to me and whispered, "What do you think we ought to do, Miss Flavia?"

"I was about to ask you the same question," I said.

Dogger looked me straight in the eye. "I believe we ought to take on the case."

"That's what I hoped you'd say. And at no cost to Mrs. Mullet. We owe her that, at the very least," I said.

Dogger nodded. "I thought you might treat yourself to a casual stroll in the neighborhood of Moonflower Cottage. I believe the air there is especially invigorating."

Of course! The obvious place to start was Moonflower Cottage. I needed to get my eyes, ears, nose, fingers, and toes onto the property there, and I needed to do it before Bob Cratchit dotted another *i*.

Precisely seven minutes later, Gladys and I were barreling toward the village as if all the furies of Hell were snapping at our heels—and perhaps they were. The rain had let up and the sky was beginning to brighten.

·THREE·

JUST PAST THE CHURCHYARD, Major Greyleigh's cottage was the only property on the narrow lane. Moonflower Cottage looked nothing like its name. Rather than romantic, it was a somewhat sad affair, hunched and penitent, in the deep shade of some trees at the end of Brambling Lane: a rutted track that petered out at the northeast corner of St. Tancred's churchyard. The house itself had seen many rains and had accumulated an indefinable air of sogginess. *Perhaps the summer home of King Neptune,* I thought.

There were as yet no police warnings in place, and no signs of anyone alive standing guard. Well, I knew where Inspector Hewitt was, didn't I? He was at Buckshaw, giving Old Hob to Constable Bunce, and he hadn't given me explicit instructions not to leave. It was a gift from above, and I offered up to Old Mother Providence a silent prayer of "Cheerio!"

Since the front door was visible from the road, I strolled casually round the back of the house and tried the windows. But alas, they were all latched, as was the garden door.

My skills as a cat burglar were considerable, as anyone with an older sister will understand. With *two* older sisters, I was near legendary.

I shinnied up a convenient pear tree and let myself in at a surprisingly beautiful Georgian casement window, which stood out, even from the ground, like a Cinderella of windows amid a wall of ugly stepsisters, its panes, tinted green with age, glowing as if with pride in their own beauty.

For a moment, I paused in my tracks to listen. I could hear nothing but birdsong from outside. Most notable about the place was its smell of sadness: an inextinguishable whiff of distant and not-so-happy times.

It's strange, isn't it, how sadness is first detected by the nose? One would expect the eyes to lead the way, but it's invariably the nose that triggers the earliest alarm. Sadness is much like smoke, I've decided: an odor raised at the very doorstep of the brain.

I made a mental note to investigate this as soon as I had an opportunity, even to write a trifling monograph on the subject, perhaps. Goodness knows I'd had enough sadness in my life to provide material for a fat volume—or several fat volumes if I really wanted to wallow.

I wiped my nose on my sleeve and looked around the room.

How I wished Dogger were here. Our two sets of eyes combined—to say nothing of our noses—

I had not asked Dogger to come with me to Moonflower Cottage because in housebreaking, two's a crowd. And besides, I did not want to lead him into iniquity. Not that barging into a stranger's house was strictly an iniquity, but you know what I mean. And, after all, since he was older, Dogger would be expected to know right from wrong much more than I would ever be.

Despite the temptation to go rooting about in a dead man's goods and chattels, I needed to have a good squint at the scene of the crime before it—or I— was disturbed. First things first. Dogger would be proud of me.

So down to the kitchen I crept, down a dark and narrow staircase that had been designed to keep the household staff out of sight of their betters: a wood-paneled cloak of invisibility right out of *The Arabian Nights*.

The kitchen, by contrast, was as surprisingly bright as a painting by Vermeer. Despite the recent rain, tall many-paned windows let tentative shafts of new sunshine fall onto the dark slate of the floor, which was illuminated in a chessboard of light.

In the very center of the room was a small but sturdy square table with a single chair. This, obviously, was where Major Greyleigh had met his maker.

Mushroom poisoning is a messy business at best: not something that Elizabeth Barrett Browning, for instance, would ever choose to write a poem about. A mushroom going daintily in on a fork is a very different thing than a load of fungus coming out in a spectacular gush.

And yet there wasn't a trace of it.

You could never have guessed what had happened here. Someone had obviously taken a great deal of trouble to clean up the residue, and I wondered why.

How had the police allowed this to happen? Or had they mopped it up themselves? Had one of their members bungled? The unfortunate Constable Bunce, perhaps? I hadn't even met him yet, but my heart had gone out to him on wings of gossamer.

I dropped to my knees and crawled under the table, craning my neck to inspect the underside of the table-top. If there is one element of criminal poisoning that is frequently overlooked, it is the examination of back-splash on the underside of furniture. *Taylor's Medical Jurisprudence* doesn't mention it; nor, for that matter, does Agatha Christie.

It's always darker under a table than it is topside, and this one was no exception. I hadn't thought to bring a torch, but that's not an obstacle. A kitchen, after all, is a toolroom, whose drawers and cupboards are—or ought to be—full of implements.

I scrambled to my feet. The answer was in the third drawer: a set of electroplated silver spoons. I chose the brightest and polished it on my skirt, then back under the table I went. Aiming the bowl of the spoon at the nearest checkerboard of sunlight on the tile floor, I angled the reflected beam of my improvised spotlight until it produced a bobbling little ray of light on the underside of the tabletop.

I ran a fingertip along the rough bottom of the boards. They were faintly damp: not the dry-as-dust surface you'd expect to find in an old country kitchen. I held my finger to my nose. The smell of bleach was obvious. Someone had done a job of cleaning. And quite recently, too.

I wiggled my way out from under the table and overturned the chair.

Aha!

I had found the elusive particles: not, like Marley's ghost, a bit of undigested beef, but instead a fine spatter of undigested mushrooms. I scraped at them with my fingernail.

There were times when I was grateful that I'd given up biting my nails, and this was a perfect example. The residue was semisolid, and not yet hardened to be beyond analysis. As I picked at it, a tiny flash of light caught my eye: almost microscopic, but certainly not imaginary. It was like the flash of a distant lighthouse, caught by the watch of a ship at sea.

A quick return to the spoons drawer and back with a mate of the soup spoon already in my hand. This would be tricky: using the first spoon to focus the sunlight on the scrapings. I turned over the second spoon and used its backside as a convex mirror to reflect the image.

I felt like the Girl with the Ten Thumbs in the fairy tale, but by gosh and garters, it worked!

As I had suspected, the pinprick of light *was* a crystal: minute, but unmistakable. I could hardly wait to get it home and under the lens of my powerful Leitz microscope.

To be a good chemist, you must have keen eyesight and a strong stomach, and I have both. I ought to mention, if I haven't already, that although I have a pair of black-framed NHS reading glasses, I do not really need them. They were foisted upon Father by an unscrupulous optician in a dark little court just off Covent Garden, and I wore them only when I needed to gain sympathy and time was short.

I thought just for a moment of stealing one of these silver spoons and having it engraved: *Necessity is the mother of invention.* It would make a ripping souvenir of this most unusual case.

But how to get the late contents of the dead man's stomach back to Buckshaw? A soft carrier was required to prevent damage: something to protect it from the air and avoid further dehydration.

The inspiration came to me in an instant, as if delivered direct from Heaven by a flock of scientific angels.

I flipped up the back of the starched white Peter Pan collar that Mrs. Mullet had insisted on my wearing, wiped the remnants of Major Greyleigh's breakfast on the underside, and neatly folded it back down into position. No one was likely to find the lethal specimen there.

A sudden shadow blotted the light from the room. Someone had walked past the window! Rather than dropping to the floor or flattening myself against the wall, I froze in position, like a rabbit hunted by a hawk. *Any* movement—even the slightest—could draw attention to your presence.

Weren't the police taught not to walk in front of windows? I'd have thought it would have been drummed into their heads on the first morning of Police College.

I hardly dared move even my eyes.

"Caught you, you devil!" rasped a hoarse voice at my ear as my elbow was roughly seized. My spine almost fell out.

I spun round and found myself nose to nose with Undine.

"I followed you," she said cheerily, before I could tear her limb from limb.

"What are you doing here?" I hissed, afraid to raise my voice.

"Trespassing," she said. "Same as you. Let's get on with it."

Several thoughts crossed my mind—none of them nice.

"You go stand watch at the front door. Find a window. Don't let anyone see you. Call me if somebody comes."

"Yes, O Mighty One! Thank you, O Mighty One!" Undine said, dropping to her knees and clasping her hands.

I walked out of the room, leaving her to stew in her own stupidity.

I made my way through a drab passage to the front of the house. Taking my own advice, I peered out through the curtains of what I took to be the drawing room, from which there was a clear view of the gate.

There was no one in sight.

I turned slowly, taking in my surroundings.

Compared with the bright kitchen, this dark little drawing room was a dungeon. A sickly-colored paper covered the walls: the color of the young man's skin described with such precision by Gilbert and Sullivan:

A pallid and thin young man,
A haggard and lank young man,
A greenery-yallery, Grosvenor Gallery,
Foot-in-the-grave young man!

On the walls hung numerous framed paintings of horses and hounds, all of them frozen in a kind of glum and oily twilight. A small, dark, shabby desk lurked in the shadows.

The room was dominated by an outsized leather chesterfield of a yellowish-gray color, which reminded me of certain species of the more interesting mushrooms. It had come, no doubt, from one of the artistic gentlemen's clubs in Pall Mall and was meant more for a committee room than for a private home. I wondered how such an enormous piece of furniture had found its way to Bishop's Lacey. It was much more grand than anything at Buckshaw.

I reached out and touched the thing. It was softer and more pliable than ever you could have imagined—like the cheek of the teenage Virgin Mary. Leather like this could not be faked. It could only be produced over time through being polished by a billion bums, if you'll forgive the expression.

After a quick examination of the red Turkey carpet (you can learn much more about a room's inhabitants by examining both sides of the carpet and the floor beneath it than you can by examining, say, the ceiling), I turned my attention to the dark desk in the corner. Standard Army & Navy Stores issue: plain, durable, and cheap. No hidden compartments and no secret documents in a cache on the underside. Just a desk.

I opened the drawers. They were empty.

How odd, I thought. Drawers were made to hold things. An empty drawer meant either that nothing had yet been put in it, or that things had been taken out of it.

Perhaps the desk had just recently been acquired. Perhaps the major was tired of dealing with his correspondence at the kitchen table. If so, where did he keep his papers?

With a daily cook coming in (dear, innocent Mrs. Mullet), he probably kept them in his bedroom. I thought I'd better have a look up there before I did anything else.

But before I could take a step, there was a "Hssst!" behind me. I spun round.

Undine again.

"I searched the loo," she said. "It seemed too clean. *And* it *reeked* of Slippo."

Good old Slippo—the bleach found in all the best-regulated bathrooms.

"Hmmm," I said, but I could almost have hugged her.

"Look!" she whispered, pointing over my shoulder.

Not daring to make any sudden movement, I craned my neck slowly around and saw a car sliding to a silent halt at the gate. I muttered a curse that must have made my ears go slightly red.

Confound that man! He kept turning up like chewing gum on the sole of a Sunday shoe.

I remembered something the vicar had once told me: "Coincidence is bosh."

My life was becoming a chessboard. Perhaps the squares of sunlight on the kitchen floor had been a sign: Undine had followed me to the churchyard. Inspector Hewitt had made his move at Buckshaw. I retaliated by coming to Moonflower Cottage. Undine had followed me here. And now Inspector Hewitt again. I felt as if I had fallen through Alice's looking glass, and that it would only be moments before the Red Queen materialized in front of me saying, "Hullo, Flavia. Got any bread and butter on you?"

But it wasn't the Red Queen standing almost on my toes: It was Undine.

"Quick!" she said, tugging at my elbow. "We have to hide!"

But where? We were just feet from the front door, through which the inspector might come at any instant. Doors and windows were out of the question. There were only two pieces of furniture in the room, the desk and the chesterfield.

The desk was too small to hide us both.

"Follow me!" Undine said. She dived for the couch and vanished as effectively as if a conjuror had made a sweep of his cape and waved his wand.

"Where are you?" I asked, trying not to panic.

"Inside," she said, her voice muffled by leather and horsehair. "Climb into the crack at the back of the seat."

I stuck my hand into the joint behind the seat cushions. To my amazement, there was a surprising amount of space in the guts of the thing.

"That's my ankle." Undine giggled. "Come on, before we get caught."

I lay down and forced a leg into the interior of the couch.

"They had one of these at the Officers' Club at Mandalay," Undine whispered. "I used to hide inside it when I'd pinched their loose change."

"Shhh!" I said. "Someone's coming."

I rolled as far back as I could into the hidden space, forcing my way with my elbows and my backside. It was, as Daffy would have said, surprisingly commodious.

And it was dark.

As footsteps came closer and closer, I held my breath. I could feel Undine's foot on my shoulder and her toes seemed to tremble.

The footsteps came to a halt, by the sound of them, just inches away.

"Hello?" said a voice. It wasn't Inspector Hewitt's. It must have been one of his constables.

"Hello?" he said again. "Anyone here?"

Had he sensed our presence? Or had he seen movement through the window?

Scarcely breathing, we waited

Ages passed. Eons. Glacial ages glided by in magnificent review.

I was beginning to see spots in front of my eyes. Oxygen deprivation, I decided. I needed to relax and breathe deeply, like some Tibetan lama or Indian holy man.

Slowly, silently, and with perfect control, I was drawing in a measured breath when—*pfft*—close to my head—as if a fairy had dropped a little posey . . .

But then the stink struck me like a sudden sledgehammer.

This was no fairy. This was no delicate daisy.

It was Undine! That rotten, putrid villain, Undine.

She had let off a silent broadside: one that was going to kill all the cattle within a radius of a mile and cause the greenwoods beyond first to sicken and then to die.

I suppressed a shuddering choke, and cursed Carl Pendracka for teaching her his malodorous tricks.

"Who's there?" the Unknown Constable demanded.

"I know you're here somewhere," he said.

Full marks, Constable, I couldn't help thinking. *You're destined for bigger things.*

And then I got the giggles. They started in my throat, then spread to my chin and my chest, and from there to my stomach. I simply couldn't suppress them.

"All right, then. Out you come. Hop it."

A hand reached into the space, grazed my nose, and seized Undine's ankle.

"Out you come," the constable said again.

There was nothing for it but to obey. I fought my way out of the upholstery, still chuckling, but unable to stop.

"Sorry about that," Undine said apologetically. "That was the Silent Assassin. It got away on me. It must have been my increased cabbage consumption."

Which set me off again. I couldn't help it.

What a scene it must have been: two girls convulsed in waves of helpless giggles and a large police constable, whose enormous, pale, looming, and unfamiliar face seemed to provide the only light in the shadows of the room. He was in no mood for levity.

"Guv'nor wants to have a word," he said in a flat tone. "In the car. Outside."

"I don't believe we've met," I said, sticking out a firm professional hand. "I'm Flavia de Luce."

"I know well enough who you are," he said, jabbing his thumb toward the window and the Vauxhall. "Guv'nor wants to see you. In the car. Outside."

I withdrew my offered hand haughtily and wiped it on my skirt, and without another word, turned and walked out the front door.

I'd be leaving Undine behind, of course, but since she had already made the acquaintance of one of Inspector Hewitt's constables at Buckshaw, she might well be able to extract further wagonloads of information. She would be quite safe with a policeman. In fact, if anything, it was he who was in danger.

Outside, I shot a glance back over my shoulder and saw that the constable was now standing in the open doorway, watching me walk away. And the look on his face was not that of a policeman. It was something else entirely: the look of a rival skunked. Resentment regurgitated.

Was the constable going to parlay his sniffing us out into a promotion? Was he using Undine and me to satisfy the fondest wish of his agèd and doting mother? Would he regale her, off duty, with the story of the smelly chesterfield? Would she laugh? Would her old heart burst with pride in her clever son?

But there was no time for that: The inspector was waiting.

I strolled casually toward the Vauxhall. Inspector Hewitt sat inside, looking straight ahead, unmoving. It was a pose, and I knew it. I opened the door on the driver's side and got in beside him.

There was a long silence. One of my specialties.

"Flavia, Flavia, Flavia," the inspector said at last.

I smiled brightly, as if noticing him for the first time.

There had been a day when Inspector Hewitt and I had been better friends. In fact at one time, his wife, Antigone, whom I adored, had invited me to tea. But when they had a baby, the fires of friendship had turned to ashes, and I didn't quite know why. Was it the baby—or was it something I had said or done?

"Yes, Inspector?" I said eagerly, as if panting for a new assignment.

There! I'd done it. The ball was in his court again.

"Flavia, Flavia, Flavia," he said again.

"Yes, Inspector?"

I could keep this up as long as he could, and I think he knew it.

"This interference has to stop," he said. "I've told you before, nicely, to keep your nose out of official business. Now I'm telling you again, and not so nicely."

Now the cow was out of the barn, or the horse out of the stable, whatever you want to call it. The gloves were off.

"Is that a threat, Inspector?"

"It's a warning," Inspector Hewitt said. "A caution. The next step is a steep one. A *very* steep one."

"Thank you for the suggestion, Inspector," I said. "I shall take it under advisement."

I opened the door of the car and stepped out without looking back, closing it behind me with maddening delicacy, slowness, and greatly exaggerated care. And then with all the nonchalance I could muster, I retrieved Gladys from where I had parked her behind a tree, gave her a light dusting-off with my skirt, raised my chin, and pedaled off in a radiant cloud of righteousness.

I could almost hear the crackling of the flames of frustration behind me.

"Don't faff with Flavia!" I should have shouted back.

But I didn't need to, did I?

*

As I pedaled along heading home, I realized how anxious I was to get there. My chemical laboratory was my kingdom, and away from it, I was a mere husk, like something shed by some disgusting insect, or the paper wrapping on a sweet. Although the rationing of sweets had only just ended at the beginning of this coronation year, I found that I had completely lost my taste for them. Daffy said it was true what they said about forbidden fruit, and that I would need to train myself to crave something else. She suggested crooked rum cigars from Cuba, or Gordon's Gin, but I think she was joking.

But as I was saying, I had become aware that there was an "inner me" and an "outer me," and at the moment I didn't much care for the outer one. I was only truly myself when I was alone among the glass flasks and retorts in that dear chemical lab in the otherwise abandoned east wing of Buckshaw.

When my great-uncle Tarquin—or "Tar," as he was called—died, twenty-five years ago, he had left behind a laboratory that caused the chemists of Oxford and Cambridge to weep with envy.

He had also left behind a treasure trove of his notebooks and journals, which, despite being placed under strict embargo by some obscure and shadowy government department, had remained at Buckshaw, where I had been devouring them for years.

Uncle Tar had been involved in certain researches

that seized the mind, turned it upside down and shook it, then wrung it out and hung it up to dry. I hardly dared even think of some of these for fear of being whisked away by night, tortured in a stone chamber, and hung from some salt-corroded yardarm at dawn.

My family had almost always, since the dawn of time, been involved in ultrasecret operations. My own mother had been connected with a shadowy governmental coven called the Nide.

It had been hinted to me on more than one occasion (once by Winston Churchill at my mother's funeral) that I, too, might be marked for membership—like it or not. Aunt Felicity, my late father's sister, was also en-tangled with the Nide, but to what extent, I did not really know. She had contrived to send me, for a time, to a wretched school in Canada, which I had guessed to be a front for some enormous power. When Father had died suddenly after my return home, I thought I had been tested and had failed. But now, as life unrolled, I was beginning to suspect that what I had once taken for failure was, in fact, a most peculiar sort of success.

It was all so confusing. Which was why I was always on the lookout for signs and portents. I'm not a super-stitious girl, but something big was lumbering this way down the road—I was sure of it. I could feel it in my bones.

This topsy-turvy world, and my place in it, needed to be set straight for once and for all.

Or maybe I was just becoming a woman.

That thought had crossed my mind on one or two

occasions, and although it chilled me silly, I'd managed to dismiss it.

On the one hand, it was the most terrifying thing I had ever faced.

The instant you become a woman, you become a captive. You are sucked up into that mysterious state that, like a person seen across a lawn through drifting smoke, is partly real and partly vapor. I had seen it happening to Feely and her friends, and it scared me almost to witlessness.

On the other hand, the prospect was deeply and strangely satisfying. It was as if in a way, I had already crossed the finish line and was home at last, and yet in another way as if I were back at the beginning, waiting for the starter's pistol.

Becoming a woman was not part of my plan. The thought of becoming a lady was even worse.

It was like being reincarnated, I suppose. Was there really such a thing as reincarnation? I should no longer be Flavia de Luce. What would I become? Even worse, *who* would I become? Would I be the wife of a provincial scrap-iron merchant, sitting at a leaded window composing poems of frail sadness, while gazing out upon a field of poppies? Or a slave, perhaps, in ancient Egypt, milling corn on a slab for the flatbread that would feed the slaves who were hauling stones for the pyramids?

But perhaps not. The world was changing, and I was changing with it. By the time I managed to reincarnate again I might well be a scientist—a chemist, of course—calibrating the controls of some new and yet-undreamed-of device that would allow me to peer personally into the secret heart of the universe. I would be able at last to prove my theory that we all of us are but ancient light.

But what would I be giving up?

A girl of my age is utterly invisible. Nobody gives a fig—or anything else—for us. But once a woman, we become targets, unless we buy joke-shop teeth and stick-on warts, and steal our clothing from hedgerows. And even then—it is simply too horrible to contemplate.

Perhaps that was part of the reason for my love of chemistry: Perhaps one day I would be able to concoct and patent an elixir of perpetual adolescence.

Gladys's chain squeaked happily at my ankles, and I knew that she agreed. For her, the promise of perpetual greasings; for me, I began to bellow the words of that old, old hymn: "Just where I am, oh let me be . . ." And Gladys's tires hum-hummed happily along, bound for Buckshaw.

Home at last, and because I didn't want to be disturbed, I shinnied up the vines, climbed over the sill, and let myself into my laboratory. At the eastern rear of the building, I was unlikely to be spotted.

First things first is my motto—at least, one of them.

I locked the door and carefully removed my Peter Pan collar. Setting it on a glass dish, I switched on a strong light and flipped over the lacy stuff with a pair of tweezers. My stomach took a sudden step back as I realized that my sample had taken a turn for the worse.

Better get to it!

Mushrooms are not very substantial things at the best of times, and one that had been picked, cooked, eaten, partly digested, then shot like a cannonball through the air, bounced off the floor, stuck to the bottom of a kitchen chair, and scraped onto a lacy collar for transport was not the tastiest thing to gaze upon.

With a razor blade, I scraped the sticky residue onto a glass slide. The stickiness was a good sign: proof that the liquids in the stuff had not entirely evaporated.

I had already formed in my mind a plan for the analysis.

The glint in the darkness under the table had been the clue. I reviewed my line of reasoning: that there had been some crystalline substance in Major Greyleigh's *vomitus* was beyond a doubt. If Mrs. Mullet—or anyone else—had poisoned him with such fast-acting precision that he never got away from the breakfast table, it could only have been through administration of the death cap mushroom (*Amanita phalloides*).

The catch was this: *Amanita phalloides* contains no crystalline matter.

Therefore, the cause of Major Greyleigh's demise was some other substance, the mushrooms being no more than mere cover.

Which let Mrs. Mullet, at least partially, off the hook. But until I could provide a complete and unassailable chain of chemical evidence, everything must remain in doubt.

I knew of only a few such fast-acting poisons. At the

top of the list were those blitzkrieg cyanide capsules, such as the one with which Hermann Göring took his own life after the fall of Nazi Germany. They worked within minutes.

Was there—could there be—any connection between Major Greyleigh and the trials at Nuremberg? Had the major, by any chance, been one of those executioners called in to apply the canvas caps, the cuffs, and the noose to those condemned to dangle to death for crimes against humanity?

It was possible. I had pored again and again over the grainy photographs in the piles of newspapers and musty magazines stored under the stairs: the *Suns* . . . the *Stars* . . . the *Mirrors* . . . the *Expresses*.

All of them stuffed to the gills with what Dogger called "mountains of mayhem." No unprintable photo had gone unpublished. Vivid pen-and-ink drawings provided close-up views of a bounty of blunt weapons, wickedly sharp razors, and bloodied beds. I shivered a bit with excitement at the thought of going through them all again: all the murders, all the investigations, all the trials and all the hangings. All of them grisly but instructive.

But I was not looking for brute power.

There is a poison that makes cyanide look like the tortoise in the fable. It is so powerful that an amount of it equal in size to just one-eighth of a grain of sand can kill in seconds.

So lethal is this substance that few people, even now, including chemists, know of its existence.

I had come across the stuff in one of Uncle Tar's secret notebooks: a small, scuffed pocket diary that looked like something ready for the rubbish bin. At the time, I had wondered why those things with the most power were so often in the most plain packages. The Holy Bible, for instance: traditionally black.

As it happened, this notebook was bound in black also, and at the top reverse of a middle page was written the word "Saxitoxin."

Ha! I had thought. *Saxitoxin. The most toxic of the known shellfish poisons.*

Uncle Tar's notes made it clear that this was a top-secret matter: that the military was investigating this swift and powerful poison as a matter of greatest urgency and under a veil of the greatest secrecy. That had been more than twenty years ago. Could they still be keeping it under their collective hats?

Even more interesting was the fact that Uncle Tar had devised a test for the presence of saxitoxin, which involved oxidizing a sample at a slightly elevated temperature in the presence of hydrogen peroxide: a substance known to every mother in the British Empire for the cleaning out of her little darlings' ears.

This was going to be a piece of cake: a dirty, deadly one to be sure, but a piece of cake nevertheless, or "notwithstanding" as Dickens would have put it.

I couldn't help rubbing my hands together in the classic expression of glee—*before,* of course, I put on my rubber gloves.

The proof in the pudding, if any were needed, lay in

the fact that saxitoxin, unlike the death cap mushroom, did indeed contain its death-dealing payload in crystalline form.

And I was about to prove it.

I positioned the prepared slide on a small glass scaffold, which I placed, with tweezers, into the center of a glass beaker, before setting it on a ring tripod, held rigidly in place by a clever rubber clamp and a heavy-duty support stand.

I was keenly aware that I probably had enough poison at my fingertips to kill in an instant the entire membership of the Bishop's Lacey Waterloo Memorial Lawn Bowling Club.

Not that I would want to, of course. But still, I couldn't be too careful.

Beside my sample on the little stand, I dripped a few drops of hydrogen peroxide, then capped the beaker with a white ceramic disk.

And then, ever so gently, I lit and applied a thin and gentle flame from a Bunsen burner to the bottom of the flask. *Easy does it, Flavia. We only need a temperature of 100 degrees C.*

Fortunately, saxitoxin, according to Uncle Tar, has a melting point of about 420 degrees F, so I didn't need to worry much about destroying the evidence.

It didn't take long, and while the glass was heating, I took a quick turn around the laboratory, lowering all the blackout blinds.

With the room now illuminated only by the flame of the burner, I pulled up a stool and peered into the flask.

"Flavia! Flavia!"

A series of staccato thuds came from the door.

"Who is it?" I said in a disinterested voice, although I knew the answer well enough.

"Skinless Jack! I've come for your soul and your liver!"

Even in the darkness of my locked lab, I found myself shivering to the very core. What was it that shook me so?

I gripped the edge of the bench.

"Flavia! It's me! Let me in!"

"Go away," I growled.

"It's important! Let me in."

The thudding continued.

There's only one way to deal with a persistent pest, which is to remain perfectly silent. Silence is more effective than a thousand swear words.

"Flavia, let me in. I've got a present for you."

I closed my eyes and banished my brain to Antarctica.

"I found it in Moonflower Cottage."

I opened the door.

"Give it here," I said, extending my hand around the door jamb.

"Only if you let me in," Undine said. "I have the upper hand and you might as well admit it."

"A cauldron of curses," I said, glaring at her.

"Kiss my bewtocks," she replied.

"Your what?"

"My bewtocks. The part you sit on."

"That's pronounced *BUT-tocks*," I said. I had to give the child credit. If she couldn't pronounce the word, it meant she had read it somewhere. According to Daffy, there is a grace that can be attained only from reading the printed page. It is a grace that *must* be acknowledged, no matter what. It was once known as the benefit of clergy, by which the ability to read aloud, in Latin, the third verse of Psalm 51 could save you from the gallows. Even though the practice has been dead for centuries, it's still alive in secret ways.

I was glad that I was keen on chemistry, rather than creeds or canon law.

"Well, kiss them, too, however they're pronounced," Undine said, squeezing herself between the door and the frame and oozing into the room.

I turned away from her and focused on my heated beaker.

The little stage seemed unchanged, and my heart sank a little.

But then as I watched with disappointed eyes, the magic began to happen. The crystal matter began to glow a bright, unearthly blue.

"Fluorescence!" I sang the word aloud. "Fluorescence! Fluorescence!"

The poison was there! The saxitoxin was there! And I was here!

I found myself hugging the repellent Undine.

"That's more like it," she said.

But I had proved my point. Major Greyleigh had died not by the poison of the death cap mushroom, but by saxitoxin: a substance known to only a handful of people—including me!

Were all the facts known, I myself would be a suspect—or perhaps even the next victim.

A wet, Draculic kiss was being planted on my cheek. I shook myself loose.

"Have a gander at this," Undine said, holding out what appeared to be a plain wooden box and shoving it in my face.

"More light! she shouted. "More light for the Infidels!"

I shut off the flame beneath the beaker and swept open the nearest blackout curtains.

"Give it here," I told her, setting the box on the windowsill. "Now then, where did you find this?"

"At that cottage. In the kitchen."

"I searched the kitchen. I didn't see it."

"That's because you're not the Amazing Me!" she crowed.

This child was getting on my nerves. She reminded me of someone I had once known.

"It was *under* the box of silverware." She giggled. "Who would think to look *under* the silverware?

"No one except me," she added in a horrid cackle, wringing her hands diabolically.

It was true. A shallow box of precisely the same dimensions as the treasured utensils above would be the safest place in the house. Who would think to look beneath the silver?

So *that* was where the major kept his valuables.

This was going to be interesting. What on earth could be worth hiding with such devilish cleverness?

I eased open the lid.

I recoiled slightly, though whether from surprise or shock, I could not tell.

A number of miniature figures—human figures—made from empty spools and painted flesh color, were tucked into small depressions in the black padded silk. They were dressed in cunningly knitted little costumes: a nanny's dress and cap, a shoemaker's leather apron, a London omnibus driver . . .

I counted them. There were thirteen.

And each had around its lolling neck an elaborately detailed noose of what could only have been human hair.

"He was a hangman," Undine hissed at my ear. "A hangman, Flavia!"

In my mind, I went to the sun and back.

"See?" Undine shouted, dancing on the spot. "Do you see, Flavia?"

"I see," I said. And I did.

Or so I thought. But I was also thinking, *I have been outdone.* This little monster had elbowed into my investigation and uncovered a prime piece of evidence. To her would go the glory.

I was simply sick.

"What do you think?" Undine said.

"Hmmm," I said. "Not without interest, but not directly involved in the man's murder."

"How do you know?" Undine said.

I improvised a flimsy answer. Perhaps she wouldn't spot it.

"Because if they were important, the police—or someone else—would have searched for them and found them and taken them away, wouldn't they? Now that you've removed criminal evidence, they will likely come to Buckshaw in the night with hounds and burning torches, and we'll both be charged with being accessories after the fact."

"Baloney!" she said, with an irritating grin.

"Well, in any case, I'll see that you get all the credit for finding a key clue that the police missed. They'll be too embarrassed. Or else they'll name a bank holiday after you. It's hard to say."

"I thought you'd be happy," Undine said, her grin falling into a pout.

"I am happy," I said. "It's just that you can't tell. I've trained myself to suppress emotion, and you ought to do the same. If you're a good girl, I might give you a few tips.

"Leave this box with me," I told her. "And I'll check it for fingerprints and so forth before we hand it over to Inspector Hewitt. He'll be livid that his men missed it."

It was not just me who hadn't thought to search under the silverware. The police ought to be ashamed of themselves.

"Now scoot," I said. "I've got things to do."

As soon as she was gone, I wrapped the box in a threadbare lab coat and started for the greenhouse. Dogger would be beside himself.

· F O U R ·

"OH DEAR," DOGGER SAID when I handed him the box. He opened it and looked inside. "Have the police seen this?"

I shook my head.

"We shall have to turn it over at once. No point in dusting for fingerprints: It already has yours and mine."

"And Undine's," I said. I could have sunk straight down into the earth.

"We must make the most of the time we have," Dogger said. "May we retire to your laboratory?"

Within minutes we were facing each other across a chemical workbench. A gooseneck lamp cast a strong light on the box. Dogger put down a magnifying glass.

"No writing, no engraving, no obvious scuffs or gouges."

"What does that mean?" I asked.

"That it is relatively new," he said. "Boxes tend to be banged about over time. Their function is to protect the contents, and we would expect some sign of their having done so.

"The wood is mahogany, which would suggest some importance. It is not a cheap wood. Someone has valued the contents enough to pay for quality."

"And the little dolls inside?" I asked.

"Fetishes," Dogger said. "Souvenirs with ritual power."

"Witchcraft!" I said. This was going to be no ordinary case of murder.

"An interesting idea," Dogger said, lifting the lid with a metal buttonhook he produced from somewhere about his person. "But I think not."

He bent over until his nose was almost touching the little figures.

"No smell. No hint of wax or candlewick. No incense. If anything, they smell of the kitchen drawer and silver polish. We may be certain, though, that they were all produced by the same hand."

"How?" I asked.

"By the stitching on their little costumes," Dogger said. "A straight in-and-out stitch. The hand of an amateur. Not the needlework of an experienced seamstress. Very crude. The work of an enthusiast: someone who had a sentimental attachment to the figures. Almost— a kind of love."

I could see that with my own eyes. As Dogger spoke, everything fell into place. And how pathetic it was!

"They're effigies of the people he hanged," I whispered.

"Yes," Dogger said. "Just one of them a woman. Notice the crude spider's web stitched into her little shawl. Made from a bit of sackcloth, by the look of it. And I suspect the miniature wigs were made of hair snipped from the head of each of his victims."

"Victims?" I asked. "He hanged them."

Dogger nodded. "Even Justice has its victims," he said. "And they are sometimes more greatly wronged than even the victims of crime."

"I shall have to think about that," I said. I felt as if my brain had had the wind knocked out of it.

"We *all* need to think about that," Dogger said.

"Now then," he went on, "tell me the outcome of your chemical analysis."

My eyes widened. How could he have possibly known?

"The smell of saxitoxin oxidizing in the presence of hydrogen peroxide is unmistakable, don't you find?"

I couldn't hold back a grin.

"So, it wasn't mushrooms," Dogger said. "That much we have established. And Mrs. Mullet is cleared of suspicion."

"But who—?"

"Ah," Dogger said. "That is the question."

"Have you given it any thought?" I asked.

"No," he said. "It's early times yet and the facts have been coming at us all askew, don't you think?"

"Absolutely," I said.

"So for now, our evidence amounts to the sample you

found and the thirteen dolls in this box. Thirteen is, I believe, the number of clients that Major Greyleigh dispatched."

"Clients?" I asked.

"So they are called," Dogger said. "Everything is reduced nowadays to a business transaction—even death."

"But wasn't it always?" I asked. "What about Mr. Sowerberry, the undertaker in *Oliver Twist?*"

"Mr. Sowerberry was a humble servant, as were so many of Dickens's characters. He never aspired to be an equal of his customers. Today it is pretended that the men on both ends of the rope have the same status, even if only for those few moments between the slamming of the cell door and the springing of the trap door. It makes other people feel better."

"Does it make the hangman feel better?"

"Possibly. Probably. Otherwise, the major wouldn't have gone to all the trouble of crafting his little puppet show."

"Was it guilt, do you think?" I asked. "A way of bringing them back without undoing what he had done?"

"Another interesting idea," Dogger said. "Certainly, a set of souvenirs. Perhaps each an unusual *memento mori*: a token to remember the dead. He might have also used them as *aide-mémoire*, to help him recall the grisly moment when each of them plummeted through the trap."

I'm afraid I gulped. I'm *not* afraid of death, but deliberate death, sudden and violent at the end of a rope, seems so unfair. I can't imagine how the relatives must feel.

"Dogger, do you think Major Greyleigh was murdered by a relative of one of his . . . clients?"

"That would be a valid assumption," Dogger said, "and one that we must either prove or eliminate."

"And how would we do that? Where would we begin?"

"With the newspapers," Dogger said.

"What?"

"I am told," he said—and I didn't ask who told him, but I strongly expect it was Alf Mullet—"that today's *News of the World* contains a list of all the hangings this century, with 'real eye-poppers' of photographs."

"Crikey!" I said. Then: "Thank you, Dogger. I'm going to go pick one up. It might save us a lot of work."

"My thoughts precisely, Miss Flavia."

That was another thing that I loved about Dogger. He was easy to take leave of. You didn't have to invent any elaborate goodbyes or polite conclusions. You simply took to your heels, and that was what I did.

A minute later, Gladys and I were flying down the avenue of chestnuts, out through the Mulford Gates—whose mossy green griffins gaped their beaks at us in astonishment as we passed—and into Bishop's Lacey.

We slowed just before we reached Miss Cool's confectionery shop. I dismounted daintily and leaned Gladys—with greatest respect—against the red pillar box at the door.

I paused to look in the window at a handwritten notice: *Lost, Strayed, or Stolen—Gray cat, brown collar, red bell. Answers to Jackanapes. Do not feed apple-peel: Vomits.*

I recognized the name of the owner as one of the ladies of the Cluck and Grumble, a monthly meeting for the female parishioners of St. Tancred's. If I needed further information, a missing cat would be an ideal excuse to visit her there. "I think I spotted your cat, Jackanapes, behind the church. He"—I assumed it to be he—"was nibbling on a bit of apple peel and vomiting, and I thought of you at once."

The bell jangled cheerfully as I stepped into the shop. There was a dramatic pause before the postmistress, Miss Cool, swept aside the curtain to her living quarters and made her entrance behind the wicket that served as the post office among the mints and humbugs and the superannuated prewar chocolates.

"Yes?" she said, turning from profile to face me. "Oh! Flavia, it's you, dear."

She seemed surprised.

"Have you had any mail from your sister Ophelia?"

She knew perfectly well that I hadn't. Every parcel, every letter, every postcard addressed to Bishop's Lacey went through her hands, and was thoroughly examined, shaken, sniffed, and held up to a powerful lamp before being handed over to the recipient.

"No, I haven't, Miss Cool. She's somewhere in Germany, I believe. She's still on her honeymoon."

"Hamburg this week, paying her respects to Mendelssohn. She wrote to Sheila Foster a few days ago."

"Oh, did she?" I tried to sound surprised. I couldn't possibly let this woman know more about my sister than I did myself. "She didn't mention that when she rang me the other day."

"Rang you? Rang you, did you say?"

"Oh, yes. She rings me quite often. We're very close, you know."

If liars turned instantly to dust, I'd be settling between the cracks of the floorboards.

"Well!" Miss Cool said. "She must be very well off now. Overseas calls are very dear. Very dear."

I smiled smugly and said nothing.

"Well, then, how can I help you today? Stamps? Sweets? Souvenirs?"

"No, thank you, Miss Cool," I said. "Just a copy of *News of the World.*"

Her eyebrows shot up like a runaway lift. "Oh dear. That's not . . . I mean to say . . . *News of the World* is not what you would call . . ."

"It's all right, Miss Cool. I just want it for the coupon. They're having an essay contest on the topic 'Young Britain and the Modern Brain.' Do you see the similarity of the words Britain and Brain? You take 'it' out and they're identical. I'm going to win. I just know it."

"If it's just the coupon you want, I can cut it out of my own copy. Or Mr. Brock's copy. He only takes it for the pictures."

"That's so kind of you, Miss Cool. I really appreciate it, but the rules state that you must purchase a copy."

I picked up a copy of the paper from the wire rack,

folded it under one arm in a businesslike way, dug in my pocket, placed sixpence on the counter, and waited for my change.

"Oh, and I'll need a receipt."

She locked eyes with me.

"As proof of purchase," I said.

After an eternity she took my coin and rummaged noisily in her change box.

"I expect the police will be visiting Buckshaw, if they haven't already. Your Mrs. Mullet is in a nice pickle. How's she bearing up?"

"Oh, she's assisting the police with their inquiries," I said, with a dismissive wave of my spare hand. "A misunderstanding."

Miss Cool snorted nastily through her nose. "Misunderstanding? She was seen leaving the place hours after the poor man's body was taken away."

"Oh?" I said casually. "By whom?"

"Neighbors, shall we say. We call ourselves the Neighborhood Watch. The world's a cesspool, Flavia. One can never be too careful—or too observant."

"My thoughts precisely," I said.

"It was Mary Belter found the body, you know—his charlady."

This was a precious nugget of information and not one I would likely get from Inspector Hewitt.

"Shocking, she said it was. Vomit sprayed everywhere—like a fire hose. She had a hard time mopping it all up before the police arrived. Said she wasn't going to have them docking her wages for work not carried out.

Mary's a real stickler for dust and dirt. Has a bit of a bee in her bonnet about soil and whatnot."

"So I've heard," I said, although I hadn't. But I needed to keep Miss Cool's tongue wagging. I nodded knowingly.

"This Major Greyleigh affair is a nasty business," she went on. "I've heard it said—and I'm not mentioning any names—that he had more than one visitor yesterday. One of them in a jeep."

In a jeep! Be still, my heart. Here was another connection to Leathcote. Could this be the particle of information that would save Mrs. Mullet's neck?

I froze my face to hide the frantic activity in my brain.

"You're quite right, Miss Cool. You ought to offer your services to Inspector Hewitt."

Careful, Flavia! In a game of jackstraws, even the slightest breath too much can result in complete collapse.

"Oh, I've no time for that since I got the television. I like to watch the test card in the daytime. It's so restful, and they play music you don't have to listen to. Will there be anything else?"

"No, thank you, Miss Cool. I'd better be on my way. I'm expecting Feely to ring me again."

I waited for her final thrust. I knew it was coming.

"Someone said you and that little girl were seen at Moonflower Cottage," she said, in a casual, offhand way, as if she were not really interested: as if she were only commenting out of concern for our welfare.

"Oh," I said. "Like Mrs. Mullet, I was assisting Inspector Hewitt with his inquiries. He was anxious to have my opinion."

"Police don't generally ask for opinions," she said, with a nasty little leer.

I looked surprised. "Do they not?" I said. "Thank you, Miss Cool, I shall tell him he's a naughty boy. I shall tell him you spotted his mistake."

And with that I was out the door. It had been as refreshing as a brisk game of croquet.

Gladys squeaked a little melody as she bore me home. The sun was shining, the birds were singing, and I had a fresh copy of *News of the World* under my arm.

Robert Browning's poem came to mind, and I couldn't help bellowing it to the wind and whoever might be listening:

"I sprang to the stirrup, and Joris, and he;
"I galloped, Dirck galloped, we galloped all three . . ."

The unfortunate Miss Gurdy, our former governess, had made Feely and Daffy and me memorize the stupid thing and recite it in unison at a picnic before issuing our cucumber sandwiches.

Would the news I brought to Buckshaw be the key that cracked the case? I remembered how, in the poem, the rider gave his horse the rest of the wine.

"Steady on, Gladys," I told her. "We have no wine,

but I shall give your chain a good swig of Castrol when we get home. I promise."

Did I imagine it, or did her squeaking almost disappear?

I was already beginning to bask in the thought of spreading the paper on a table and poring over past executions with Dogger. I could barely wait to hear his thoughts.

I found him in the butler's pantry, fiddling with the wires inside our ancient electric toaster.

"It somehow keeps getting egg inside it," Dogger said. "I suspect someone has had the idea of omelettes on toast."

"Not me," I said. "I'm sometimes emotional about omelettes since Esmeralda—"

Esmeralda had been my pet Buff Orpington hen, who had accidentally, I liked to think, been eaten, and of whom I still had vivid dreams and nocturnal stomach uprisings.

"I understand," Dogger said. "I shall ask Mrs. M to henceforth make the toast in the kitchen and ease the gumming up of the electrical apparatus."

I shot him a radiant smile of appreciation.

"Shall we retire to the Long Gallery?" I asked. "Less traffic."

The Long Gallery occupied the entire ground floor of Buckshaw's east wing. Its walls were hung with portraits of long-dead de Luces, who gazed down their cold noses at nothing, for the most part. The gallery was never used nowadays. It froze in winter and stank in summer of varnish carelessly made from egg whites and various Mediterranean bushes. Old paint buckets were stored there as well, and in summer, the atmosphere could be volatile.

The fact that Uncle Tar had participated directly in the experiments leading to the atomic bomb intrigued me. *Did he ever,* I wondered, *consider the explosive power contained in the room directly beneath his feet? Could the war have been won more quickly and at much less cost by putting a match to a collection of country-house portraits?*

Well, no matter. The gallery now was derelict. It did, however, hold several attractions: a couple of rickety wooden chairs and a long, sturdy map table that had been stowed there because it was too big for a growing library, and because none of us still read maps. And it was private; no one ever went there.

Dogger and I spread the *News of the World* on the table with room to spare. The light from the east windows was dusty but good.

I turned a few pages to get an overview of the contents. I didn't have far to look.

"Here it is, Dogger," I said excitedly.

There in a long list were all the usual names, many of them household words—at least in my household: John Christie, Edith Thompson, John Haigh (the Acid Bath Murderer), Herbert Rowse Armstrong, George Joseph Smith (the Brides in the Bath Murderer).

"It's interesting," Dogger said, "that Christie, Smith, and Armstrong were all sent to eternity by the same hangman, John Ellis, a former newsagent, barber, and hairdresser who also hanged the notorious Dr. Crippen. Yet Ellis was so badly shaken by his bungling of Edith Thompson's hanging that he went on to alcoholic decline and eventual suicide. Haigh was dispatched by Albert Pierrepoint, a former grocer's drayman.

"The profession of hangman tends to run in families: Albert's uncle Thomas Pierrepoint was also an executioner, and Pierrepoint's own father, Henry Pierrepoint, was struck off the register of approved executioners after a formal complaint from John Ellis. Hanging is a highly competitive profession."

"What about Major Greyleigh? Do you suppose he has any hangman relatives?"

"It's possible," Dogger said.

I pointed with my forefinger to the newspaper.

"There are so many names here," I said. "I've never heard of most of them."

"Not all murderers are famous," Dogger said. "Some have lived—and continue to live—exceptionally quiet lives. As do most hangmen."

"Look at these," I said, and began reading them off. It was a roll call from the scaffold: "Martin Mayer, Stanley Pothouse, Ellen Gamage, Dennis Stout, Brian Kelly, Nancy Blankenship, Mary Jane Osler."

"How many of them hanged by Greyleigh?" Dogger asked.

"None," I said. "So far."

"We must remember," Dogger said, "that he hanged thirteen. And, as I recall, several of those took place abroad during the war trials."

"Wait," I said. "Here he is: He hanged a William Kennedy at Strangeways Prison in Manchester . . . let's see . . . six years ago. And look, here's another. He hanged Nigel Mogley, also at Strangeways, the previous year."

"Yes, I remember the Mogley affair," Dogger said. "Very nasty indeed. But if we're to track down the relatives of a hanged murderer, it's going to be a lot easier to find a Mogley than a Kennedy. Assuming that they have the same surname, which we must not do."

"Shall we forget about Major Greyleigh's murderer being one of his own relatives?" I asked.

"We must look first into those things which are within our abilities," Dogger said. "In the words of that excellent Franciscan philosopher John Punch, 'Things are not to be multiplied without necessity.'"

"Look under our noses first," I said. "That's what he meant, isn't it?"

Dogger nodded. "But not entirely," he said. "Although this case is not necessarily what we would call a domestic homicide, there may be certain similarities. Most domestic victims are female and most of those are committed by a spouse. Since Major Greyleigh had no spouse—"

"That we know of," I interrupted.

"That we know of." Dogger smiled. "Well observed, Miss Flavia. Shall we return to the lists?"

I nodded eagerly and picked up a pencil. "Rather than the names of the condemned killers, let's draw up a separate list of those executions that were carried out by Major Greyleigh."

Dogger nodded. "We won't find all thirteen," he said,

"but we ought to be able to identify those that took place in this country."

It took longer than I thought, dodging back and forth between various lists of prisons, prisoners, wardens, justices, lord chief justices, and executioners.

In the end we had eight names.

"Shall we arrange them in alphabetical order?" Dogger suggested.

"Save us some time," I said, although I didn't really want to save time. I wanted to sit here across the table from Dogger in the milky light of these ancient windows until the stars faded and the sun went out.

I shoved the list across the table. "Does anything strike you, Dogger?"

Dogger reached into his vest pocket and extracted a pair of spectacles. He wiped the lenses gently with his tie and pulled the wires over his ears. He read the list aloud.

"Gilbert Ash, Patrick Boniface, Dolly Camber, William Kennedy, Nigel Mogley, John Planer, Richard Regent, Anthony Speck."

"Dolly Camber," I said. "The poisoner. Wasp spiders. She gathered clusters of them from the grasslands near Rye. Distilled their juice and dripped it into her drunken husband's ear with an eyedropper while he was sleeping off an old boys' reunion."

"Yes," Dogger said. "A seven days' wonder, in her time. I didn't remember Major Greyleigh had been her executioner. That would explain the spider's web on the female doll."

"You're right!" I said.

"The others are quite anonymous."

Dogger removed his glasses and tucked them away. "And Richard Regent," he said. "We must pay particular attention to Richard Regent, whoever he may have been."

"May have been?" I asked.

"Yes," Dogger said. "The name is an obvious concoction. A nice bit of handiwork by the lads of the Department of Concealment and Obfuscation, I should say."

"MI5 and MI6, you mean?" I asked. Alf Mullet had often curled my childish ears with hair-raising tales of trickery and deception, far beyond the knowledge of the general public. "Mustn't breathe a word," he had always told me, his forefinger to his lips. "Hush-hush stuff. Written in the black books. Known only to God and perhaps the home secretary."

Dogger nodded. "And other, higher, more exalted integers," he said, with a slight shake of his head.

I waited for him to elaborate, but he did not.

"This particular Richard Regent," I said. "Why must we pay attention to him, especially?"

"We mustn't," Dogger said. "He's in the past. It's not the person, it's the name. We must be alert to *all* the Richard Regents we encounter. But we must first learn to spot them."

"Like counterfeit banknotes," I said.

"Precisely. Few people realize that there are Oxford Firsts kept busy day and night creating aliases. *What's in a name* and so forth. But names are power. As you will recall, the Lord remarked to Jacob, 'I have called thee by thy name; thou art mine.'"

"That's interesting," I said, "but what does it mean?"

"It means that when you know a person's name, you have very great power over them. Very great, very *deep* power: power even at a cellular level. Or so some believe."

"Really?" I said.

"Quite." Dogger smiled. "Which is why those who forge identities are so careful to ring all the right chimes, so to speak. To be credible, they must choose a surname that hints at money, power, nobility, or luxury goods. In this case, they have gone a little too far and reached for royalty."

"But why?" I asked. "Why create a whole new identity and then allow it to be destroyed?"

"Ah!" Dogger said. "Think of Dr. Frankenstein and *his* failures. Sometimes the beloved child must be destroyed."

"Sacrificed to a higher cause?" I asked.

"Precisely!" Dogger said. "And in the end, one waits upon the day when our Maker gathers up the parts to restring his puppets and set them dancing in a better world."

"Do you really believe that, Dogger?" I asked.

This was probably the most important question I had ever asked in my brief life.

"Some of us believe it," Dogger said, "and some of us must." He stood up and dusted an imaginary speck from his cuff. "And now if you'll excuse me, Miss Flavia, I must go butter my boots. I promised the vicar I'd help him replace the bell ropes in the church tower, so I mustn't appear shabby."

After he was gone, I thought over for a long time what he had said. At last, I made my way to that claustrophobic cupboard under the stairs with its hoard of long-outdated newspapers.

A hundred years of murder at my fingertips. There was so much to do.

I was still at it after midnight when I fell asleep on my stool and banged my head on the corner of an old tin campaign trunk.

"Curses!" I said. (Actually, I didn't say "Curses!" I let fly something much more daring, but since I don't want to be thought of badly, I've softened it considerably.)

I put out the light, removed my shoes, and crept up the staircase to my inviting, although moldy, bedroom.

I undressed quickly and climbed into bed. If I'd been the type for teddy bears I'd have grabbed old Theodorus, or whatever his name might have been, and tucked myself in. Instead, my cuddly companion was a copy of the first volume of Sir Robert Christison's *A Treatise on Poisons*.

After a time, I put aside the book and stared at the water stains on the ceiling. One of them was boot-shaped and looked like Italy. The smaller stain, just to the south of it, must be Malta, and I pondered for a while on how it came to pass that Saint Paul, while visiting there, was shown to be immune to poisons—or at least to snakebite—as described in the book of Acts.

I could not sleep. I tossed and turned for what seemed like hours, and then, as the sky outside began to grow light, I climbed out of bed, shrugged myself into my favorite old brown dressing gown (it had belonged to Father, and was now all of him that I had left), went quietly into my laboratory, locked the door, and with a beaker and Bunsen burner, boiled some water for tea.

I poured the boiling water through a filter paper filled with tea leaves. Tea is said to be an antidote to almost everything, and it would help me clear my mind.

As I sipped, I thought how refreshing it was to be alone. I remembered the words of that idiotic and wrongheaded old song "Tea for Two." To my mind, tea for one is infinitely more enjoyable. Just me and a steaming cup of tannic acid.

Somewhere nearby, I heard the flush of a W.C. Who could be up at such an hour, and what were they doing in this part of the house?

I stood up and moved stealthily to the door. I was skilled in opening doors without a sound, and thankful when it came open in silence.

I tiptoed into the hall. A sliver of light was showing under the door of the necessary room.

"Who's there?" I demanded in a coarse and throaty voice in case it was a burglar.

"It's me," came Undine's cheery voice.

"What are you doing?" I asked crossly. I wasn't thrilled about anyone using my private part of the house, much less this excrescence of a cousin.

"Making hot cross buns!" she shouted with excessive volume. "I'm cross and they're hot."

"Go back to bed," I said, as the door opened and Undine appeared, flapping her hands.

"Foof! That was a real four-flusher," she said, waving her arms, then miming falling over dead with her tongue hanging out. "Don't light any matches!"

I froze the muscles of my face.

"I knew you were awake," she said. "I could hear you moving around in there."

"Could you? Really?" I asked. "Moving around? In there? How awfully clever of you."

But sarcasm is wasted on the young. They haven't yet learned to bleed under such deadly wit.

"Now I'm hungry again," Undine said. "Got any grub in your lair?"

"No," I lied.

She rubbed her hands together enthusiastically. "I smell tea," she said. "Let's make some toast, too. You can fire up the old Bunsen burner. I'm famished—after that," as she waved a hand weakly behind her.

I was still too sleepy to protest. As Undine dashed off to raid the pantry for bread and jam, I settled onto a lab stool with my head in my hands.

I needed to come up with a plan. It was time to track down the families of Major Greyleigh's "clients." But where to begin? I wondered. Had I bitten off more than I could chew? How could I possibly locate—let alone investigate—so many people? How could one girl, with no resources but her wits—

Suddenly Undine was back, arms full of food. "I brought some bacon and eggs, too," she said.

The very sight of her made me cross.

"You can't cook bacon and eggs on a Bunsen burner," I said grumpily. Actually, you can, and I had often done so. But young girls like Undine need to meet occasionally with contrariness. It builds backbone and gives the speaker time to get her wits together.

"Oh, you'll find a way." She grinned. "Carl says you're resourceful. Carl says he can cook bacon and eggs on the radiator of his jeep. He says it's commando tactics."

As it turned out, Carl was right. A burette clamp and a stainless-steel dissecting sheet served as an admirable grill, and the laboratory was soon filled with the mouthwatering smell of crisp bacon and sizzling eggs.

"Let's add some jam!" Undine shouted. "I love damson jam on bacon. It reminds me of Ibu."

I managed a smile at last.

This, after all, was home.

We gobbled more or less cozily away, the Beast and I, until the sun was fully up and the gurglings and groanings of Buckshaw's ancient plumbing told us that the household had come at last out of its suspended animation.

After a while, I heard a clumping on the stairs and Mrs. Mullet's voice filtered through the panels of the door.

"Breakfast!" she shouted. "Come and get it before I feeds it to the cat."

The fact that we had no cat never kept Mrs. M from creating and enjoying the drama of her daily life.

"Shall you tell her we've already eaten, or shall I?" Undine asked with a wink.

Like it or not, we were co-conspirators, co-cogs, and the machinery of life would go rolling merrily along at Buckshaw.

As we descended the east staircase, Undine plucked urgently at my sleeve. "Can I ask you just one question?"

Softened, I suppose by our shared and secret breakfast, I nodded.

"Who is Asterion?"

Somewhere inside my head, something froze. I pretended it hadn't.

I knew the name well enough. Asterion was the name of the Minotaur in Greek mythology. Hadn't I mimicked him myself one winter evening during a compulsory Girl Guides game of hide-and-seek in the crypt of St. Tancred's, after which one of our lily-livered members had to be taken to hospital for observation?

"I don't know," I said. "Is this another of your stupid riddles?"

"No," she said. "I'm disappointed in you. I thought you knew everything."

I said nothing. I did not want to admit that somewhere in the coils of my brain, a tangled string had been plucked with unsettling force.

I could not let Undine know how badly she had

shaken me, but I walked down the remaining stairs like a poker.

We were now seated in silence at the breakfast table. Undine had brought the toaster in from the kitchen and was using it, along with a few pieces of cutlery and some strips of toast, to form a kind of poor man's Meccano set, with which she had constructed a miniature gallows.

"*Kerchunk!*" she shouted, flipping the door of the toaster and dropping to his death a poor little man pinched out of Hovis bread. "Is that the sound the gallows makes, do you think, Flavia? *Kerchunk?* Or would it be a *kerboom*? It's made from lumber, you know."

I shrugged.

"Major Greyleigh was a hangman. I could have asked him. Too bad he's dead."

"How thoughtless of him," I said.

"*Kerchunk!*" the gallows went again, this time sending a little bread lady plummeting into eternity.

Undine popped the crumbs into her mouth and began shaping a new victim from a fresh piece of toast.

I tried to be casual by stifling a yawn. "Your question," I said, "about Asteroid . . ."

Undine snorted. "Asterion," she said. "An asteroid is an unearthly body . . . like Marilyn Monroe."

"Who told you that? About Marilyn Monroe, I mean?"

"Carl. Carl knows practically everything."

"He was pulling your leg."

"Carl possesses a vast and comprehensive knowledge. He told me so. He's a polymath. It's an easy word to remember because it's like a parrot doing arithmetic. He also has an eidetic memory. That means 'photographic.' He never forgets anything."

"Then why is he peeling potatoes on an airfield?" I asked.

"Because they're keeping him in *reserve!*" she crowed.

Talking to Undine is like dealing with a rogue cuckoo clock. The bird keeps popping out until you remove the weights.

"Asterion," I said casually. "Where did you hear about this Asterion?"

"From Mrs. Mullet. I just happened to overhear her on the telephone."

Mrs. Mullet on the telephone? Our telephone was kept in a small cubicle under the stairs, and Father had always strictly forbidden its use except in the direst emergency. Even after his death there was still no chitchat at Buckshaw, and I could never recall Mrs. Mullet using "the instrument," as Father called it, in my lifetime.

"You couldn't have," I said. "She never goes near the thing."

"Not *here,*" Undine said in an exasperated voice, blowing through her nose like a startled horse. "It was at *her* house. On *her* telephone. She was talking to her friend Mrs. Waller."

That explained it—at least in part. When it came to

trumpeting things aloud, Mrs. Waller wasn't far behind the BBC Home Service.

I shook my head.

"Tell me exactly what happened. I need to know the context. Do you know what context means?"

"No."

"It means I need more details. Describe the scene. What were you doing at Mrs. Mullet's? What was she doing? And so forth."

"I can't tell you," Undine said. "It's a secret."

I almost bit through my lip to keep from swearing.

"I'll tell you anyway," she said. "Because you and I are chums now. But keep it under your hat. We were planning a birthday surprise for you."

"Para-Dimethylaminobenzaldehyde!" I expostulated.

It was my favorite chemical cuss word. It was not only melodic, but like Walt Whitman, contained multitudes. The substance was used in drug tests, such as the one for opium, and in detecting the indole alkaloids, such as physostigmine, the active poison in the seeds of the Calabar bean. It had been used notably by the famous Nobel Prize winner Paul Ehrlich to detect the difference between typhoid and diarrhea.

Edward G. Robinson had played the role of Ehrlich in the film *Dr. Ehrlich's Magic Bullet,* which Father refused to allow me to see. I begged and I pleaded—I even cajoled—but Father refused to give in. "It is unsuitable for a girl of your age and upbringing," he had said. I had even tried jollying the vicar into booking the film for his Friday Night Famous Film series for the boys and girls of the parish. But Father had somehow got wind of my plan and put the kibosh on it.

"But Dr. Ehrlich is a famous chemist," I had pleaded.

"I know who Dr. Ehrlich is," Father had said, "and Nobel Prize or no Nobel Prize, he's not to be trotted out for public view in a decent parish church."

"Para-Dimethylaminobenzaldehyde!" I said it again for emphasis, and Undine grinned from ear to ear.

"Gesundheit!" she said, and I was instantly in a better mood.

"Now then," I told her, rubbing my hands together, "*without* giving away any more secrets, tell me about Mrs. Mullet's cozy phone chat with her friend Mrs. Waller."

"Well, I went up to her front door and rang the bell—"

"Skip the bell, kid," I lisped in my best Humphrey Bogart voice. "Get down to the dirt."

It's sometimes best to inject a bit of humor when you're manipulating people. It's not much different from masking the taste of cod liver oil with a sickly sweet fruit, such as cherries or oranges or lemons.

"The dirt?" Undine said. "You mean Asterion, don't you?"

I patted her on the head. "You got it, kid. Now spit it out."

By now Undine was fairly glowing. She was at my mercy as effectively as if I had hypnotized her.

"Well, Mrs. Mullet and Mrs. Waller were at Lady Rex-Wells's together, years and years ago. They were al-

ready on the phone when I came in. They were gabbing
about Elsie, one of the maids at Lady Rex-Wells's who
used to go hysterical and roll herself up in a rug."

"I think I've heard about Elsie," I said.

"Mrs. Waller's so *loud*! I could hear her even when
Mrs. Mullet had the phone pressed tight against her
ear."

She mimicked an annoying tinny-sounding voice I
took to be Mrs. Waller's: "Well, Elsie's had an opera-
tion. She hasn't been herself since. She can't work
anymore. Cookers give her the fantods."

I grinned. Undine had all the makings of a cracker-
jack mimic. Encouraged, she went on, bubbling away
like a roadside spring.

"Mrs. Waller's daughter Madge supports her," she
continued. "Madge is a wizard typist, you know. She
types at a hundred and twenty words a minute and
takes Pitman shorthand at two hundred. She was offered a job at Leathcote. Confidential secretary to Mister Big Britches. Confidential! She doesn't even know
his real name. He goes by the name of Colonel Crane,
but some of the other bigwigs call him Asterion. Not to
his face, of course."

"Of course," I said. But my mind was partly dis-
tracted. Did Mrs. Waller and her daughter Madge realize the consequences of bandying gossip about with
Mrs. Mullet on a country telephone line? Probably not.
Father had been quite right to think "the instrument"
deadly.

"Of course," I said again to regain control of the conversation.

I have found that when listening, agreeing now and then builds the bonds of trust with the speaker, and often results in a whole fresh flow of scuttlebutt.

"You overheard all this?" I asked. "Jolly good show!"

"I pretended to be asleep at the kitchen table." Undine grinned. "I even drooled a little."

How could you hate a girl like that?

"Mrs. Waller said Madge told her some of the things she reads and writes would curl your hair, toes, and fingernails."

"Such as?" I asked.

"She didn't say. But Mrs. Mullet said 'I know' as if she actually *did* know."

"Remind me to buy you a pair of brass knuckles, Sluggo," I said. "You're a marvel."

"May I go now?" Undine asked. "I've got some scores to settle."

I waved her away. Well, no, I didn't actually *wave* her away, I blew her a kiss before I could stop myself. And then I was appalled at what I had done.

Is this what happens when you're becoming a woman? I wondered. *Do you suddenly start blowing kisses to your antagonist as if you were onstage in the West End at the curtain call of* Peter Pan?

"I'm your crocodile," Undine had told me in the churchyard. "Tick-tock. Tick-tock."

But instead, she had saved my bacon several times in

just two days. Was it possible that your nemesis could also be your savior?

Undine seemed to be developing the ability of disgorging the most unexpected information at the most unexpected times.

"Don't throw out the baby with the bathwater," Dogger had once advised me when I scoffed at the idea of communion wafers and sacramental wine being the literal body and blood of Christ.

And he was right. Sometimes it pays to listen to one's soul.

Why was I blocking the name Asterion? Why was my mind resisting even thinking about it?

The very sound of the word rang deeply, and always had, somewhere inside my brain: like the bells of a distant country church.

Asterion. Asterion. Where had I heard that name before?

I racked my brain, but nothing special came to mind. Whatever the memory, it was deeply buried.

Rather than Asterion, my mind threw up the name Marcel Proust.

Marcel Proust? I thought. *You must be joking.*

Marcel Proust, that boring old scribbler lounging in his bed full of crumbs?

Daffy had insisted upon reading aloud to me from *Remembrance of Things Past*: the part where Proust nibbles on a madeleine and releases a mind-numbing torrent of memories that will gush on unplugged for seven soggy volumes. Madeleines, she explained, were little shell-shaped cakes named for Mary Magdalene and a French word meaning "little girl."

"Which is far more than you need to know at present," she had added.

The only part of this sludge that interested me was that smells have a high speed and high priority railway to the brain: particularly those parts of it involved with memories and emotions.

And believe me, I had a surplus of those! I needed only to set them free.

I had rifled through a shelf of Mrs. Mullet's cookbooks, a few still bearing the stamp of Lady Rex-Wells's domestic library.

I had almost worn my fingers to the bone on these grease-spotted pages before I finally came across the recipe for madeleines. The secret ingredients were flour, sugar, baking soda, and either lemon juice or vanilla.

Eureka! Here comes chemistry to the rescue.

I knew from my own analysis of one of Mrs. Mullet's lemon pies that the essential oil in lemons is one of the most common terpenes, limonene. Lemons also contain eight of the chemical elements: sodium, calcium, potassium, magnesium, phosphorus, copper, iron, and zinc.

The lemon's shape is no accident: It is Mother Nature's hand grenade.

I remembered from my laboratory work that the very smell of lemons raised from the back of my brain scenes of polished furniture and floors, and of those uck-making pies.

I had not yet investigated vanilla. Alone in the

kitchen, and with the pantry at hand, there was no time like the present.

A few steps and I had in my hand a jar of sugar with vanilla pods embedded in the granules. I unscrewed the lid and held the jar to my nose.

I breathed in the scent, scooping the air toward my nostrils.

My legs quaked and trembled, baby-like. I had to sit down on a stool.

In in an instant, I was transported from the pantry to the Visto.

It was a warm summer's day, and I was bundled, too warmly dressed, into a hooded wicker pram. The sky overhead was a limitless blue.

A large red face blotted out the sun.

This was my very earliest memory.

"No tantrums from you," the red face said. It bore an uncanny resemblance to Aunt Felicity. A large spoon was being forced into my mouth, and on it was a disgusting white mess.

I tried to pull away. My head recoiled and hit a hard wooden backstop. I began to cry.

I would later learn that this horror, looking like a load of maggots, was Nesselrode pudding, speckled with pieces of pulverized chestnut like the dead flies on the white paper in a butcher-shop window.

And then Father's face appeared.

The wicker creaked alarmingly as the two of them bent over me, their faces like twin moons blooming, hiding the sky.

I looked from one of them to the other.

"She's dead," one of them said in a bare whisper. "You are now Asterion. The Nide has spoken."

I spat the unholy mess out of my mouth and onto my yellow wool jumper.

The memory ended there abruptly, like a needle knocked from a gramophone record by a clumsy dancer.

And yet the scene had remained seared into my soul: so private and so obscene that I had never told anyone— not even myself.

Who was the "she" they whispered about?

They could only have been referring to the death of my mother, Harriet.

But which of them had then become Asterion? Was it Father or Aunt Felicity?

And more to the point, with Father dead, who was *now* Asterion? Who was leading the powerful Nide?

Shaken, and with my head spinning, I pressed the vanilla pods deeper into their nest of sugar. *The jar of memories*, I thought, *ought to be labeled with a skull and crossbones.*

I needed some fresh air.

· F I V E ·

GLADYS WAS OVERJOYED TO see me. I could tell by the little squeak of delight she gave as I seized her handlebars. She frets when I'm too long at breakfast, eager to hit the open road.

The fresh air of the outdoors cleared my mind marvelously. I knew precisely what my next step ought to be. Why hadn't I thought of it before?

It wasn't more than a few minutes' ride to the home of our neighbor Maximilian Brock. Max was a retired concert pianist of what he called "diminished verticality." He had once confided in me that he was the president of the Royal Society of Dwarfs, but I wasn't sure whether to believe him. Max was, above all, mischievous.

I found him fiddling at the front door with a fistful of wires.

"*Haroo, haroo, mon prince*," he called out as I approached. "*On me fait tort!*"

This was Max's traditional greeting: the famous hue and cry, as raised by injured parties on the island of Alderney.

"I'm rerigging my doorbell," he explained as I drew nearer. "I've had Bach and I've had Mozart, but now, by Jove, it's time for something scintillating by Scriabin. One of the preludes, perhaps?"

He touched the ends of two wires together and from somewhere in the depths came the sound of a cascading piano passage. I recognized it at once as a piece that Feely had worked up. Max had tutored her in the keyboard arts until Feely called it off. "He's far too personal," she said. "Too *forte* in the fingering department, if you know what I mean."

I had appreciated Feely sharing this information, as it was a sign that I was growing up. Max had never been a pest with me, and now I needed information, which he had by the bushel basket.

Among his other accomplishments, he—or so it was said—had written lurid tales of love and betrayal for certain American confession magazines: "Lust in the Timberland," "I Was a Child Taxidermist," and so forth.

"It pays the bills," he had once told the vicar's wife, "and can be done in bed, unlike playing the piano." It was also the vicar's wife to whom he had confessed compiling a series of scrapbooks on judicial hangings.

"Justice must not only be done, and *seen* to be done,"

he had told her, "but documented in great detail as a deterrent to our young ones."

"And with that he laughed," she told me. "A most peculiar giggling laugh. I didn't know what to make of it."

"I need a favor, Max," I said. "I believe you once mentioned your collection of hanging scrapbooks."

"No, I didn't, dear girl. Not to you, at least."

"Can I have a squint anyway?" I asked. "I'm awfully keen on the scaffold, the gallows, and the drop—whatever you want to call them."

Better to be up-front about things.

"Delighted!" he said. "Come in and lock away the weary world."

I followed him into the depths.

"Investigating the death of Major Greyleigh, are you?" he asked over his shoulder as we navigated a zig-zagging series of alternating dark and white passages before stepping at last through an oak-paneled door and into a surprisingly sun-drenched library.

"Yes, but keep it under your hat, Max," I said.

"Wild horses," he said, drawing an imaginary zipper across his mouth. "Flaming toothpicks under finger-nails, cannibal snails in ear canals, that sort of thing. Safe with me.

"Now then," he said, turning and pointing to a wall of scrapbooks. "What do you think of that?"

There must have been scores of the things—possibly even hundreds: scrapbooks bound in linen and in oil-cloth, scrapbooks bound in cardboard and in leather,

each a different color, a panorama of Harlequin costumes with their lozenge-shaped labels, scrapbooks
bound in silk and sailcloth, in canvas and in crepe, in
taffeta and tinsel—scrapbooks bound in, for all I knew,
human skin, and all lovingly homemade.

I wanted to think something appropriately solemn
and noble at this moment; something I could remember
in my later years: "a National Gallery of the Gallows,"
perhaps.

But I was overwhelmed and disgraced myself.

I hissed through my teeth. "Hangings, Max?" I asked.
"All this?"

I gaped around the room and let out a second hiss.

Scraping bashfully at the carpet with a small pointed
shoe, Max stuck out his chin, almost defensively, then
pulled it in again. "It's just a hobby," he said. "A mere
hobby. Trifle heaped upon trifle, and so forth."

"It's magnificent!" I said. "I'd kill to have a library
like this."

"Some have," Max said, almost under his breath.

What did he mean by that? Surely Max hadn't—

"Were you acquainted with Major Greyleigh?" I asked.
It slipped out before I could stop it.

Surely a man of Max's tastes would have made the
acquaintance of the only public hangman for miles
around.

"No, I'm afraid I was not. Never had the pleasure."

"But you both attend—attended—St. Tancred's!"

"And so do you," Max said. "Odd, isn't it?" he went
on, picking delicately at an invisibly flawed fingernail.

"But one doesn't just go galloping up to strangers demanding all the dirty details, does one? At least not at the beginning."

"You first need to be introduced. Is that it?"

"Something like, yes. Rather like those two Englishmen in the play . . . but go ahead. Help yourself."

He made a sweeping gesture with his hand toward the rows of books.

"Dig in. I bestow upon you the freedom of the parish, as it were."

But where to begin? It was like being told to grab a handful of ocean.

"The volumes are arranged chronologically and alphabetically," Max said. "It takes a bit of getting used to. But once you've got the *hang* of it . . ."

He giggled. "You must forgive my enthusiasm," he said.

"Enthusiasm begs no forgiveness," I told him, quoting something Father had once said when criticized about his stamp collection.

Max beamed and turned away for a moment. I was astonished to realize he was close to tears.

He used the moment to fetch down a large apple-green volume. "Here's Hanley," he said. "As good a place as any to start."

He placed the scrapbook on a table and opened it gently. "Fragile," he said. "Old newspaper reminds us vividly how close we are to dust."

I was going to enjoy this. I could tell.

Max pointed to a grainy black-and-white photograph—

a newspaper clipping—of a man in a high-winged collar standing alone in the dock. Facing him, a judge in a white horsehair wig was raising a frozen finger.

"Percival Hanley," Max said. "Like so many others: a rainy night, a girl, a drink, a cruel laugh, a knife, a slash, a pool of blood. The old, old story."

I found myself gaping at the man in the yellowing photo who was so soon to become a corpse. There's something weirdly magnetic about knowing such a thing. It forms an instant and invisible bond: a secret kind of love—and perhaps even forgiveness.

I let out my breath slowly, already feeling the noose around my neck.

"And then," said Max, "the cuffs, the cell, the stony bread. The dock, the walk, and then the drop."

"The *treasured* drop," I said. "Stop it, Max. You're making my elbows cold."

And it was true. A creeping gooseflesh was already halfway to my armpits on its way to my neck. Such sudden insight could be handled only in small quantities.

"And look here," Max said quietly, turning a page to reveal a pleasant-looking portly gent stepping out of a rain-wet automobile and away from its shining nickel-plated radiator. His face was not smiling nor was it grim. He was just another face in the crowd. Just another pedestrian carrying a black case.

"The arrival of the hangman," Max said reverently. "The moment of truth . . . almost."

"Is that him?" I asked. "Major Greyleigh, I mean?"

"Yes."

I hugged myself and rubbed my shoulders.

"The rest of it carried out behind barred doors, of course," Max went on, his voice changing almost to a chant.

"Fortunately for us, there is one final shot. It was obtained by Freddie Leaper, an enterprising photographer from *News of the World,* by concealing a bulky press camera in an artificial hunchback made of wicker and strapped to his shoulders. He even went so far as to manufacture a built-up boot, which he dragged behind for sympathy *in a most pathetic manner*—or so it was said. I'm quoting now from his own newspaper. They covered the ensuing trial in astonishing detail and with even greater relish.

"*He pulled the wool over the eyes of the Law!* they wrote. *No one dared question him! Not even the governor!*"

"The photographer?" I asked. "The photographer was put on trial?"

"For dusting the dignity of the court," Max said. "Freddie was sentenced to nine months, I believe."

Max turned the page to reveal a large photo of black iron bars and bolts, and behind them a small and forbidding metal door.

Killer's last walk, the caption read in bold black letters.

"The bourne from which no traveler returns," Max intoned, "but in a wicker basket."

"Wicker seems to play an important role in the Dance of Death," I said, proud of having joined the game.

"A keen observation!" Max said. He was about to clap me on the back when he stopped.

"Is that it?" I asked. "The final photo? I don't see anything much."

"That blurry bundle of rags on the left," he said, "is the elbow of the condemned, Percival Hanley. His final public appearance."

"And the hangman?"

"A quick look at his handiwork for the record, then hustled out a back passageway in a news-seller's getup. Bundle of newspapers in his arms. Hard to spot. Gone before his subject's eyelids have stopped flickering. Another fine job. Money in the bank and a nice fishing trip in the offing. British justice."

"Wait a minute, Max," I said. "I'm British to the bone, but this stuff gives me the jimjams."

"It's meant to." Max grinned. "That's the way it works."

"Is it the same in every prison?"

"Pretty well," Max said. "Governments, and especially the judicial system, cling to cut-and-dried. The illusion of strict decency, you know."

"And what do you think, Max? Do you think it's decent?"

"Dear girl," he said. "Would I have given up so many hours of my short life"—he laughed extravagantly as he reached out to stroke the spine of a purple scrapbook—"to labor so with scissors and paste pot, if I didn't?"

He left a moist silence hanging in the air.

"Yes, well, then . . ." he said at last. "Do you want to see more?"

I gulped and admitted that I did.

And for the next couple of hours, I sat in silence as Max turned the pages of the scrapbooks, commenting briefly on a few and leaving the others for me to read by myself. Talk was unnecessary. Photos flew by in a numbing procession.

"That's Annie Embers," he said, pointing. "Poisoned her three children and died of heart failure on her way to the chamber. Cheated the law. Law not pleased. Steps taken. Behind closed doors, of course."

So, *this* was the world in which Major Greyleigh carried out his deadly duties. I could imagine him speaking softly to the condemned, gently holding the elbow of Annie Embers to make sure she didn't trip and injure herself.

Max turned another page, and here were photos of an actual noose, with printed arrows pointing to the splice and eyelet, and a typed table of the required fatal drop lengths based upon the prisoner's weight.

And then there was the trolley, a stout businesslike cart to receive the body of the condemned once it was removed from the grip of the noose. It looked like the carts you see in Covent Garden for apples or potatoes.

"The Tram to Morgue Street," Max said in a quiet voice. I noticed that he was watching me closely. He had stopped turning the pages.

"Yes," I said. I was not going to play at this private game of his, whatever it was.

"Look, Max," I said, "I have to go."

He nodded sadly—or did I imagine the sadness?

He walked me to the front door and held it open for me ceremoniously.

I stepped outside, then turned back to face him. "I expect you'll be adding Major Greyleigh to your cuttings," I said.

"Yes—I expect I will," Max said after a long pause. "Listen, Flavia—" he added suddenly.

I realized I had been standing there nibbling at a hangnail.

"Yes?"

"Look after yourself," he said as he closed the door, as if barricading himself against some evil lurking in the forecourt.

How ridiculous, I thought as I seized Gladys by the handlebars and pushed off homeward. Who else was there to look after me? I was an orphan with two remote and glacial sisters, and an aunt who seemed to live on another planet. Aunt Felicity was an odd old bird who flew aeroplanes and hinted at a vast correspondence with some obscure and secret masters.

"For all we know, she might be a theosophist," Daffy had once said. But whatever she was, Aunt Felicity ruled whatever roost she happened to find herself in.

I could speak of none of this, of course, even if my tongue were burning. There are secret obligations thrust upon us all, but none more than those we are forced to grow into.

They are like awakening from a dream in quicksand. Who could possibly throw you a rope?

The answer came in a flash. Dogger!

Dogger, of course, my shield and protector.

"Gladys," I said, when I got to the gate, "make haste, and don't spare the old gutta-percha." Gladys knew what I meant.

· S I X ·

IF THERE IS ONE place on earth where I am truly at home, besides my laboratory, it is sitting on an upturned bucket in the greenhouse at Buckshaw. It is here that Dogger and I solve the problems of the universe. It is a place of safety where we can speak freely, and with no danger of being overheard.

Facing each other, we have a three-hundred-and-sixty-degree view of the approaches; no one can catch us unawares. No one can eavesdrop on our deliberations.

"Did you have a productive outing, Miss Flavia?" he asked.

"I did," I said. I needed to warm up to this conversation slowly: to collect my thoughts. "I went to Max's house. Did you guess where I was?"

"Guesses are for amateurs, Miss Flavia," Dogger said with a slight smile.

"I'm sorry," I said. "I take it back."

"No need to do that. Friendship, I believe, transcends the odd banana peel."

I felt warm all over. "Go ahead, tell me how you knew," I said, giving him an especially generous smile.

"You have that slightly electric look about you as if you have been in conversation with Mr. Brock. It's quite unmistakable."

"Really? It's that obvious?"

"To me it is," Dogger said. "Besides, he is the only person I'm aware of with a library on judicial hangings. I should have been disappointed in you if you hadn't paid him a visit."

"You flatter me, Dogger."

"No, I don't, Miss Flavia. I merely state the obvious."

"Tea?" I asked. We kept an old enamel teapot on an electric hotplate for those days—especially rainy ones—when we felt like a sip and a chin-wag.

"The making of a pot of tea is a blessing," Father once told me in a rare moment of revealing his thoughts. "A blessing upon both the one who prepares it and those who drink it. A small sacrament, to be sure, but it must never be done frivolously or unthinkingly."

Father and Dogger had both partaken in solemn tea ceremonies while in captivity during the war, and although they never spoke of it, you could tell by the way they handled their cups and saucers that it was a kind of communion: a matter of life and death combined.

"It's like lending a book, isn't it, Father?" Daffy had asked, breaking the spell.

"Precisely, Daphne," Father had told her, and I saw her begin to glow with a new, raw pride.

Oh, how I missed him. It was a kind of ache that cannot be put into words.

"I feel as if we're going round in circles," I said to Dogger. "We haven't even seen the victim. We haven't access to the evidence except a quarter teaspoon of splatter and some dolls. We're working at a great disadvantage."

"Do you think so?" Dogger asked. "The days of village crimes being solved by dotty old ladies on tricycles are almost over, save for the occasional Agatha Christie at Christmas. The man in a white lab coat with a microscope is the new Sir Lancelot. Science has overthrown both native wit and the tingle of spinster intuition, so that you are, Miss de Luce, as the Americans say, 'sitting in the catbird seat.'"

"Do you really think so, Dogger? If that's true, drawbacks have become doorways. But perhaps I was reasoning ahead of the facts. Didn't Sherlock Holmes warn against that?"

"'It is a capital mistake to theorize in advance of the facts,'" Dogger quoted. "'The Adventure of the Second Stain.'"

"Do you read Sherlock Holmes, Dogger?"

"Of course," he said. "Doesn't everyone?"

The tea had done its work and we were now in that warm, companionable state that others seek at church: bliss and brains—an unbeatable combination.

In the church, the graveyard provides the background aroma of earth. I have often thought that all great detectives ought to have their office in a church-yard since the smell of the decaying dead is so much more stimulating than that of cigarettes and coffee.

In the greenhouse, of course, we have the potting tables to provide that stimulus. No wonder God created us in a garden! I'd bet a shilling that it was actually in a greenhouse but was crossed out by our Bible's early editors as too posh.

"We'll not be able to manage a look at the remains of Major Greyleigh," Dogger said, pursuing his own line of thoughts. "Nor will we have access to the pathologist's report. The major will be put on ice and parked there until it pleases Her Majesty. I suggest that your best line of pursuit lies much closer to home."

"Mrs. Mullet!" I'm afraid I shouted.

"Just so," said Dogger.

"Come along, Mrs. M," I said heartily, rushing into the kitchen at speed to create an impression of determination. "I hereby free you from your bonds. It's Girls' Day Out. The monstrous regiment of women is about to march!"

"I've work to do," she said, pushing a pail of water across the floor with a mop. "Mind your feet."

I could see that she was determined, so I did the only thing I could think of: I got down on my knees and began wringing my hands.

"Oh beautiful maiden," I said in what I thought was

a princely voice, "oh charming girl, oh lovely one, oh marvel of unequaled beauty, come with me to the church, where we shall be wed, and raise a flock of children with green hair and amber eyes."

"Get away with you," she said. "You're in the way of my mop. Church indeed," she sniffed.

"Well, that part's true," I said. "The Cluck and Grumble is today. I was hoping to do a spot of the old cloak-and-dagger. You know—pump the ladies of the parish about Major Greyleigh. I could use your skills."

I saw her eyes begin to light—and then to fade.

"You want to pump *me*, you mean."

She said this with a slight smile to show that she wasn't being impertinent, and that there were no hard feelings.

The vicar was the only male allowed at the Cluck and Grumble, and then only for ten minutes, during which he sipped his tea from a Spode cup adorned with angels and strawberries, before making his excuses and escaping. Once he was gone, the ladies got down to it with a vengeance, and there were no holds barred. Rich picking grounds for a little pitcher with big ears and acute hearing such as mine.

"No . . . no . . . I promise, Mrs. M, no questions. Cross my heart and hope to die."

I faked a few magical gestures and kissed both my thumbs.

"Well, all right," she said. "But no monkeyshines, mind."

*

The sunshine had returned as we walked toward the village, although to the east, rain still slanted down over the hills in that way once described as "like pencil lead."

"I'm worried about our young Undine," Mrs. Mullet said out of nowhere.

"In what way, Mrs. M?" I asked.

"She's 'angin' about with a bad lot. She needs to be taken in 'and."

Mrs. Mullet was never one to beat about the bush.

"By whom?" I said, and the moment the words slipped my lips I regretted them.

"By you, for one," she said. "She needs more of a big sister, like."

"Well, she has Daffy," I said, not very convincingly.

"Miss Daphne's goin' up to Oxford. She already 'as 'er papers filled out. The vicar's putting in a word for 'er."

"What!"

"It's true," Mrs. Mullet said. "She's goin' to read English and teach somewhere swanky, she says."

I couldn't believe my ears. Why hadn't I been informed? Why couldn't my own sister have told me first?

"Well, she might not go, after all," Mrs. Mullet went on. "'I 'ave three strikes against me,' she told me. 'My religion, my wantin' formal eddication, and bein' the sister of Flavia de Luce.' I'm sure she was jokin', but that's what she said, dear."

Daffy? Joking? When senses of humor were being handed out, my sister had been standing at the tail end of the queue with her snout stuck in a copy of *Paradise Lost*.

I was about to spit in the dirt when I realized that the last item—the one about being my sister—was a compliment. The fact that Daffy acknowledged living in my shadow should have given me an inner glow, and it almost did.

Mrs. Mullet had slowly swiveled her face toward me, not saying anything, like a gigantic toad.

"Well, you know what I mean," I conceded. "Daffy and I are both still here. We share the same blood."

"Blood don't count. You 'ave to care."

Her words hurt because they were practically true. As I have said, I loved Undine, but not in any useful way. My love was remote and nearly mythical: like the king's daughter in a fairy tale.

Mrs. Mullet went on. "She needs someone to teach 'er to clean 'er teeth, to wash 'er 'ands and 'air, like. She needs someone to get 'er into the Girl Guides: somebody who can teach 'er to start a campfire and not to whistle in church."

"She seems quite fond of Carl Pendracka," I said.

"Pfffssshhh! 'E's an American," she scoffed.

"Nothing wrong with that. The Americans are on our side, especially the ones at Leathcote. They're more like neighbors."

"But he's also a man," she said, and there was no arguing with that. "I've tried to do my bit, God knows. I've took 'er to the cinema in Hinley. Thought she'd enjoy some of them Gene Artery and Roy Rochester pictures. Teach 'er to know good from bad. You can tell 'oo's good and 'oo's bad in the pictures by the color of their 'ats and 'orses. The good 'uns get the white and the bad 'uns get the black."

"I'll never forget that, Mrs. M. And she came home whistling 'My Adobe Hacienda' through her teeth. It went on for weeks. Everywhere. Day and night. Maddening."

"That's what I was talkin' about," she said.

"I'll have a chat with Carl," I promised. "I'll remind him that Undine's a very impressionable child. I'll ask him to take care what he puts into her head."

We strolled in silence for a minute. A pair of robins hopped up and down in a hedgerow as if they were playing a rowdy game of Snakes and Ladders. If they could have such courage, why shouldn't I?

"Mrs. M," I said, "why do I have the feeling that you're keeping something from me?"

Did I see her blanch?

She stopped walking; lifted a foot and pretended to examine an imaginary stone stuck in the sole of her shoe.

"About what?" she asked.

"About Moonflower Cottage. About the death of Major Greyleigh."

Had I fancied it, or did she breathe an enormous sigh of relief?

"Ah," she said.

We walked on in silence for another full minute. I kept quiet to allow her to gather her thoughts.

And then she spoke: "I might as well tell you. I've

known Tommy Greyleigh since I was in pinafores," she said. "'E took me to the promenades when I was just a girl."

It was as if she had seized her own face and ripped it away, revealing an unsuspected stranger beneath the skin. Who was she, really? I had always taken Mrs. M for little more than a kitchen appliance. How wrong— how very wrong I had been, and how stupid.

My mouth must have made an enormous O.

"It's true. 'E bought me a gardenia and a nice stick o' Blackpool rock. 'Land of 'Ope and Glory,' the band played. Them days is gone."

I nodded like a bobbing bird. I didn't want to break the spell.

"Later, I used to see 'im in the papers. Whenever 'e did, you know, a big job. I knew well enough 'e was an 'angman. Once, I wondered if 'e ever thought o' me when 'e was turnin' off one of them poisonin' wives 'e used to do away with. Oh! I oughtn't to 'ave said that."

"It's all right, Mrs. M," I said, touching her arm. "I'd have thought the same thing. This is fascinating. Do go on."

"Well, when 'e retired an' moved to Bishop's Lacey, I ran smack into 'im one day in the butcher's shop. Knew me right away, 'e did. Called me by my name straight-away. ''Ullo, Meg,' 'e said. 'E's the only one as ever called me Meg. Even Alf 'as always called me Margaret. 'Fancy meetin' you 'ere,' 'e said. 'E called me by my old name, of course, not my married name, cause 'e didn't know that, did 'e?

"We got to talkin', mostly about old times, and then 'e said as 'ow 'e'd just bought Moonflower Cottage and was lookin' for someone to do a bit of light cookin'.

"Well, I told 'im as 'ow—what with your father—sorry, Miss Flavia—and now Miss Ophelia bein' gone and married, I wasn't as busy as I used to be—"

"It's all right, Mrs. M," I told her. "You're perfectly free to make whatever arrangements you like. It's your life, after all."

She swung her head slowly round and looked me in the eye. "Yes," she said. "Yes, I s'pose it is."

"And so, you agreed to cook for him."

"Just breakfasts," Mrs. Mullet said. "No more than breakfasts."

"And what did Alf think about that?"

Mrs. Mullet flushed and wiped at a couple of loose strands of hair that had somehow escaped her brushed neatness. "Alf never knew nothing 'bout it," she whispered. " 'E'd of been outside hisself."

"So that's the secret you've been keeping," I said.

She nodded eagerly, and I accepted eagerly.

"But I understand why you didn't want to tell me," I said. "It must have been a shock to run into him like that."

Mrs. Mullet seemed suddenly somehow lighter. After being reined in for so many years, something had been loosed.

"We 'ad some lovely mornin's," she went on. " 'E told me of 'is younger years, after I flew out of 'is life. That's 'ow 'e put it: 'You flew out of my life,' 'e said, 'like a bird of paradise.'

"We both laughed at that. 'E met a lovely girl called Marguerite. Almost the same name as me, but in French. It means 'a pearl.'"

I registered surprise, as if I didn't already know that fact. I had once dissolved my mother's pearls during a scandalous—but informative—chemical experiment. Pearls and I were old acquaintances.

Mrs. Mullet went on: "Marguerite was the daughter of a painter in Primrose 'Ill. Sounds too pretty to be true, doesn't it? But it was. She was so beautiful she sucked all the light out of the room and made it come back out of 'er face and 'er 'air. 'Er father painted 'er as Guinevere—King Arthur's wife, you know? 'Er face was so famous she used to get stopped in 'Arrods and asked to sign people's shoppin' bags.

"'E courted 'er for seven years, till she was twenty-four. 'Er father was against it. Said 'e was no more than a common tobacconist, which was true enough at the time. But 'e 'ad given 'er 'is 'eart, and 'e couldn't take it back. 'E wanted to elope, but she was dead set against it. Said 'er father would 'ave 'er 'unted down and killed. Artists are like that. So 'e did the honorable thing and asked 'er father to go for a drink with 'im. Told 'im 'e was putting in 'is name for 'angman, and if 'e succeeded, why 'e'd be sittin' pretty, and would the father allow 'im to 'ave 'is daughter's 'and?"

"It's like *The Arabian Nights*, isn't it?" I said, wishing that life could always be like this. "And did he?"

"'Er father was dead set against murder. Believed murderers should be put to death. Said that 'angman was a noble calling, and all that. Said that if Tommy got the job, 'e'd foot the weddin' bill hisself."

I breathed out heavily. My frail body was not designed for drama like this. I could feel my heart accelerating.

"Go on!" I said. "Please!"

"Well, 'e got the job right enough. Took a apprenticeship from a cabinetmaker in the trade. 'Elped out with a couple of 'angin's in 'is spare time, studied all the lengths and weights—ropes and bodies, that is—and finally got the all clear from the 'Ome Office to go out and do it on 'is own.

"And the father kept 'is word. 'E built them a nice 'ouse in Battersea. Weddin' in 'Anover Square and an 'oneymoon abroad. Night train to Dover and on to Paris. Suite at Claridge's."

She stopped abruptly, and I noticed a tear forming in her left eye, immediately followed by another in the right.

"She was so beautiful," she said. "Beautiful," she whispered. "'E showed me a picture of 'er once."

"What is it, Mrs. M?" I asked. Was it merely sentimentality that made her weep?

She shook her head and took a shuddering breath. "When 'e woke up in the mornin' on the first day of their 'oneymoon, she was stone-cold dead in bed right there beside 'im. The most beautiful creature in the world."

"I'm sorry," I said. What else could one say?

Even secondhand, this was the most awful thing I had ever heard. I wanted to cry myself.

"'E never married again. 'E lived in that 'ouse in Battersea till the day 'e retired. The Battersea 'Angman, they called him."

"Yes," I said. "I've seen it in the old newspapers."

"'E was famous," Mrs. Mullet said, "an 'e was a lovely man, in spite of what 'e done. 'You're gentle and you're tender-'earted,' I told him. 'Yes,' 'e says, 'I believe I am.' As if 'e'd never thought of it before. So, when I found 'im dead—"

"You found him dead?" I asked. "*You* found him dead?"

"Yes, I did."

"Why didn't you tell me?" I said, too loudly, with exasperation in my voice.

"Alf," she said simply.

Ah, yes. Alf. The jealous husband.

"I should 'ave run 'ome and got 'im. Alf always knows what to do. But I didn't. And then it was too late."

"So, what did you do? When you found his body, I mean."

"Well, I checked that 'e was dead. I'd seen this 'appen before, remember, at Lady Rex-Wells's. Didn't want to make the same mistake again."

"And then?" I asked, hardly daring to breathe.

"I took out my notebook—where I keeps my grocery lists—an' my pencil, and I made a few sketches."

"*Sketches?*" I almost ruptured my vocal cords.

"They aren't much to look at," she said. "I've been takin' them Tuesday classes at the Buttercross. Drawin' from Life. Alf says it beefs up your brain to study coordination of the 'and and eye. Would you like to see them?"

Would I?! My imagination was positively slavering.

"Yes . . . please. If you don't mind." I had suddenly gone all polite and formal.

"I'll show you them sometime," she said.

I had to bite my tongue.

What was she holding back? Surely, she must have left Major Greyleigh at his breakfast of mushrooms and then returned to find him dead. But why? She said she ought to have rushed home and told Alf, but she hadn't. Where had she gone? Where had she been in the meantime?

"Mrs. M," I said, "I think we ought to—"

But by now we were at the church, and even from the road I could hear the hum of daggers from inside the parish hall. Character assassination is not a particularly silent art, and the ladies of St. Tancred's were masters whose murmurs and hissing tones drifted out to escape in the churchyard.

"*Dear* Mrs. Mullet!"

It was Elaine Chicory, of course.

"I said as soon as I heard, it wasn't her, didn't I, Delvina?"

"*Poor* you! *How* could you *bear* it?"

Delvina Patt had joined in.

Mrs. Mullet put on a face of hardship lightly borne.

She distributed a wan smile to the entire room before plowing her way through the crowd to the tea bowser.

"She's a rock," Delvina said. "Isn't she a rock? A fortress in a sea of evil."

Why, I wondered, *do people always drag out the oldest clichés first?*

"And she's one of us, isn't she?" I added, knowing full well that my words would be repeated again and again, which would do me no harm among the ladies of the Cluck and Grumble. My name among them would be Golden, which just happens to be one translation of the name Flavia.

Life's a game, isn't it?

I stared studiously up at the ceiling; because nobody talks to you when you're staring at the ceiling, it's a useful pose for listening intently.

"That old basket of bones," Mrs. Parmelee was saying. "And a mouth on her like Pinocchio's whale."

"But in her case," Miss Goody replied with a smirk, "there's no fire inside."

They both giggled shamelessly. No point in further eavesdropping: This was garden-variety gossip; a waste of time on both our parts.

From my left came a whisper. I heard the word "police." This was more like it.

"Police," someone was saying. I shifted my head as if for a better view of the ceiling, but the better to aim my ear. I raised one hand to form a listening cup, pretending to scratch my scalp in puzzlement.

"They called round her house and gave her a good

grilling. She was one of the last to see him alive—apart from—"

I could see from the corner of my eye that she jerked her head toward Mrs. Mullet, who was still getting her tea to her taste. Four scant teaspoons of sugar and just the barest ooze of milk.

It was Laura Candy speaking. I could recognize her voice even when she whispered, due to her adenoids. Laura and I had a history that extended back to vengeance within the Altar Guild, a history of which I was not particularly proud.

"She picked him mushrooms just after daybreak. Probably didn't want to be spotted."

"Did she have designs on him?" another voice whispered. "A fungal flirtation?"

They both giggled nastily.

"Oh, no . . . he's not—wasn't—inclined that way at all."

They both giggled again and changed the topic to hairdressers and their quirks.

"Mine's in South Kensington. Very posh. She came from California and did Joan Crawford. Did James Mason once, and he tipped her fifty pounds. In banknotes! Fifty pounds! In California! Fancy!"

I remembered a theory once stated by Philip Odell, the fictional detective on the BBC wireless series, that in times of crisis, people are compelled to speak about the incident, but deflect their words instead into other, and sometimes more curious, channels. Even though

Philip was fictional, he was often right, and I had on more than one occasion taken his advice.

"Flavia!"

It was Cynthia Richardson, the vicar's wife.

"How good to see you, but whatever are you doing here?"

"I came with Mrs. Mullet," I said, lowering my voice. "You know . . . moral support."

"Oh dear, yes," Cynthia said. "She does soldier on, doesn't she, just when she ought to be soldiering off."

"Well, actually," I said, "I brought *her*. I thought she needed a break."

"So considerate." Cynthia smiled, not because she thought so, but because she was married to a vicar.

"Actually, I was hoping for a scoop," I said. I had discovered that disarming frankness succeeds where fine words fail.

"Oh dear—yes," Cynthia said, looking round. She had taken my meaning instantly.

"What have you heard?" I asked, before she could mount any defense. The art of being a vicar's wife is learning to pick other people's brains, rather than your own. Because of that, vicars' wives know things that would make your hair curl, but you had to be quick-witted and strike while the iron was hot.

"Well, I . . ."

"Out with it, Cynthia," I said, with a light chuckle and a cheeky grin.

"Well . . ."

"*Cynthia!*" a voice boomed at our elbows.

It was Elaine Chicory. Who else?

"This *shocking murder*," Elaine hissed. "*Surely* you . . ."

Her tone was loud but confidential, and she glared round as if to make us all feel like eavesdroppers.

"I'm afraid I must fly," Cynthia said. "The parish leaflets are due today and the mimeograph's gone bust again. It's back to that dirty old jellygraph, I suppose. I shall need a jolly good percolation in the bubble bath."

She cast down her eyes in modesty. The very idea of a vicar's wife steeping in a bubble bath was enough to make a horse blush, and Cynthia knew it.

"Ta-ta, Flavia," she said. "Lovely to see you. We shall catch up later."

And with that she was gone.

Had she given me an invitation, or was she practicing her skilled evasion techniques?

"She's tinting her hair," Mrs. Parmelee said. "Looks like a wet dog hung on a clotheshorse."

Mrs. Mullet, meanwhile, appeared to be meditating Buddha-like beside the tea urn. Everyone seemed too shy to approach her. Although they suspected she was innocent of Major Greyleigh's murder, they had become suddenly reluctant to be seen too close to a person who had been fingered by the police—even briefly.

I knew that she had transformed herself into a listening post, and that not a word spoken in the room had escaped her elephantine ears. Not that they were larger than anyone else's; the difference was in the way she used them. When it came to gossip and the gathering of it, Mrs. Mullet could have sunk that little tittle-tattle William Connor, who calls himself Cassandra in *News of the World.*

Not to insist too much, but Mrs. Mullet's ears ought to have been a military secret.

One of her greatest assets was the ability to look, even at a distance, as if she were thinking about tea, which was what she was doing now. Even as our eyes met, she gave not the slightest flicker of recognition, as if her entire being—her whole soul—were focusing intently on the inner workings of the tea-making mechanism and its proper place in the Christian church.

It was a lovely performance and a pleasure to watch.

I quickly scanned the hall, looking for possible fruitful conversations. Most of the women had clustered in groups of three and four, and all appeared to be smiling. Murder would not be the topic of such cheerful chatter.

In the far corner sat an old woman on a wooden pew: a relic of the Sunday School furnishings that were being replaced gradually by ghastly plastic chairs. It was Mrs. Skinnett, who had once, in another era, been confidential secretary to the president of one of the major motorcar companies, or so it was said.

She was the very picture of placid contentment, obviously intent on her own inner world. She looked neither to the right nor the left, but stared, unfocused, straight ahead into her world of memories.

I picked up a cup of tea from the trestle table and sat down beside her.

"Tea, Mrs. Skinnett?"

She did not reply immediately. As I waited, I noticed a bulky Bakelite box hanging round her neck from a lanyard, from which wires or tubes ran upward to her ears.

Of course! Mrs. Skinnett was profoundly deaf: victim of a bomb blast in a London volunteer canteen during an air raid.

She suddenly turned and smiled up at me. "Thank you, dear," she said. "How thoughtful. Mmmm."

I perched dutifully beside her on the edge of the pew, looking ready to spring into action at her slightest wish.

"You're one of the de Luce girls, aren't you?" she asked.

"I'm Flavia, the youngest," I told her.

Mrs. Skinnett pointed her free forefinger at the marbled box hanging on her breastbone. "Speak into this thing," she said. "I'm a little hard of hearing. Rodney rigged this up for me. My nephew. He's in Signals, you know. Clever with electrical gadgets."

"I'm Flavia, the youngest," I repeated, louder and closer to the metal grille of the device.

Mrs. Skinnett nodded. "You're famous, you know," she said. "I heard all about you and that business with the postage stamps. They say King George himself came down to Buckshaw to thank you, though I don't believe everything I hear."

"Very wise, Mrs. Skinnett," I said, "and nor do I."

Dogger had told me that one does not repeat what a king has said to you, nor is it in good taste to repeat what one has said to a king.

Mrs. Skinnett went on. "When William and Matthew died, as they say, 'for King and country'—they were in the RAF, the two of them—I was told at first they'd both gone down in the Channel, but that turned out to be untrue. I prayed they hadn't, but then I prayed they had."

Everyone in Bishop's Lacey and far beyond had heard about the Skinnett boys: separated because they were brothers and posted to two different squadrons as a safety measure, and yet, against all the odds, shot down at the same time on the same day during the same raid on an enemy airfield in France.

I put my hand on the back of hers. "They will never be forgotten, Mrs. Skinnett," I said. "They are legends."

"I know they are, dear. You don't have to tell me."

I looked into her faded blue eyes and recoiled almost physically. I had to brace myself. Their depths were indescribable: beyond compare.

In her eyes were other worlds and other times. The past was still alive in her! I could see it!

In those pale blue irises were births, deaths, and loves; successes and failures; tragedies and comedies; and, yes, hates. I had never seen anything like it, and in a way, I hoped I never would again.

It was a kind of nakedness I could not yet understand.

The nakedness of age.

"Murder is all they want to talk about," she said suddenly. "Look at them."

She raised a veined, unsteady hand to indicate the ladies in the hall.

"I can hear them," she said. "At least some of them. Rodney wired in some kind of superheterodyne circuit that amplifies certain frequencies of the human voice. It cuts in and out. In wet weather I get the BBC Overseas Service and the occasional police call. The static is often merciless, but you'd be surprised at what I sometimes hear."

"I'll bet I wouldn't." I grinned. "I have acute hearing myself."

She patted my hand and looked me straight in the eye. The years dropped away and she was instantly the same age as me.

"This Greyleigh business," she said. "Nasty. I picked up a call on my hearing apparatus, you know, at about the time the major died."

I had to wait until my heart settled.

"It must have been close by for you to hear it," I said. Mrs. Skinnett lived at The Laurels, just to the west of St. Tancred's. Probably less than two hundred yards.

"That's what I thought," she said. "It was quite clear. No static. A man's voice. 'Lima Charlie Bravo returning.'"

I remembered my brief wireless training at Miss Bodycote's Female Academy.

And I knew that Lima stood for *L*, Charlie for *C*, and Bravo for *B*. Could *LC* stand for Leathcote? It was certainly possible. And *B* for Base?

So someone from Leathcote may well have been at the scene of the crime. Perhaps even Asterion, the resident Mister Big Britches at Leathcote, was involved in the major's death.

My head was spinning.

"Sorry, Mrs. Skinnett," I said. "One of my ears plugged. Wax."

I gave it a vigorous reaming out with my little finger to reinforce the fib. "Now, what were you saying?"

"The voice seemed oddly familiar. Someone I've met before. Couldn't quite place it. Oh, well . . ." Mrs. Skinnett gave my knuckles a sudden squeeze. "Over there, look: Ursula Grimsdyke and Nancy Poe. They're talking about your Mrs. Mullet."

She saw my eyes widen.

"She says she saw the Mullet woman talking outside Moonflower Cottage with someone else—a man in uniform—not long before Major Greyleigh's body was discovered."

"Who was it? Did she say?"

Mrs. Skinnett fiddled with a knob on the side of her listening device. "Superheterodyne regenerative feedback control. Raises the 'Q' of the resonant circuit, Rodney says, but also narrows the bandwidth and increases the risk of feedback, in proportion."

She gave the knob another hopeful twist, then wrinkled her face. "Sorry, dear. I'm no good with the electrical impulses."

"It's been lovely speaking with you, Mrs. Skinnett. We must talk again sometime."

She wasn't letting go of my hand. Her grip was firm.

Again, I looked into her remarkable eyes, but only for an instant.

"If you don't mind my saying so," I said softly into her apparatus, "you're very beautiful."

"Yes," she said.

Feeling for a moment as if I were a ballet dancer, I walked almost on tiptoe an invisible tightrope toward the tea urn and Mrs. Mullet.

"Got the goods?" I asked out of the corner of my mouth.

She smiled. "Yes, dear," she said.

My ears were already itching in anticipation. We could natter happily all the way back across the fields to Buckshaw.

"I've got to go 'ome, dear," Mrs. Mullet said suddenly when we were outside. "Today's our anniversary, and Alf gets in an awful 'uff if I don't make 'im a suet pudding. 'I do fancy a suet pudding,' 'e always says, an' I know 'e means 'e 'asn't forgot our anniversary. But *I* forgot with all this . . ." She waved a forefinger in a circle, trying to bring a word to mind. "Hurley-scurry," she said at last, looking proud of herself. "I shall see you later."

And with that she walked off.

"But Mrs. M," I called after her, "what about—"

"Later," she called back over her shoulder. Such determination in a single word! It was almost a barked command, and it froze me on the spot.

I was standing there dripping with cold disappointment when I heard the whine of a motor, and an excited *toot-toot-toot* of a horn. I spun round just in time to see a jeep coming directly at me, its occupants waving their hands madly and shouting words I could not hear above the roar of the engine.

I leaped not-very-gazelle-like to one side, and as the jeep shot past, I had a quick impression of bare toes wrapped round the steering wheel. Someone was driving the thing with his feet!

Before I could make sense of the scene, the jeep shot into the opening of the lych-gate, where it came to a grinding stop. With its heavy old timbers, the gate was too sturdy and too narrow for the jeep to pass through. Steam began jetting from beneath the bonnet, and a cloud of ancient dust rose up before settling on the lych-gate.

Ashes of ancestors, I thought.

The driver was Carl Pendracka, who still sat gripping the wheel with his bare feet and a look of amazement on his face. His knees were folded up under his chin like a defective penknife. How he had managed to get into that position boggled my mind. I did not recognize his passengers.

"Flavia!" Carl called out, followed by a loud wolf whistle. "Where's your Sunday bonnet?"

I ignored him.

Also, I had become suddenly shy. There were two strangers in the jeep with Carl: two American servicemen in fatigues, both of them good-looking in various ways.

"This here's Eugene Cobb," Carl said. "But we call him Jeep after Eugene, the Jeep in *Popeye*. Jeep's teaching me to drive Texas-style And this here creature in the back is Rinso White. Rinso's from Rochester, New York, U.S. of A. Rochester's where Kodak calls home. You know . . . Kodak? Cameras? Rinso used to work there in the summers when he was a schoolboy, didn't you, Rinso? Used to take the girlies into the darkroom to see what would develop."

Rinso grinned modestly from ear to ear, as if it were true.

"You know why they called it Kodak?" Carl went on. " 'Cause that's the noise the shutter makes when you take a snap."

He made a clicking sound with his tongue: "*Kloclack* . . . *Kloclack* . . . *Kloclack.*"

To accent his sound effects, he reached over and tooted the jeep's comical little horn.

Poop-poop-poop!

It's a pity, I thought, *that Undine isn't here to enjoy it.*

He kept on doing this, still seated in the jeep as casually as if they had not just collided headlong with the property of the Church of England.

"Why would you want to drive Texas-style?" I asked. "You're in England."

"Commando tactics." Carl grinned. "Never know when you're going to have to escape from some moated old castle in a straitjacket. Isn't that right, Jeep?"

Jeep turned slowly in his seat and regarded Carl as if he'd never seen him before.

"If you say so," he said.

"Jeep's what we call laconic. That means he's a man of few words. Aren't you, Jeep?"

"If you say so," Jeep said.

Carl laughed. "See what I mean? But it's okay. Loquaciousness is frowned upon in the military. Isn't it, Jeep?"

"If you say so," Jeep said.

Carl cackled. "I get such a kick out of him," he said. "Eugene's from the Ozarks: the mountains. Shot squirrels with slingshots, bows and arrows, and Springfield rifles. Natural-born killer, aren't you, Jeep?"

I waited for Jeep's inevitable reply, but it didn't come. His attention had drifted away to somewhere on the other side of the churchyard.

"Where's your old friend Mordecai?" I asked. Mordecai had been Carl's shadow: a whispering know-it-all who always insinuated himself to be an overflowing fountain of inside information.

"Went AWOL," Carl said. "Cashiered. Sent off. Rode the painted pony into the sunset. Jeep's his replacement in certain respects, but not all. With Mordecai gone, I'm the brains of the outfit now—the Human Encyclopedia."

"So I've heard," I said.

"Ask me a question," Carl said. "Anything. Go ahead. Try me."

It was an old parlor trick, and I had used it myself. If the person asks a question you can't answer, make one up that they can't possibly check.

"What's the temperature, in centigrade, of the seventh circle of Hell?"

Carl scratched his head. "Beats me," he said. "What is it?"

"One hundred and seventy degrees," I said. I didn't just pick this number out of thin air: It was the melting point of cyanide, one of my greatest enthusiasms.

"Well, I'll be dog-washed," Carl said. "I never knew that. I'll have to add it to my repertory. Ask me another."

I don't know to this day where the inspiration came from. I can only guess that it sprang from saxitoxin: the fact that saxitoxin came from butter clams, which are prevalent, as is the United States Army Air Force, in the Pacific Northwest regions of the North American continent, such as Alaska.

Stripped to its essence, my thought was this: Where had the fatal saxitoxin come from? How had it made its way to Bishop's Lacey?

"What do you do at Leathcote?" I asked. "The war has been over for donkey's. Most of you Americans have gone home, but I still see the bombers come and go."

Carl scratched his nose busily, and I knew instantly that he knew something he didn't want to tell.

"Well," he said, "we've got a couple of hundred acres of war surplus that we don't want to bother carting home. You know: warehouses full of chewin' gum, cigarettes, K rations, potatoes, boots, helmets, grits, greatcoats, beans, beer, banjos . . ." He grinned.

"And you sell them to the highest bidder," I guessed, half laughing.

Carl's heart stopped. I could see it in his face. For just an instant his eyes went dead, and the blood rose in his cheeks.

"Oh, it's big stuff, too," he said, forcing a half-hearted laugh. "Airplanes, tractors, trucks, bulldozers. Not much call for the likes of *them* at the village pub."

"I suppose not," I said. "You'd have to sell them overseas."

Again, Carl went into a sudden brain freeze, as if he'd been hit in the middle of his forehead by a firework.

I'd had enough. Carl knew more than he was telling, and the planes that came and went at Leathcote were not all carrying soothers to orphans.

Time to change the subject. I put on a smarmy smile that meant nothing. "What brings you boys to Bishop's Lacey?"

"We call ourselves Five-in-a-Jeep," Carl said. "Kind of like Enid Blyton, but older and with tobacco and petrol. And wilder."

He gave a low growl that ended in a bark.

"But there are only three of you," I pointed out.

"Yeah, well, nobody's perfect," he said, swiveling round in his seat to see if his pals were appreciating his witty repartee. "Besides, the extra two are metaphorical."

"Oh, go soak your head," I told him. I wasn't expecting the light round of applause from the back seat, which left me nothing to do but spin on my heel and walk away, like a music hall comic leaving 'em wanting more.

"Hey, little lady," Carl called. "Don't get your frock in a knot. I was only teasin'."

Which made things forty-five times worse. It was time to bring out my most devastating weapon.

If there's one thing a girl needs to know to succeed in the world, it's the ability to turn on the tears at will. Tears are the only known acid that eats away at the male ego, and it's important to know how to summon them in seconds. Delayed tears are no good: They go off quicker than even the dampest cheeses.

It's a simple trick, and easy to learn. One simply turns away, as if hurt beyond all hope of healing, opens the eyes as wide as they will go, then stares fixedly, without blinking, at the brightest part of the sky. The eyes, drying rapidly, will begin to irrigate themselves in well under a minute, until they are flooding like the Nile in monsoon season.

There isn't a man alive who can resist such a scurvy attack, but who am I to say that it is wrong?

"Grow up," I said, turning back and wiping at my eyes. "And stop showing off. You might be impressing your cronies, but you're not impressing me."

"Tcha!" Carl said. "Did you hear that, buckaroos?"

There was a notable silence. He had definitely spotted the tears.

"Do you know what I believe I've gone and done?" Carl said in a grave and mournful voice. "I believe I've gone and overstepped myself. Sometimes I'm stupid, and sometimes is now. C'mon, Flavia, forgive and forget. I throw my cloak in the gutter. I beg you to step on it. Please!"

I gave out a merry, ironic ringing laugh and left him to sort it out.

"Pretty please?"

It was the ultimate beggary.

"Move the stupid jeep," I said, "before someone spots us."

I included myself to tighten the noose.

"I can't," Carl said. "There's no room. We're wedged in."

"Eugene, climb over the bonnet," I said. "Rinso, you come over from the back."

"Jeep," Jeep said, scowling.

"Jeep," I said, and his eyes relaxed. "You and Rinso can push from the front here, and I'll help you. Carl, you'd better drive."

Rinso gave me a sheepish look, but without protest he climbed from the back seat, between Carl and Jeep, over the bonnet and stood beside me, as Jeep followed.

Carl put the jeep into reverse and let in the clutch as the three of us put our hands on the grille and pushed.

"Oh! It's hot!" I said.

Carl laughed. "It's called the Go Devil, that engine. Runs on fire and brimstone."

Despite what it ran on, the jeep refused to budge. The rear wheels spun, but the nose was well and truly wedged in a vise of ancient ecclesiastical timber.

Rinso, Jeep, and I pushed until our eyes were bugging from our heads, as Carl raced the engine and hammered at the clutch with his bare heel.

"Wait," I said, raising a hand. "Carl, you get out and push. You're much stronger than I am."

"But—" Carl managed before I cut him off.

"Don't say it," I told him, scowling.

I was not unfamiliar with motorcars. Dogger had taught me to drive my mother's old Rolls-Royce around the estate, and I had become actually quite an accomplished motorist.

Carl climbed out without a word, and I scrambled into the driver's seat. The steering wheel was on the wrong side, but I wasn't going to be intimidated by that.

"On three," I told them. "One . . . two . . . three!"

The three of them pushed and strained. I let in the clutch, and the jeep, wheels spinning, shot back out of the lych-gate like a stone from a catapult. I braked, shifted from reverse into first gear, and brought the jeep round in a circle to face in the opposite direction. No one who hadn't seen the accident would ever know what had happened.

I jumped down to inspect the damage. There were two fresh gouges on the posts of the lych-gate. I picked up a handful of soil and slathered the wooden wounds.

"Good as new," I said. "Or as good as they were in seventeen-hundred-and-whatever-it-was."

Carl made a deep bow as he swept the air with an imaginary cavalier's hat.

"In your debt, milady," he said.

"Yes, you are," I said, keeping a solemn face.

"Name your price," he said. "Alas, I am not a genie. I regret that I cannot offer three wishes. Uncle Sam permits only one."

I pouted, trying to look pensive, eyes rolled up toward the Heavens. I put my finger on my chin.

"I'll tell you what," I said after an agonizing pause. "Can you get me onto the base at Leathcote? Without being spotted?"

Asterion, I had decided, could be tracked down only by a girl of apparent innocence and naïveté: mainly me.

Carl was taken aback.

"I could be shot at the stake," he said, suddenly solemn, if not frightened to death. "What do you want to do that for?"

"Oh, it's just a game," I said. "Efficiency badge for Girl Guides. It's called Stalking."

This was only a partial truth. There *had* been a Stalking badge once upon a time, but it was now called Naturalist. Also, I had been sacked from the Girl Guides several years ago after a practical joke went wrong and required special counseling for one of my fellow Guides. The fact that I had refused a direct order from Miss Delaney to sit for punishment on a stool in the corner wearing the "Crown of Thorns" meant that it was unlikely I should ever be begged to come back.

"Someone has bet me I can't earn it," I said, just to sweeten the pot.

"What is it, this badge?" Carl asked.

"Oh, it's like a scavenger hunt—only in the dark.

You must get into a place like a castle or a fortress, and escape with something unique, like the flag, for instance, or a signboard or the headmistress's shoe. It's a game. It's meant to teach resourcefulness and initiative. *You* know what resourcefulness and initiative are, don't you, Carl?"

"C'mon, Carl, give her a break," Rinso said. "Smitty's on guard duty tonight. He could let her in and out again and nobody'd be the wiser. Let the little girl earn her badge. They've been through a lot, these English. What do you say, Jeep?"

Jeep said, "Well . . ."

"C'mon, Jeep. You were a Boy Scout yourself, weren't you? Back in Arkansas?"

"For a while," Jeep said.

"And you must've had merit badges," Carl persisted.

"A few," Jeep said.

"What were they?"

"Plumbing and Ornithology," Jeep said.

"Well, there you go," Carl said. "What time shall we pick you up?"

"It has to be after dark," I said. "Otherwise, it doesn't count."

"Harsh," Rinso said.

"Midnight would be perfect," I said brightly, as if I had just thought of it.

"See you at zero hours Zulu," Carl said, letting in the clutch. Their three heads shot violently back—and then forward. It's a wonder their spinal columns didn't snap.

Poop-poop went the tinny horn as they rode out of sight.

I looked around, then let off a grin.

This was going to be a piece of cake.

Actually, it almost went off without a hitch. I prepared myself by relaxing in the evening on my bed. Although I couldn't possibly visualize what was to come, I picked out a dramatic soundtrack: Grieg's mighty Piano Concerto in A minor. As I dredged the disks out from under my bed, I was already humming the melody: a grand and haunting panorama of mountains, glaciers, and peaks to be scaled and conquered. In the hands of Clifford Curzon, the white keys were walrus tusks, while the black were the bleak and yet thrilling rocks and boulders of Norway's remote mountain passes and fjords.

I might have dozed a bit as Clifford scaled the harmonic heights, faced certain danger, and yet descended safely at the end in triumph, as he always managed to do. I had long ago selected this piece to be played at my funeral, with my sister Daffy at the keyboard and the London Philharmonic, brought in by special train for the occasion, fiddling and trumpeting like mad, and everyone shedding scalding tears for poor, dear, dead Flavia. This was classical music at its finest.

When I awoke, it was half eleven: just time to find a black wool cardigan and a sturdy waterproof mackintosh. As I examined myself in the cracked cheval glass in the corner, I realized I looked like one of the black bishops from a chess set, but without the wound in my head. *Miter!* That was the proper name for a bishop's hat, and although I knew it was thought by some to look like the fish of Christianity, it always looked to me like someone who had been attacked from one side by an axe murderer.

·SEVEN·

In the Belly of the Beast

I AM SHOCKED, EVEN now, to see my own hand forming these words on the paper, as if I were being commanded—or is it *bidden?*—to write what I am told.

Why should this chapter be given a title and set apart from the others?

I haven't the foggiest idea, but I do know that this part of my account is so deep, so dark, and so dense that it is completely unlike the others.

I feel that I have been diminished, and yet at the same time magnified. I'm beginning to understand why people's brains can sometimes become addled like egg-nog, without their even noticing the change. One day you're Flavia de Luce and the next you're not, and pre-sumably you will have to wait through patient eons, like an evolving caveman, to discover who it is you're in the process of becoming.

I know I'm not the girl I once was, but I'm not yet sure who I really am. Nor, when it comes right down to it, am I now even sure who I used to be. I'm like a tight-rope walker teetering on the edge of some vast, but still invisible, abyss.

It's all so bloody frustrating!

What happened that night at the American base at Leathcote was like a lightning bolt in the darkness, il-luminating what had once been unseen and unsus-pected, and I still cannot make out whether I'm the better for it or whether I'm accursed.

To return to that scene makes my skin crawl, and yet at the same time fills me with a kind of glory that I can't explain.

But let me try anyway.

It had been raining, the kind of cold, thin, persistent rain with occasional flashes of distant lightning that have for centuries licked the British into what we are: bold, defiant, and shaking in our soggy boots.

Carl, as arranged, had picked me up at Buckshaw at midnight, and driven me, mostly in silence, to Leath-cote. Was he having second thoughts? I wondered. What-ever the cause, he seemed subdued as we splashed and bounced between the dark hedgerows, glancing only occasionally round at me in the back seat of the jeep, as if disappointed each time that I was still there. He was already distancing himself from me.

At the air base, he had seen me safely past the guardhouse, where we were waved swiftly through with a hooded torch by a silent black-caped figure I took to be their friend Smitty, or some other accomplice, then he dropped me in the shadows of the nearest building, which I guessed to be a hangar.

It was almost too easy.

Does "easy" often come before disaster? I am now inclined to think so, even if it smacks of superstition.

"Remember," Carl said. "We don't know you. You're on your own.

"And don't take any wooden nickels," he added as I stepped down onto the puddled tarmac. Then suddenly his jeep jerked and growled away into the night.

I don't know how long I stood alone in darkness, pressing myself against the corner of the looming hangar, afraid to move and afraid to keep still. After what seemed like an eternity, the sound of wet tires on tarmac came to my ears.

Was it Carl coming back, or had he abandoned me? Had he been discovered and forced to flee?

Or was it the sentry: the dark-caped figure I had supposed to be Smitty?

But what if it was someone else? Some other sentry?

I forced myself to close my eyes. If he caught a glimpse of my whites, I'd have a quick bullet through the brain. Sentries, I remembered, were chosen for the excellence of their marksmanship and not for their loving kindness.

I pressed more tightly up against the wall, hoping that would somehow help me blend with it. I prayed to whoever was listening that a sudden flash of lightning would not give me away.

I also held my breath.

The sound of footsteps suddenly stopped—came a bit closer—and stopped again.

I didn't dare open my eyes.

"Who goes there?" asked a voice in the age-old challenge. It was an American accent.

What was one to say? "It's only me" seemed feeble and insufficient.

"Who goes there?" the voice said again, in an impatient and even more demanding tone.

"Friend," I said almost instinctively, and opened my eyes, which were blinded instantly by the beam of a torch so intense it must have been powered by distilled sunlight.

I threw my hands up to shield myself from the glare. I was thinking of begging for mercy when the light moved slowly downward from my eyes, and over my wet, bedraggled raincoat.

I must have been a sight in this baggy, oversized outfit, which hung from my shoulders like a personal thundercloud. The smell of its synthetic resin was gagging me, as inside this makeshift tent, cold perspiration was already beginning to trickle down unpleasantly from my underarms toward my feet.

The phrase "secret agent" crossed my mind, and in a parallel world nearby, I was already dead.

"Advance to be recognized," the sentry said, and I took a small step forward.

I knew that the next step was to establish one's cre-
dentials, and I almost said, "I'm a friend of Carl and
Rinso," but realized just in time that could put their
necks in a noose, as well as mine.

"My name is Flavia de Luce," I said, speaking slowly
and enunciating clearly. "I live at Buckshaw, in Bishop's
Lacey, and I am the daughter of Colonel Haviland de
Luce."

There was a long silence, during which the beam of
the torch moved back up to my face.

"Please," I said. "The light's painful."

The beam hung on my face for a moment and then
dropped to the ground.

"Thank you," I whispered. I still couldn't see the face
of the sentry.

"State your business," he said.

There was no point in beating around the bush.
Honesty was all I had on my side.

"I've come to see someone," I said.

"Who?" he demanded, shifting the beam of the torch
up to a point just under my chin. My breastbone began
to heat.

"I don't know," I said.

The sentry spun suddenly on the sole of his boot and
made a quarter turn before slamming the other foot
down with a frightful crash, which echoed instantly from
the wall of the hangar.

I almost leaped out of my skin.

"Walk ahead of me," he said. "To your left. Slow
pace. Don't try anything stupid."

"Left," he said, touching my elbow with something hard and metallic, and it was only then I realized he had a weapon in his hand, and that it was pointed at me.

I could see a glint of light reflected from the rainy tarmac on the underside of its barrel. *Probably an M1*, I thought. Carl had brought one of these to one of Feely's musical soirees to be handed round and admired, and I remembered that it could fire up to fifty rounds a minute.

"You can't outrun 'em," Carl had said, and I was grateful for his advice.

Not that I had any intention of making a break for it. I was in the dark, in the rain, with an armed sentry whose face remained invisible.

But I was almost there! I had almost reached my intended goal.

I hadn't planned, of course, on being caught; but that hadn't been my fault.

Sheer stupid chance had done me in, and I was counting on sheer stupid chance to set me free.

I shuffled along from puddle to puddle, letting my shoulders hang limply. I didn't want to look threatening.

"Where are you taking me?" I asked. Surely, he couldn't take offense at that.

"You'll see," he said. "Keep moving."

I had visions of this nice young man sitting at home in his mother's parlor in Plainville, Kansas, the Stars and Stripes on the wall and the Andrews Sisters on the wireless—radio, they called it—singing "Don't Fence

Me In." The evening meal was on its way to the table and there was an apple pie browning and bubbling in the oven.

"Where are you from?" I asked.

"None of your business," he said in a voice so flat my heart sank like a stone.

Down the long dark side of a hangar we made our way, the only sounds our soggy feet on the hard tarmac.

"Go right," he said, and I obeyed.

Now we were shuffling along the side of another hangar. I could smell the aeroplanes inside: a sharp but exciting mix of leather, aluminum, and high-octane aviation petrol. "Gas," they called it. It wasn't, of course, a gas at all, but a liquid—up until the very instant it vaporized and exploded in the cylinders of the mammoth motors that drove these machines through the night air to rain death and destruction on other people, other hangars, other lands.

Where have these bombers been? I wondered. *And what have they done?*

Don't let it thrill you, Flavia, an inner voice said. *It won't be long before you will be required to find it sickening.*

"Halt!" the sentry said, slamming a booted foot down with an alarming noise. "Guardhouse," he added, as if that would explain everything.

I hadn't spotted the guardhouse. Its blacked-out windows gave away nothing.

"Inside," he said, opening a door from which a flood of light caught me like an insect on the stage of an illuminating microscope.

"Inside," he repeated, and I tripped on the doorstep.

I squinted against the light, even though it was dim. The room was small, the walls painted buff below and green above. It was divided into two areas by something resembling a wicket, with wire cage and a counter formed by a plain plank.

In the corner, a small, overfired stove was almost incandescent. The room was suffocatingly hot.

On a table was a green-hooded lamp, behind which a man in American army uniform sat smoking a cigar and swigging at a tin mug of what I guessed was coffee.

He would be the good guy, I thought: *the one in the white hat who played against the flinty exterior of the sentry.*

The man behind the desk—judging by the single bar on his shoulders, he was a lieutenant—began pulling out drawers, rifling through invisible papers. At last, he gave up his search and looked at me directly.

"Trespassing on a military base is a very serious matter," he said.

"Yes, sir," I said. "I'm sorry."

"Are you?" he asked, his gaze suddenly piercing.

"No," I admitted.

"Then why lie?" he asked with a wave of his cigar that he might have learned from a Noël Coward comedy.

"I am trying to get up the courage to tell the truth," I said.

He crushed the cigar savagely in an ashtray and snatched up a pen, which he held at the ready over a blank sheet of paper.

"Well, out with it." He raised his eyebrows into expectant inverted Vs.

"Yes, sir," I said. "I was thinking that myself."

"Well?"

Now his eyes had become gimlets.

"Well, sir . . . I was looking for someone."

He put down the pen and touched the corner of his mouth with an index finger, as if stifling a smile.

"Unusual place and time to be looking for somebody, isn't it?"

"Yes, sir. I suppose it is."

"Well, tell me who it is. This person you're looking for, I mean."

As he touched the corner of his mouth again and picked up the pen, I noticed that his fingernails were bitten to the quick.

Here was a person I could relate to.

This was the moment of truth. I had a choice: Either tell him the facts or play the innocent and slink away defeated. I would never get this chance again.

"Please, sir," I said, nodding toward the sentry. "May we be alone, sir?"

"A . . . lone?" He stretched the word out as if it were a rubber band.

"If you please, sir."

He chewed at his lip for a moment.

"I think I heard a dog barking," he said to the sentry. "Better check on it."

"Yes, sir!"

The sentry clicked his heels and made an elaborately geometric exit.

"Now then, who are you looking for?"

"Well, I don't know his name for certain, sir—"

He threw down his pen. I had gone too far.

"He goes by Colonel Crane, but some people call him Asterion."

There was silence. A *vast* silence. The universe held its breath.

The lieutenant looked at me as if I had just told him that the Houses of Parliament and all their inhabitants had been hoovered up by a flying saucer.

"Don't say that name!" he hissed, leaping to his feet. "That name must never, ever, be spoken aloud. Got it?"

I nodded.

"God in Heaven!" he whispered, getting up from his desk and crossing to the blackout blinds, which he lifted an inch to peer anxiously out into the night.

"Who did you say you were? *What's* your name?"

"I didn't say, sir. I told the sentry—the guard—that I'm Flavia de Luce, that I live at Buckshaw, in Bishop's Lacey, and that I'm the daughter of Colonel Haviland de Luce."

"God in Heaven!" he said again, this time louder. "And what brought you here?"

I decided to test my theory and see how he responded. "I'm looking into the death of a Major Greyleigh. He was murdered. I believe his killer may have been acting on the orders of the person named Asteri—"

"No!" he shouted. "I told you."

Sorry, I mouthed.

He ran his fingers through his hair, picked up his cigar, and put it down again. "And what makes you think that—that this particular person is here?"

"Logic," I said. "Because he can't be anywhere else."

"Look," he said. "I'm going to close my eyes and count to twenty, slowly. When I open them again you will be gone. We'll forget about the trespass. We'll pretend it never happened. You'll put the whole thing out of your mind, and we'll all be happier in the morning. I'll even throw in a driver and a ride home in a jeep. Wouldn't that be something?"

"No, sir," I said. "I've ridden in a jeep several times before, and so have most of my friends. And I can't leave until I speak to As—to that person who mustn't be mentioned."

The lieutenant let out such a long heavy breath, it might have been the death sigh of a dragon.

He picked up a pen and scribbled a short note on a piece of paper. It couldn't have been more than ten lines.

He went to the door, opened it, and handed the folded note to the sentry, who had been lurking suspiciously close to the door all the while. With a few whispered words, the messenger was on his way.

"Sit down," the lieutenant said. "This could be a long wait."

And indeed, it was. Although I don't wear a wristwatch (vanity, practicality, and the danger of it being snagged or stolen), I judged the wait to be somewhat more than an hour, with the lieutenant pretending to read over and over the same piece of paper, while occasionally shuffling things in the drawers of the desk and twice in the filing cabinet.

He said not a word, and I returned the favor. Two silent stones we were, on opposite sides of a vast and empty sea. The room was stifling. We might as well have been waiting with Moses in Moab for the promised land.

In my head I recited the periodic table of elements: one of the chief benefits of being a chemist. One is never bored in the presence of deadly dainties such as arsenic.

Some people pull out a paperback and lose themselves in tales of holidays at the seaside: of endless saltwater taffy under a hot sun with octopus lovers.

But not for me, thank you all the same. I'll take arsenic every time.

I thought of Giulia Tofana, who, in the 1600s, concocted an arsenic cocktail that was believed to have killed as many as six hundred people. Today she'd probably be running a nightclub in Soho and singing on top of a piano, or so Daffy said.

Seen in its raw state through a magnifying glass, arsenic looks like the White Cliffs of Dover, except that it is yellow and smells like garlic.

I was working my way toward polonium, which was named in honor of Poland, the native country of the brilliant Marie Curie and her husband, Pierre, who discovered the stuff in 1898. Polonium is a quarter of a million times more poisonous than cyanide, and ought to be studied at a distance, although I keep a small sample of the stuff in a lead-lined box as a sentimental relic. Madame Curie had sent it to Uncle Tar as a memento of their rich correspondence, and in the end outlived him by several years. It looked like nothing so much as a slab of seaside toffee.

The lieutenant got anxiously to his feet as a jeep drew up outside with a squeak of brakes. Boots clumped at the door and a large person in a black rain cape entered the room. He glanced at me, then with a jerk of his head beckoned the lieutenant. They retreated behind the wicket and began a low palaver. I could not make out the words but knew by the rising and falling volume of their voices that they were looking at me every few seconds, and then away.

I was beginning to feel like a slave girl being auctioned in *The Arabian Nights* when I heard my name:

"Miss de Luce . . ."

I looked up and saw that it was the lieutenant addressing me.

"Go with the sergeant here."

The sergeant, whose face was as blank as the arsenic-white cliffs of Dover, had already opened the door upon the darkness and the drizzle.

He extended an arm to give me leave to pass, although he did not touch me.

I marched past him without a word and climbed into the jeep. After the hot funk of the guardhouse, the cold night air was a blessing and I inhaled it deeply.

"Onward!" I said and gave him my most dazzling

grin. He scowled as he slid dramatically into the driver's seat.

The jeep started up reluctantly, and the sergeant gunned it several times against the wet weather.

"Choke," I suggested, but he did not respond.

At last, with a jerk, we moved off and the guardhouse vanished behind us into the night. We followed a single road with black-water-filled ditches on either side until we came to another windswept area of the tarmac. Here were more hangars and a few utility buildings.

The sergeant turned abruptly in to a passageway between two hangars, each of them equally dark and looming; then an abrupt right in to another passageway and then left again.

Despite our hurry, we seemed to be getting nowhere, and I thought I recognized a water stain on a hangar wall in the shape of an Erlenmeyer flask.

I kept it to myself.

We veered onto a perimeter road, then jounced along monotonously, apparently going nowhere much. The jeep's headlights were of the hooded blackout type, so there wasn't much to see but the bottoms of the heavy rainclouds overhead. A small flock of Canada geese feeding in the uncut grass at the roadside looked up at us scornfully but seemed unafraid.

I glanced over at the sergeant. In the glow of the dash light, he was gripping the wheel with white granite knuckles, his square chin pointed straight ahead as if he were pursuing it like a thrown axe. Only now did I get a glimpse of his badge peeking out from beneath his rain cape: *Police,* it said, with an eagle, a cloud, and what might have been a fistful of thunderbolts.

Now, appearing here and there through the rain, looking like abandoned windmills, were several square structures with high glass windows. During the war, these would have been control towers for the fighters and bombers. Everyone in Bishop's Lacey had flocked like ducklings to the cinema in Hinley to see Gregory Peck in *Twelve O'Clock High* and we all knew what control towers looked like. It could well have been filmed at Leathcote.

Tonight, those same elevated windows, encrusted now with sun-baked grime and bird droppings, and looking like blind, clouded elderly eyes, stared out over the cracked and overgrown runways with a leering, even malevolent look. I shivered and pulled my waterproof more tightly around my shoulders.

The sergeant, looking ever more determined, drove on.

I thought to lighten the mood; perhaps even to cheer him up.

"Sergeant," I asked, "with you way out here on the perimeter, who's guarding the fort?"

He shot me a half-contemptuous look. "Military secret," he growled.

I had to give him credit. Until now, in the short time I had known him, he had played his role to perfection. He hadn't shown a pinch of humanity.

I rewarded him by laughing at his joke, perhaps too loudly.

"Where are we going?" I asked. "Or is that a military secret, too?"

I watched the corner of his mouth for a telltale twitch, but his stern look was pure perfection. This lad was good!

We bounced on through the night and the puddles, before slowing and turning off at last onto an abandoned taxiway, its tarmac stained with ancient oil and rubber and goodness knows what else. At the far end was another control tower, tumbledown, derelict, and all in darkness.

I realized with a shiver how late it must be.

The sergeant steered the jeep round in a tight circle in front of the structure, coming to a jerky stop to face in the direction from which we had come. For a moment we sat amid the metallic ticking of the cooling vehicle. The sound of the wind was a moan.

"Are we there?" I asked.

The sergeant pointed with a horrid forefinger, like the Ghost of Christmas Future in the story of Scrooge.

"Toc seven," he said.

I knew from Alf Mullet that "toc" was code for the letter *T* in the British military alphabetic code books, but not the American, in which, according to Carl, it was "tare" or "tango." The *T* most likely stood for "tower," but I was not going to show my ignorance by asking. I gave him a quick, businesslike nod.

"Roger," I said, and clambered daintily down from the jeep.

The sergeant didn't stop me. He unwrapped his knees from the steering column and walked round the bonnet of the jeep to join me. He dug into his rain gear and, after a brief fumble, produced a ring of keys.

We waded through wet weeds toward the tower. The sergeant fiddled with the keys, selected one, and with some difficulty, tried unsuccessfully to insert it into a Yale lock.

He wiggled it vertically, then horizontally, but it simply wouldn't fit. I thought of asking him to try the others, but it had become a matter of mastery.

"Let me try," I said, holding out my hand. With a savage look, he handed me the keys, which I cradled in my palm, keeping the selected key separate from the others, then lifted them to my head and rubbed both sides of the chosen one into my hair.

It was a trick Dogger had taught me, so I can't take any credit except for remembering the dodge.

With a twist and a click the door was open. I handed the keys back to the sergeant.

"Military secret," I said, and I thought he was going to hemorrhage right there on the spot. He whispered a coarse word, but I pretended not to hear it.

Producing a torch from a pocket, he lighted our way slowly through the open door.

The interior of the tower was a shambles. Broken panels hung from the ceiling by bare wires and the floor was littered with shards of shattered glass, some of it from smashed liquor bottles, some of it from broken windows.

"Shall we go up?" I asked, pointing to a narrow staircase.

"Not safe. Condemned."

Pity, I thought. *It might be as close as I ever got to Gregory Peck.* Feely and Daffy would be simply writhing with jealousy.

The sergeant led the way to an oblong room with a small platform and a greasy blackboard. He put the heel of his boot against the edge of the platform and pushed.

In surprising silence, the platform slid to one side, revealing the top step of a ladder.

"Are you taking me to Asterion?" I asked.

"Shut up," he snarled, and I realized I was skating on very thin ice.

"You first," he said, shining the beam of his torch into the abyss. I crouched down and managed to get one foot onto the ladder.

"Down," he said, and I felt like a dog. I wasn't used to being spoken to in this way, and I didn't like it a bit. For all I knew, the man could be a mass murderer leading me to some subterranean chamber of horrors from which I would never emerge alive. There would be a search, but I would never be found. Perhaps in some future century someone would happen upon a pitiful pile of dust and say, "By Jove—I believe those are bones!"

By now we were at the bottom of the ladder in a pit with earthen walls, which had the sharp, rich pong of acid earth of all soil cellars beneath an area where human beings have lived for ages: an acrid and metallic mixture of vinegar and dead, exhausted dirt. It was like an auger thrust up the nose.

"Phew!" I said.

"Turn around," the sergeant ordered.

Slowly I did as I was told and found myself facing the entrance to a dark tunnel. The threshold was of strengthened concrete. I could tell by the remnants of hinges there had been a door here once. Now all that remained was a steel sill and blackness beyond.

Someone meant business.

The sergeant turned the beam of his torch toward the wall, revealing a switch in a red-painted box. He flipped the toggle, and ahead of us a corridor appeared, lit by dozens of little lights, each in a small metal cage, disappearing like a pathway of fireflies into the distance.

"After you," the sergeant said. Was he suddenly sounding more humane? Had something changed now that we were in the depths—or was it my wishful thinking?

I decided to test him.

"Is it safe?" I asked.

"Safe as Superman's socks," he said, and the man actually laughed.

His earlier anger had vanished abruptly. Did he think he was putting one over on me by referring to an American comic book hero?

Carl and I had pored over his stack of comics (of which he seemed to have an endless supply) and I was aware of the possible presence of a supervillain whose hand was everywhere.

Was I, in fact, on my way to meet him in his subterranean lair? Was he the dreaded Asterion?

The windings and meanderings of this underground maze suggested the presence of a Minotaur: the bull-headed man who breathed flames and smoke and consumed all comers.

A sudden chill ran up my spine and ended in a shudder. The next instant I was flushed as if by the fires of Hell. Had I contracted some filthy tropical disease, or was this what adult responsibility felt like?

To keep away such thoughts, I began to pay careful attention to my surroundings, looking for clues . . . or discrepancies: anything to occupy my fevered mind.

The first thing I noticed was that there was no dust on the floor. *How odd,* I thought: *The place ought to be ankle-deep in the stuff.* The tower had been abandoned for more than eight years. It ought to have been a dustbin, but it wasn't.

Someone was keeping it swept.

Which led to another bout of shivering on my part. Who—or what—were we about to meet?

The lieutenant and the sergeant wouldn't be taking me to this place if there was nothing here. This was no picnic.

My naming of Asterion had shaken them badly, and this was their response. If he had alarmed the American 8th Army, what would Asterion do to me?

What would I say to him when we met? Would I demand that he immediately explain the murder of Major Greyleigh, or would I lead him into a trap of words, like Odysseus and the Cyclops?

I took a deep breath to strengthen myself. The smell

of the place had changed as we moved along the corridor: It was now more metallic and piercing; less earthy and more alive with ozone. My mind summoned up gunpowder and electrical sparks: somewhat like the tower laboratory in Dr. Frankenstein's castle must have smelled. Oddly enough, this made me feel more confident. There was nothing supernatural about this underground fortress.

"Huh," I said, more to assert myself than anything else. I looked back over my shoulder to see if the sergeant was following. He was, but I couldn't help noticing the tension of his face muscles. He had the look of a man riding a rocket.

We had covered a distance I judged to be a quarter of a mile when the tunnel—or passageway—came to a sudden end. In front of us was a round steel hatch that might have been the entrance to a tank—or a submarine.

The sergeant motioned me out of the way and began to twist the mechanism that held the thing shut. It was rather like an oversized water faucet. Oddly enough, it didn't squeak.

In silence, the great round door swung open.

"Step inside," the sergeant said.

"It's dark in there," I said as I stepped across the steel threshold.

"No one ever died from darkness," the sergeant whispered in my ear.

I scrambled over the lip of the hatch and felt with my toes for the floor on the other side. It was farther than I thought, and I slipped and fell, and it knocked the wind out of me.

As I was raising myself on my hands, the hatch slammed shut with a horrific metallic *clang*!

Wherever I was, he was not staying with me—nor was he taking me back with him.

"Sergeant!" I shouted.

But there was no reply.

·EIGHT·

I WANTED TO CRY. For the first time in ages, I wanted to cry. I wanted to have a good old-fashioned wail: a healthy old heartbreaking howl.

But why bother when there was no one here to hear it?

Cries were evolved by humans to summon help. But with no nearby ears to hear, they were useless, and a waste of strength.

"Crumbs!" I said to the darkness, which struck me as funny, and I began to laugh. Perhaps the reptilian part of my brain was automatically suggesting the classic solution to mazes: a trail of crumbs. I stopped my hand from reaching for my pocket.

It really was too amusing when you thought about it. Fearless Flavia led willingly into an underground bunker by a silent American he-man. Feely and Daffy would have laughed themselves silly.

But Feely and Daffy weren't here. I was on my own.

It wasn't as if this was the first time I'd been in such a predicament. There had been that nasty business with being bound and tied in the Pit Shed at the library in Bishop's Lacey, but that was positively civilized compared with this.

My laughter faded to a chuckle—then stopped. How can you be resourceful in the dark? The sergeant had said that no one ever died from darkness, and he was probably right. But had anyone ever done anything truly useful in a complete blackout?

Had they?

You might not believe this, but the first thing that came to mind was the poet John Milton. He had written much of *Paradise Lost* and all of *Paradise Regained* after going blind. Daffy had told me how remarkable it was that Milton was able to recall so much: that loss of sight had resulted in a truly magnificent feat of memory. The story of the struggle between God and Satan had been recorded for once and for all by a man who couldn't see his own fingertips. This was the truth of the struggle between light and darkness.

And now I was seeing exactly what Milton saw. What sense of it could *my* brain make?

I focused intently and ordered my thoughts. This had been Uncle Tar's advice to himself for sleepless nights. His notebooks were dotted with helpful but random suggestions, which I found occasionally useful, and this was the one that sprang to mind.

Darkness.

Well, in the first place, you can *hear* the darkness. In it, sounds are distinctly different, as if they are being amplified and focused. Could it be that when sight ceases, your brain turns up the volume on your ears? I made a mental note to formulate a set of experiments to prove this theory, and perhaps win a Nobel Prize.

But there was no time now.

My second observation was that things smell different in darkness. Perhaps on the same principle as vision, that sharper acid odor of the air had also increased and was now almost suffocating me.

I thought of oxygen deprivation.

But even now another idea was taking shape, and I acted upon it at once. I stuck out my tongue and licked the wall. The taste was foul: cement, soot, and oil. But I had nothing to compare it with; there was no baseline. I ought to have tasted the wall while I was still in the outer corridor in the light.

And now, here I was in pitch blackness.

At that very instant the lights went on: as before, a chain of fairy lamps disappearing into the distance.

Blinded by the lights, I smiled.

The vicar had once preached an entire sermon explaining the proverb *A merry heart maketh a cheerful countenance,* and I am not exactly what you would call a girl of cheerful countenance. I don't go around gaping and grinning like the village idiot just to make myself look holy. Although I'm not unhappy, I generally try to keep a serious expression on my face in the presence of others. It's cheap insulation from the world.

But now, in this ghastly tunnel, I must admit, I grinned, even though there was no one else here to see it, and it felt so surprisingly good that I did it again.

The best smile, I decided, *is for oneself.* I know it sounds tiresome, but it's true.

It was the lights. Dim as they were, they pointed like an arrow to whatever lay ahead in the distance.

I scrambled up out of the dust and brushed myself off. The Minotaur was waiting, and I was so eager I fancied I could already taste the beef. Or something else.

As I set off along the tunnel, I noticed the multitude of doorways or closed gates on either side. They reminded me of the steel pens used for loading cattle into railway wagons. I had once seen cows herded up the ramps in the Doddingsley yards by men waving wet sacks, and I had been sick in the grass.

Walking cautiously along, I was stopped in my tracks by a droning sound that seemed to come from all around me. It grew louder and louder and there was a sudden booming and a screech of tires from overhead, then the tunnel shook and echoed before the sound diminished in the distance.

It was an aircraft landing. I was sure of it. I was directly under the runways. The doors and hatches I had seen were probably petrol bowsers.

What a relief. I was not far from civilization after all, and the image of the Minotaur faded.

It was then that I stepped on the rat. I had not seen the thing huddled close to the wall, and I expect it was playing dead—until I stepped on its tail, at which point it went scuttling off in that sinister fashion that all sneaks, including rats, have.

As for me, I almost took the train to Poole, if you know what I mean. The stupid thing had startled me more than frightened me. I do not fear rats, and I've had to deal with several of the creatures over the past few years. The underground hydraulic systems that once powered the fountains at Buckshaw are home to great colonies of rats, but with Dogger around, they know their place.

I knew already that rats, if followed, will lead you to food. If there was another living being in this network of caves, the rat would find them. Which is why I chose to follow the rat. Not that I had much choice, since it was traveling the same corridor as I was.

Still, I decided that if the rat changed direction, I would follow.

And it didn't take long. The corridor turned to the left; the rat reached the turning before I did, and when I rounded the corner, the rat was gone. It appeared to have vanished into thin air.

And then I smelled it. Wood smoke! Where was it coming from?

Where there's wood smoke there's fire, and where

there's fire there's often food and where there's food there's someone—or something—to devour it.

I might have been much closer to Asterion than I had imagined. And he to me.

The hair at the back of my neck bristled at the thought.

I moved slowly now, watching for any opening in the concrete, and I felt it before I saw it: a slight breeze brushed my ankles: a faint but detectable movement of air.

I got down on my hands and knees, and I found it almost at once: a metal grating at floor level. It had been painted gray and was nearly invisible in the dim light of the tunnel. I stuck my fingers through the mesh of the grille and gave it a tug.

It came away in my hands, and the smell of wood smoke came with it.

What was the purpose of this opening?

I knew that climbing into a drain could be deadly. But a drain—unless it was dead dry—would have water at its lowest point, and the smell of burning wood could not possibly get through it. Still, there were all those horrific stories about Victorian chimney sweeps and or-phans who had been trapped and died horribly in deadly nooks and crannies where they couldn't turn around. Their pitiful white bones might not be discovered for a hundred years.

I stuck an arm in and felt around.

Nothing. My fingers trembled in empty space.

But then, at the very limit of my reach . . . an iron rung. I stuck my head in for a quick look.

There were footholds in the wall of the opening! Would I be able to squeeze into it?

I hoisted the heavy grille and held it for an instant, like a knight's shield, across my shoulders for measurement.

There were a good two or three inches to spare.

On my knees, I lowered myself slowly into the opening, feeling with a foot for the metal rung, easing myself down into the shaft until my chin was at floor level.

One last look around before I began my descent. Would the fairy lights of the tunnel be the last things I saw on my relatively short visit to Planet Earth? Would I be gobbled up from below by some foul fiend with razor-sharp teeth and stinking breath?

Stop it, Flavia! my inner voice said impatiently. *Stop wallowing!*

Dogger had told me that our primal fears are locked away in the most primitive parts of our brains, but that they can be conquered by reason and training.

"There's nothing so fearful as the sound of a slither," he had said. "Even those peoples who inhabit the Arctic regions, where there are no snakes, are as petrified as we are. A most instructive lesson."

My inner voice, I realized, was coming from the same region in my brain as my instinctive fears. They spoke the same language.

"Go talk to someone else," I muttered, and began to climb down. Which didn't make sense, but when you're being brave, logic is sometimes lost.

The shaft was so narrow I could not look straight

down. There was nothing to do but keep descending. *It can't go on forever,* I thought.

The word "claustrophobia" (I looked it up later) is derived from the same word as "closet" and "cloister." As someone with personal experience of having been tied up and locked in a cupboard, I find it helpful to know similar instances of torture.

This shaft was no closet or cloister. It was like being tied up in a bag in a barn, like a pig about to be slaughtered. *Awaiting the knife.* I could hear my own breathing and my own heartbeat. This ought to be reassuring, but it isn't. The human body ought to be mostly unaware of its own processes; deaf to its thumps and gurglings.

The pulsing chambers of the heart, for instance—

My foot touched bottom. With a jolt I was off the rungs and standing on a solid surface. I ducked slightly to withdraw my head from the shaft.

My mouth fell open. I was unable to stop it.

I was standing in a large but dimly lit area. Although it appeared at first glance to be a workshop, it was also a mouthwatering chemical laboratory. I recognized, for instance, in a corner, an electron microscope and what could only be a mass spectrometer. There had been a most interesting article about these devices in *The Chemical Chronicle,* and I had longed to get my hands on one. With a flick of a switch and a song in your heart you could identify virtually any substance known to Man or the Chemical Gods.

I gaped as I looked around. Leathcote was no mere American airbase. How clever of someone to think of using miles of wartime runways as camouflage for a very different undertaking! How many more levels were there below this one?

My mind had never been truly boggled before, but it was boggled now.

In the area in which I now stood, row after row of bottled chemicals marched off into the distance, shelf upon shelf of elaborate glassware of every shape imaginable. Colored pilot lights and glowing meters of every hue.

It was the laboratory of my dreams.

Yes! That was it—I was dreaming. I was still sitting in that suffocating guardhouse watching the lieutenant pretend to read his papers. Without being aware of it, I had fallen asleep and fallen into the world of fantasy. The sergeant, the jeep, the rain, the runways: None of them had been real. They were all just pictures painted by my weary brain. I had been sleepwalking in the coils of my own sleeping subconscious. If I pinched myself, I would wake up in the guardhouse. I would give up on my mission—at least for tonight.

But would I ever get another chance?

Entangled in the chains of sleep, the voice inside me said, in a slow, lazy, and confidential tone. It could sometimes be quite poetic. I closed my eyes. I needed to be sure.

I reached up and applied my thumb to a point on my jawbone, just under the ear. It was one of the secret pressure points of Kano jiujitsu that Dogger had taught me. I pressed—hard.

The agony was instant, and I let out a yelp. There's no pain anything like that in the Land of Nod!

I said something naughty. But now I knew for certain: I wasn't asleep.

I opened my eyes and looked around me.

In another corner was part of an aircraft: a bomb bay if I wasn't mistaken, containing something shrouded by a silvery-gray drop cloth.

My armpits tingled. A sure sign I was onto something. I was about to lift the corner of the sheet for a quick squint when I heard an unmistakable noise: the sound of military boots on concrete. And it was getting closer!

There were no options. I was forced to take the only move open to me: I dived under the sheet and stood stock still.

The sound of the boots was coming closer and closer. I could hear the metallic click of the individual heel taps on the concrete floor.

They stopped. The wearer must be standing almost within reach.

Don't even think about sneezing, I thought. The sheet was dusty and waved slightly in the moving air of the intruder's arrival.

Intruder! I was the intruder, and if I was caught there was the distinct possibility of being hanged as a spy. An investigator of sufficient rank would have no trouble linking me to the Nide.

I would be arrested, imprisoned, tried, and hanged in secret. No one would ever know what had become of me. Stories would be fabricated.

Oh, she moved away. Took up a job with one of the minor banks. Trainee. New Zealand. Australia. One of those places.

Although she frankly hated the antipodes ("They reek of kangaroos and kiwis," she had sniffed), Aunt Felicity had strong links with both places, so that these professionally crafted rumors would all sound on the up-and-up.

My place in history would be erased with a few strokes of a pen at some anonymous building just off Birdcage Walk.

I knew from his diaries that Uncle Tar, in his day, had often taken tea there with a certain dignitary to whom he referred only as "the Gentleman in question"—and always with a capital G.

I can only suppose it was the thought of kiwis and sniffing and birdcages, but without warning, I sneezed. And it was a corker!

"*Amf-kisha-shafsha-charoo!*"

It was as if Zeus had taken up residence in my nose and decided, just for fun, to hurl a handful of experimental lightning bolts—like the ones on the sergeant's police badge—out of both my nostrils.

But these were no lightning bolts. I hastily wiped my nose on the hem of my skirt, just as the drop cloth was whisked away and I was left standing there exposed.

"Flavia!"

"Rinso!" I said, for it was he.

"What are you doing here? How did you get in here?" he asked.

"I could ask you the same," I said, stalling for time to think.

"I work here," Rinso said.

"Here? In this lab?"

Rinso nodded.

"I thought you washed dishes, or something?"

"Well, I do," he said, almost apologetically. "Petri dishes. Flasks. Beakers. And all like that."

"Here?" I could scarcely believe him.

"No—in the Emerald City. Where else?"

"Look, Rinso," I said. "There's no time to waste. It's a matter of life and death. Where can I find Asterion?"

Rinso's face went white. It actually went *white*, as if he was going to faint. He grabbed the corner of the bomb bay to steady himself.

"Where did you hear *that*?" he whispered.

"I can't tell you," I said, shaking my head. "Sorry, Rinso. Where can I find him?"

"Look," he said. "We have to get you out of here. They'll kill you if you're caught."

"Oh, come off it," I said.

"Look, Flavia," Rinso said, taking my hand, "I've taken a liking to you. I wouldn't want to see anything happen to you. But listen to me. This place is top secret—beyond top secret. Way, way, *way* beyond top secret. If they catch you here, heads will roll like bowling balls in Brooklyn—beginning with yours."

He reached out and almost touched my face, and I fancied I saw a tear start in his eye.

"You're serious, aren't you?" I whispered. "You really mean it."

He nodded his head vigorously, biting his lower lip. He was crying.

"We have to get you out of here," he said. "Now!"

My heart sank. There went all my progress. Wasted! Everything would be lost.

I knew suddenly how Job must have felt when God killed all his cattle: as if a cork in his heel had been yanked out suddenly, and his lifeblood drained out into the sand.

"Stay here," Rinso whispered, letting go of my hand. "I have an idea."

He pulled the drop cloth back into its original position.

"Don't move a muscle," he said, and his boots as he clopped away sounded for all the world like a knacker's horse treading its final cobblestones.

He needn't have warned me. I had been badly shaken, and like all animals that have been badly shaken, I froze in position.

I ought not to have followed that rat. If I had stayed in the tunnel and walked on straight to my destination— whatever it was or might have been—I'd have been safe. I had been given a virtual pass to the doorstep, almost given a map to Asterion. If the rat hadn't diverted me, I'd now be in the presence of the mystery man.

There's a lesson there somewhere, but I'm not sure

what it is. Without the rat, I'd not have discovered this secret subterranean laboratory, and credit ought to be given where credit is due.

Now the boots were coming back, and with them came a low metallic rattling.

"Right then," Rinso whispered on the other side of the drapery. "Let me make sure the coast is clear."

After a brief pause, he pulled the sheet aside. "Hop it," he said. "Get on the cart."

He had brought a metal tea cart with rubber wheels. Beneath the top was a bottom shelf upon which was an insulated urn, or teapot. It was not unlike the one in the parish hall at St. Tancred's. Oh! How long ago all that now seemed!

"Climb under," Rinso said, lifting the corner of the drop cloth. "Keep your head down, and not a peep out of you."

As Rinso lifted the tea cauldron, I folded myself like an Ordnance Survey map and squeezed onto the lower shelf. A drapery, which I judged by its smell to be a fair linen tablecloth, cascaded down around me, and the tea bowser was set down over my head with a solid thump.

Rinso began walking slowly, his sole-savers *clackety-clack*ing on the floor, and the wheels of the trolley wobbling along unevenly, as all tea trollies everywhere do.

I began to relax and enjoy the ride. Rinso worked here and knew the place well. He would wheel me to safety and release me, and I would resume my hunt for the dangerous—and now deadly—Asterion.

This way and that we went, the turnings too numerous to count. I knew by the increased brightness filtering through the tablecloth that we had left the dim laboratory and ventured out into brighter corridors.

"Ah! White," a voice said, surprisingly close at hand.

"Morning, sir," Rinso replied.

His words surprised me. It couldn't be more than five o'clock in the morning.

"What have we here? Early elevenses?"

His accent, like Rinso's, was American.

"I'm afraid not, General. Just tea."

"Tea will do," the general said. "But don't make a habit of it. Ha-ha. Don't think I'm going native. Here, I've got my own mug."

"No, sir," Rinso said. "I'll grab some coffee next time around. And doughnuts."

The sound of liquid dribbling came to my ears. My knees began to pain.

"A promise made is a debt unpaid," the general said. "And don't think I won't hold you to it."

"Yes, sir," Rinso said, and with a jerk of the cart, we rumbled on.

The pain in my knees was becoming paralyzing.

"Rinso . . ." I whispered.

Rather than speaking he began to whistle.

"Morning . . . morning . . ." he said, and there were a couple of mumbled responses.

I was ready to scream when we stopped. After a moment, I heard Rinso's clackers walking away, and the sound of a door opening. With a finger, I lifted the veil and peeked out into the corridor. It seemed to run to

Mandalay without a bend. I twisted round and peered in the other direction. Ditto.

I scrambled out of the cart and began to run. I fancied I heard Rinso's voice in the rapidly receding distance shouting "Flavia! Flavia! Come back! Come back!"

But Rinso wouldn't shout. He wouldn't raise the alarm. He would go back to whatever he had been doing before he had found me and pretend I never happened. That's the way the world works, and for once I was glad of it.

I needed to get out of this corridor as quickly as possible. I needed to become invisible again. There was a doorway on the right with a stenciled sign in ominous red letters saying *Positively No Admittance*. I smiled at the arrogance of it. Since when had I ever been stopped by a mere sign?

To my mind, a sign is—well, a sign of laziness. If it isn't important enough to have a human enforcer, it isn't important enough to obey. A few dabs of paint don't cut any ice with me.

I tried the knob, and praise be to all the saints and all the martyrs and all the angels, even the fallen ones, the door swung open, and I stepped inside. This corridor was in complete and utter darkness.

It was as if all the light had been suddenly sucked out of the universe, and all eyes had become instantly redundant.

At least I was safe in here. No one could see me in the dark.

I began feeling my way along the wall, touching it only with my fingertips on both sides to maintain my balance. Something loomed up in front of me. I could sense it before I felt it: a certain deadness of the air just off the tip of my nose. I could smell it, too: the distinct odor of wood. I stroked it lightly. It was a door—no doubt about it. I could feel one of the hinges. My hand closed on the doorknob.

Slowly, I let my fingers tighten around the knob, moving only in tiny slices of an inch.

So far, so good. The knob was turning. The door wasn't locked.

I pushed gently, and the door swung inward.

I stepped inside.

·NINE·

I WASN'T PREPARED FOR what I saw. I couldn't have been.

The room before me was a softly illuminated gentleman's study, with leather chairs and sofas bathed in low but luxurious light. Tall bookcases reached to the ceiling and on the walls were fine prints of paintings whose names and artists one couldn't quite remember.

A wood fire crackled cozily in the fireplace, and on the mantel, in the shadows, were several framed family photographs.

At the center of the room was a large, leather-topped desk of the sort usually (but erroneously) called a partners desk, lit gently by a green-shaded hanging lamp.

At the desk, a man was seated with his back turned partly to me, with only his hands in the light. At his feet was a wicker basket in which lay an Irish setter. The dog looked up instantly, then got slowly to its feet and came ambling toward me across the room.

I held my breath and waited as the dog approached. I was too afraid to move.

The animal seemed to stare at me for a very long time, then extended its nose and smelled my hand. I wanted to pet it: to stroke its head and scratch it behind the ears and tell it what a good dog it was, but I didn't dare.

I would let the dog make the decision. It was, after all, on its own territory, whereas I was a rank (literally) intruder. I could smell my own sweat. I was going to say "perspiration," but sweat is sweat, and it was running down my spine.

The dog looked up at me again, almost hopefully, and began to wag its tail slowly. In the shadows, I noticed for the first time that its muzzle was white with age, its eyes clouded.

Good dog, I mouthed. Maybe it had learned to read lips; you never know.

The dog turned at once and shambled back to its basket, into which it climbed, then circled several times before dropping with a heavy sigh onto its blanket.

The man at the desk hadn't moved. He was obviously unaware of my presence.

By the movements of his neck and shoulders, I deduced that he was writing.

Ought I to announce myself? Should I clear my throat? I didn't want to startle him.

Would he sense my presence?

And then it struck me: like a slap in the face by Fate. Was this Asterion? Could it possibly be?

The room was not a military room. The man before me was not in uniform, but rather dressed more like a country squire. He wore a tweed jacket with leather patches on the elbows, and I could tell by the collar that his shirt was of cotton and had come from Jermyn Street.

As if he had sensed my presence, the man stopped writing, and lifted his head. Was he listening?

He returned to his writing, as if he had merely stopped to think.

This couldn't go on. My time had finally come. I needed to get the upper hand, and surprise was the only weapon I had.

"Are you Asterion?" I asked, in the strongest, clearest voice that I could muster, although it wasn't much.

The man seemed to put down his pen but did not reply.

"Are you Asterion?" I asked again.

He took hold of the arms of his chair with both hands and rose slowly to his feet. For a long moment he stood there, as if he had frozen in time, and then, slowly, he turned, and I saw his face.

There are no words. I cannot describe what happened to my brain. I can only tell my feelings, which never stop. Feelings are beyond words; beyond action; beyond reason. They are the only true and constant indicators we ever have in this cruel life.

The man before me was Father. My own father. The father whose funeral I had attended. The father for whom I had cried my eyes out for weeks on end.

No! I wanted to scream. *Imposter!* But I could not.

The two of us stood there, facing each other, caught in some kind of celestial glacier, like little figures carved from ice.

Naturally, I wanted to run to him and shower him with kisses as I had done when I was a toddler. But I could not. Father was not that kind of man, and I was no longer that kind of girl. Our relationship had become one of icy respect rather than genuine love. I could see that clearly now: a gift of the moment.

And then the hate poured in, as if a dam had broken, flooding me with a riptide of resentment. How could he have done this to me? What kind of man would put his own children through such torture?

My mind was filled with visions of the long-forgotten past, brought back to life by Father's treachery. I saw again his face bent over me in my stroller—and then that other face—and that other voice: *You are now Asterion.* Was it Aunt Felicity? Their faces were remarkably alike. I had never noticed it before. But then another forgotten image came suddenly to mind: Father extending a cautious finger for me to grip; his face at the table while feeding me mush on a spoon; his face again as he lifted me high in the air, my feet kicking to be let down. It was like a film run backward and at high speed, image after image in senseless profusion.

I covered my eyes with my hand, but the torture didn't stop. These scenes were burned into my brain and would not be blocked by anything but death.

What had changed him? Was it the war?

The war may have begun the process, but I think in the end it was guilt. Guilt about his days of battle away from his daughters, and later guilt about his obsessive devotion to his stamp collecting. Time lost and time squandered—all of it.

Time stolen from children can never be repaid. That is the true bitterness.

"May I sit?" I asked.

Father stepped to one side and pulled out a straight chair. He held it for me as I sat. It was almost laughable.

He had not yet spoken a word, but stood looking at me as if I were some strange sea creature that had washed up on the shore of his private desert island.

"May I offer you a cup of tea?" he asked at last.

So that was his game! Trot out the old normality. Business as usual. Pip-pip and a stiff upper lip.

"No, thank you," I said.

Father sat down at his desk again, glancing at me once or twice as if to gauge my fury.

"Flavia," he said, "I have been dreading this moment for a very long time."

"Yes?" I said.

This was a wound that was going to take an eon to heal, like that of the king in the Grail Castle. In that tale, the king could not be healed until someone asked him the correct question, which was "What ails thee?"

Not much has changed in a thousand years.

"What's the matter with you?" I asked.

He pinched the bridge of his nose between thumb and forefinger, then looked at his hands as if to find the answer written on his palms.

"Duty," he said at last, softly.

I let the silence remain in the room. I magnified it with my own silence.

"I don't expect you to understand," Father said at last. "There are powers ineffable—do you know what 'ineffable' means?"

"Of course I do," I said, angry that he had stirred me to speech. "It means 'inexpressible.' Beyond words."

Father nodded. "Just so. There are powers beyond powers, powers beyond words. They can only be referred to in the most vague or abstract terms."

"Please try," I said. Was this *me*? *Me* talking to my own father? Was I like Job, grumbling to God?

"They have me in their grip," Father went on. "Under their boots, in a way. Yes, the powers have boots. Boots with hooks and hobnails."

I must admit I was fascinated with the idea.

"Why don't you break free?" I asked. It seemed a simple solution.

"I cannot," Father said. It appeared as if he were trying to unscrew one of his fingers.

"Why?" I asked.

"Because I am one of them," he said. "In fact, I am—"

"You *are* Asterion!" I gasped. *"You!"*

"You must let me explain in my own way," Father

said. "I've been rehearsing it for several years in case this day ever came. I prayed that it wouldn't, but it has, and I am prepared."

How like Father, I thought: *Kit bag at the ready, speeches memorized, shaved and shriven on the day of battle.*

"Do you miss Dogger?" I asked. I couldn't resist twisting that most painful of knives.

"I miss him terribly," Father said. "Without him I am no more than a shadow."

"He misses you terribly, also," I said. Had I hurt him enough? Perhaps. I was both proud and ashamed of myself.

"Go ahead," I said. "I'll be quiet."

Father folded his hands in his lap. I knew him well enough to know that it was a sign of resignation.

"For generations, we de Luces have been members of the Nide—although that name is itself a deflection and a deceit. No more than a pleasant joke, really. Uncle Tarquin was deeply involved, as was your mother. Your aunt Felicity was, until quite recently, an important and powerful figure.

"We were intentionally modeled on the Book of Ezekiel: 'Wheels within wheels,' you may remember. It is an allegory for what lies beyond: beyond government, beyond the law, beyond the Church. Someone once spoke of it as 'Justice Invisible.' Others have called it Fate. For every wheel there was another wheel. Whenever you thought you'd found the largest or the smallest wheel, you'd discover that it was either the smallest or the largest of yet another and unsuspected set."

"Sounds like Charlie Chaplin in *Modern Times*," I said. The image came to mind of the Little Tramp crawling between the turning, grinding steel gears of some great and desperately inhuman machine.

Father nodded. "Another allegory," he said. "Chaplin was one of us. A tragic little man. Rather than remaining hidden in plain sight, he tried to warn the world. He was crushed by his own cogs and spat out. He was banished just last year."

"And so are you," I said softly, my mind not yet completely caught up with my brain.

Father nodded.

"But why?" I asked.

"Duty," he said. "Duty again: the farthest-reaching shackle and the cruelest one. Look, Flavia, you must understand this: Each of us, at birth, is given what is sometimes called the pearl of greatest price. It is the one thing that will drive us from the cradle to the grave. Sometimes we choose it and sometimes it is thrust upon us. For some it's money and for others glory. For some it's love and for others it's power. It drives us as surely as water and fire drive the steam engine, and it varies not so much as a particle from birth till death. For me, it was duty. For better or for worse, duty. I had no choice. Do you see?"

"It must be horrible," I said.

"No," Father said. "That's just the thing. It isn't horrible at all. We think of it as being right: of being true and noble, regardless of the consequences. We enjoy it all the while that it's devouring us. Your curse is chemistry."

"What?"

I heard the crack of a bullwhip in my brain. How odd that the sound had escaped my ears.

"Driven!" I whispered. The word leaked from my lips like poison.

Father nodded. "I didn't want to vanish from your lives, but I had no choice. The decision was made in other rooms by other powers. I had to die. There was no other way."

I let out a long breath. My world was crumbling.

Here I was, taking tea in an underground cavern with a man whom I had seen laid to rest in the crypt of St. Tancred's; a man for whom I had cried bitter, shuddering tears.

The very thought of it made me tremble.

"At Buckshaw," Father went on, "I was no longer of any use. My position had been compromised. As well, I was now in grave danger. As were my children."

"Me?" I gasped. "Feely? Daffy?"

"Your own investigations, I'm sorry to say, brought to bear upon us a great deal of unwanted publicity."

His words were a punch in the stomach.

I! I myself had been responsible for his failure. It was unthinkable. How could he do this to me?

"I'm sorry," I said, and I hated my mouth for leaking the words.

Father nodded. "I could no longer act the faintly eccentric country squire with a passion for postage stamps."

"All those meetings . . . all those conventions . . . all those philatelic shows . . ."

"Not entirely fraudulent," Father said. "I *was* keen on stamps as a boy."

"You used them as a cloak!" I said, and I felt bitter resentment rising in my throat.

I had been deprived of my father's love—and so had my sisters—by so simple a deception.

I wanted to spit. I wanted to vomit.

"You were also a magician as a boy," I said, recalling the only other instance when Father had really taken the time to talk to me. It had been in a jail cell in Hinley. It had been raining then, too. He had told me about his school days at Greyminster, and of the fatal consequences of what had begun as no more than a schoolboy prank.

"And your old headmaster," I said. "Dr. Kissing. Was he also—"

Father bowed his head and said nothing.

Dr. Kissing was still alive, although he, too, had been long cut off from the world in a private nursing home called Rook's End. I had twice visited the old gentleman there and had twice fallen under his spell.

Suddenly it all made sense.

"Was he . . . *is* he . . . another of your wheels? Was it he who decided you had to die?"

I had never seen Father look so forlorn. I wanted to fly across the room and hug him and shower him with kisses, but I could not. How can you embrace a man who has ordered the death of other human beings?

The very idea filled me with a sickening, almost inexpressible fury.

I needed first to let the hatred boil away, and hatred, I had already learned, can be a slow, slow thing. If love was sugar, hate was lead.

Oddly enough, lead can exist in a form called lead acetate, or sugar of lead, which, though poisonous, is sweet to the taste.

Sweet poison! Wheels within wheels! Spinning . . . always and forever spinning!

"Are you coming home to Buckshaw?" I asked, my voice trembling. It was the question that was burning at the back of my brain. Did I really want him to?

"No," Father said gently. "I cannot. Heaven and earth were moved to grant me safety here, and it cannot be undone."

I knew he was telling the truth. Our whole lives had been stage-managed by unseen hands. What had been the expense of faking a funeral; of pretending probate of his will? Of leaving me the mistress of Buckshaw?

Those bridges had been burned. I could see that clearly now. You cannot call back the smoke. You cannot cram the genie back into his jar.

Wheels within wheels, most of them unknown and unsuspected.

I had to make a stand.

"Very well, Father. Or should I call you Asterion?"

"Asterion will do for now," he said with a wry smile on his face. "You may call me Father when I'm dead again."

"May I ask you one favor?"

"Perhaps," he said.

"Major Greyleigh. Who murdered him?"

"I don't know, precisely. But I do know why."

"Why?" I said, pressing my advantage, if indeed I had one.

"He saw me here. He carried out the occasional contract for the powers that be. He was a hangman, you know."

"Yes, I knew that," I said. "It was not a well-kept secret."

"He plied his trade in the wake of the Nuremberg trials. A minor, but necessary, cog."

"What did he do to deserve his death?" I asked. "Was it revenge?"

"No," Father said. "His crime was that he came to Leathcote to look up an old friend, and saw me here, walking in the rain. And he recognized me. That in itself was not necessarily a death sentence, but he made the fatal mistake of telling someone else. He had to be silenced. The order was given."

"By you?" I asked.

Father shook his head as if all the burdens of the world were on his shoulders.

"But you let it happen?"

I could scarcely believe my own boldness. This was my own father I was holding to account.

"I tried to stop it. You must believe me, Flavia. I drove to Bishop's Lacey and to Moonflower Cottage, but it was too late. The command had already been carried out."

"Whom did he tell?" I demanded, perhaps a bit too loudly. My words rang in the air like gunshots.

"I'm sorry, Flavia. I cannot say. There's a limit to everything."

"Except wheels," I said bitterly.

"Except wheels," Father said quietly. "And now you must go. Our time is at an end. You have found out what you came to find out."

He got slowly up out of his chair and came toward me. Hope sprang up in my breast.

"When will I see you again?" I asked.

His complete silence told me the truth.

"*Will* I ever see you again?"

"No," he said. "I have much to do, and when it's done, I am commanded—it is my duty—to vanish without a trace. The lives of thousands depend upon my being dead and remaining dead. Do you see? I beg you to keep this meeting secret. It will benefit no one if it becomes known and will bring great harm to many."

Kissed off! Just like that!

"So, I shall become one of the wheels," I said.

Father reached out and took my hand. He gave it a firm shake. "My dear," he said, "surely you know. You *have* been one of the wheels for a very long time."

"But—"

"But me no buts," Father said, and the devil actually smiled. "I shall ring the guardhouse and ask the sergeant to pick you up. He's waiting in the rain."

And so am I, I thought.

We British are known for manufacturing things from

iron and steel: everything from steam engines to battle-ships, from girders to garden benches, and now, apparently, hearts.

I had spent most of my life trying to get closer to this man, and suddenly I couldn't wait to get away from him.

I got to my feet and walked to the door. With my hand on the knob, I turned back.

I took a deep breath. "Father," I said, "I love you—but that's all."

And I marched out, not looking back, my heels clicking on the swabbed concrete floor like the knitting needles—or whatever they call them—of the Greek Fates.

With a squeal of brakes, the jeep drew up on the gravel sweep at Buckshaw. Had anyone heard us in the house?

We had driven all the way from Leathcote in darkness and silence, the sergeant and I ignoring each other like a couple of mutes at an undertaker's picnic. We did not like each other and there was no point in pretending we did.

I climbed out of the jeep, determined not to look back. *Give him at least a forefinger of farewell,* my inner voice pleaded. *It's not his fault. He's just a pawn in this game of gears.*

I turned and raised a hand. It could have passed as thanks, or the wiping away of a raindrop.

But the sergeant had already put the jeep in reverse

and was backing in a tight circle on the gravel, glancing over his shoulder as if he were steering a bumper car at the Brighton Pier.

With a crunch of gears and a rooster tail of white gravel, he spun away into the darkness. Was he intentionally trying to awaken the household?

"*Salmagundi!*" I called out after him, but not very loudly. It was the worst word I could think of at the spur of the moment.

A sliver of dawn was in the east, and I shivered.

What a wicked turn my life had taken! I was suddenly no longer an orphan. I had become a daughter without benefits, my father stolen by a shadowy gang of double-dealers in Death.

Had it really happened? Had I really found my dead father alive, living like an underhanded rabbit, plotting the downfall of strangers from an underground sanctuary?

It seemed unlikely. It was the stuff of drugged dreams: the chaff of a madwoman's brain.

Was I living in a lie?

But ho-hum, said my inner voice. Hadn't I been practically without a father since the day I was born? Father at first had been in Burma and Thailand with Dogger, captive to the Japanese and forced to labor on the so-called Death Railway. It had broken both of them, but in different ways. Dogger still suffered from recurring delusions that he was once again bloodied in chains, and Father from his pantomime performance of a country gentleman.

I could see it all now: the greasepaint and the lime-light; a quiet collector of postage stamps in a remote and sleepy village. How carefully it had all been planned! And how artfully acted—until now. Until today when I—his own daughter!—had broken the code and confronted him in his lair. Was I a traitor—or a heroine?

It was all too much for my brain. While I was designed by Nature to study chemistry, the endless arrangements of atoms that spell out the formulae of the universe, family entanglements were beyond my power.

As I had done before when returning home at an inhuman hour, I made my way round to the southeast corner of the house and grabbed an old familiar vine.

"Flavia of the Apes," I said to amuse myself, and I found myself grinning stupidly as I climbed hand over hand up to one of the laboratory windows—a window that I left permanently ajar for emergencies such as this—and scrambled in over the sill.

"I thought you'd never get home," Undine said from the shadows.

I nearly soiled myself. What was this nasty little nuisance doing in my private laboratory?

"I fell asleep," she said, "but that blasted jeep woke me up. Where did you go? Got a crush? Night watchman at Leathcote?" She touched my elbow confidentially. "I won't tell. Promise."

I kept my mouth shut for fear of flames shooting out. But oh, how I longed for a magic wand to turn this little nuisance into something useful, such as a chamber pot, or a spit bucket.

"Who else is awake all night?" she demanded. "Who else has a jeep?"

"Oh, dry up," I said.

How perilously close to the truth this creepy child had come! I'd have to keep an eye on her. I remembered once when I had called Daffy "creepy" to her face, she had replied that the word, in Scotland, denoted the name of the stool the pastor stood on in the pulpit to make himself seem taller. You can never one-up a know-it-all.

If belittlement were swordsmanship, Daffy would be Basil Rathbone.

I seized Undine by the scruff of the neck and shoved her out into the hall.

"Go to bed!" I hissed. "And stay there!"

And for once the little stinker obeyed.

· T E N ·

OF ALL THE MEALTIMES of the day, breakfast is the grisliest. Our brains and bodies have not yet had their chemical brakes released, and our powers are accordingly diminished. At least, that's the way I see it, based upon my own observations.

This breakfast was no different. I had come downstairs groggily, still bound in the chains of dreams and suspicions; still numb with the shock of coming face-to-face with my dead father.

I slid silently into my chair, giving only a slight nod to Mrs. Mullet. She smiled in acknowledgment of my hermit behavior.

Daffy was staring intently at the pages of a book called *East of Eden*, which was propped open with a fork and a butter knife.

Undine had already seated herself at the table, knife

and fork in hand, their butt ends planted firmly on the tablecloth, business ends pointed at the ceiling, her mouth open in a fierce and hideous display of teeth.

Mrs. M knew well enough to feed her first to allow time for my juices to stir and make me more civil.

"What do you fancy today, dear?"

"Poo Pudding," Undine said. "And a piece of Pumble-chook Pie."

"Sorry, dear," Mrs. Mullet said. "The Poo Pudding's all gone. They et it up yesterday at the Idiots' Picnic."

Like all of those who labor in servitude, Mrs. Mullet had a shrewd sense of humor when pressed.

"I'll bring you some nice toast and jelly to get you started. What kind of jelly would you like?"

"Pus," Undine said. "Plain old pus. And some toasted toenails!"

"As good as done," said Mrs. Mullet.

I could tell by the slight crinkle at the corners of her mouth that she had already laid her plan. She would slather a couple of toasted slices of bread with a spoon-ful of her abominable custard pie filling. She would snip some bits of breadcrust into passable dirty toenails: It would be almost as good as the real thing, and both the giver and the recipient would be happy.

She mimed jotting the order on the palm of her hand with an invisible pencil.

"And you, Miss Flavia?"

"I should like half a grapefruit," I said. It was the most insipid thing I could think of on the spur of the moment. The very thought of it almost made me gag, but it would set me as far apart as possible from this witlet who sat across the table from me, whom I both loved and hated with all the clouds and conflagrations of Heaven and Hell.

"And toast on the trivet," I said. There was nothing worse than water-tainted toast. I would tear strips from the hot, crispy buttered bread to form the so-called soldiers, whose fate was to march into my mouth and into the Valley of Death.

"And put a bit of poison on it," I said, more to outdo Undine than anything. Mrs. Mullet, I knew, would sprinkle a pinch of cinnamon on the toast to provide a bit of menace.

"Very good, dear," Mrs. M said. "And a nice cup of tea?"

"I'm going to start up a company devoted to tea," Undine interrupted. "Carl says that to get filthy rich you must use your noggin. He says I have a good noggin and I ought to use it more. *So,* I thought: *What is it that everyone does all the time,* and then I thought, *Tea!*

"We're a nation of tea drinkers, aren't we? Sometimes that's all we do. So, I'm going to start up a company to bring everybody tea—*in bed!*"

She shouted the last words and looked round the table at us, as pleased with herself as God must have been when He'd created the Heavens and Earth and saw that it was Good.

"I shall call it T. Ladies," she went on. "We'll go round all the houses and bring people their morning tea in bed. All my ladies will be called by the same name:

Mrs. Malcolm-Wise. It will suggest that they are posh and just oozing with brains.

"Good morning, Mr. So-and-So, or Mrs. So-and-So, we'll say to them, as we pour out the old Earl Grey or Lapsang Oolong or whatever they've ordered. *It's raining again today, and the Prime Minister is at Chequers with his dog. The king is in his counting house and I'm here with your Orange Pekoe.* That's a joke, Flavia: to start their day with a bit of humor.

"Good morning, Mrs. Malcolm-Wise, they'll answer. *Could I please have just a touch of lemon in the old brew this morning? I was making rather merry last evening and my eyeballs ache.*

"How about that, Flavia? Isn't that brilliant? Don't you admire me? I'll be rolling in the dough and driving a Bentley with louvers. Tea in bed! Think of it! Every man a millionaire! What do you think? Honestly."

I am of two minds about tea. On the one hand I adore it because it contains a healthy slug of tannic acid: a fetching stew of hydrogen, oxygen, and carbon which, just a few years ago, was still being used in cases of strychnine poisoning because of its ability to precipitate the strychnine into a harmless salt by forming hydrogen bonds. On the other hand, tannic acid, by combining with animal gelatin, converts skin into leather, and although I was born into a tribe of Leather Stomachs, I didn't really fancy the idea of having a gut like a Highland bagpipe.

"I think I'd prefer a cup of cocoa this morning," I said to Mrs. Mullet.

My encounter with Father at Leathcote had left me still feeling slightly sick to my stomach. The nitric oxide in the cocoa would produce a calming effect by reducing my blood pressure. There was a whole day ahead to be planned, and I hadn't the foggiest idea where to begin.

The Girl Guides have all those songs you're forced to sing about starting with a little step and putting your best foot forward, and so forth: poor advice, I always thought, if you were living on a ledge. The best plan, to my way of thinking, was to have a good gander in all directions before moving so much as a toe, and that's what I planned to do.

I managed to make it through breakfast by pretending to pout. As Daffy was an old hand at moodiness, she didn't notice my silence, and a tight smile at Mrs. Mullet was enough.

After a single bite of toast I pushed back my chair and got up from the table.

"Tell Mrs. Mullet I've come down with the Black Plague," I told Undine.

"Roger, over and out, Sneezo," she said.

I left the room before a murder—*another* murder—was committed. I went straight to the greenhouse. No one would bother me there.

I found Dogger mixing an insecticide of whale oil soap and an emulsion of kerosene in a zinc watering can.

"What's up, Doc?" I asked in a Bugs Bunny voice, trying to cheer myself up. Was I whistling in the dark, trying

202 · ALAN BRADLEY

to bridge the great gulf that had opened between us? I now knew something of vital importance that Dogger did not, and I wasn't sure I cared for the feeling.

"Thrips," he said, and went silent.

Did he know about Father? And if he didn't, ought I to tell him?

"It rained in the night," I said conversationally.

"Yes."

"Dogger," I said, "I need some advice."

"Yes," he said.

Was that a "yes" with a question mark after it, meaning "What advice do you need?" Or was it an emphatic "*yes!*" meaning "*You certainly do!*"?

"Are you good at keeping secrets?" I asked.

"Not particularly," Dogger said.

"Not particularly?" I repeated.

"I can keep a secret if required to do so, but I am against secrets on general principle. They ought not to be required in a truly civilized society."

"Ah!" I said.

"I believe," Dogger went on, "that I am more opposed to being *asked* to keep a secret than the actual keeping of one."

"Ah!" I said again.

"You may recall that Timycha of Sparta, when she was either six months or ten months pregnant, bit off her own tongue rather than reveal the secrets of Pythagoras to the tyrant Dionysus. She spat it out at his feet."

I was going to look up good old Timycha the first chance I got. She was a girl after my own heart.

"One signs the Official Secrets Act, of course," Dogger went on, "but that is an entirely different matter. Most of the ancient philosophers, including Confucius, Plato, and Aristotle, believed that the most important thing was a virtuous friendship."

"And is that what you believe?"

"Yes, it is," Dogger said, loading some of his insecticide into a ribbed rubber atomizer. "Those ancient gentlemen were very seldom wrong."

"Then that is what I shall believe," I said.

"Very wise," Dogger said and walked out the door toward the roses.

So that was that. The decision had fallen into my lap like Newton's apple.

I would keep Father's secret, I decided as I walked back from the greenhouse. But if I couldn't have a virtuous friendship with him, I would have a virtuous friendship with somebody else.

I waited until Undine had trotted off to St. Tancred's for a confirmation class. Aunt Felicity had insisted on it, in spite of all the obstacles.

"The girl needs guidance," she had said. "Even if it's from above." And she chuckled that warm, humorous chuckle she always uses when being ironical. I could have strangled her. Warm, humorous chuckles set all my alarm bells ringing, even if they come from family. *Especially* if they come from family.

I had been appointed to accompany Undine to her first few classes. Don't ask me why. The ways of Heaven do not come easily to me. Which is why, in part, I had decided to skip today's session. This little girl had no need of an armed escort.

At the very first class, she had piped up and said to the vicar, "Ibu said that all clergymen are beating an empty tub."

"Well, dear," the vicar had responded, with a gentle smile, "that may well be so, but many find the bucket filled with faith."

"And what is faith?" Undine shot back.

"It's a mystery," the vicar had replied.

"Ibu said anyone who tries to explain anything by claiming it's a mystery is a carpetbagger," Undine said, crossing her arms.

The vicar smiled a frail smile. "Your Ibu was being very protective of you," he said. And then, as an after-thought, "Did she say anything else?"

I could see his strategy. He wanted to clear the decks of any unsuspected explosives before proceeding with the class.

"Yes," Undine said, standing with her legs apart and her hands planted firmly on her hips. "She said if Darwin was right, how come Jesus had no living descendants?"

"An excellent question," the vicar said. "Perhaps we shall come to that in due course."

As I opened the kitchen door, my thoughts flew back for a moment to Father—then suddenly to Mrs. Mullet—and a sudden paralyzing thought: Might she, too, be a member of the Nide?

I froze on the doorstep and a shiver shook my shoulders. This thought had never occurred to me before, even though I had known her all my life.

Well, why not? I thought. For donkey's years she had been in constant and easy contact with Father, who might just be the biggest of all the big wheels. And who would ever suspect a country-house cook?

She was, like me, invisible.

My tongue was itching to ask her what she had picked up at the Cluck and Grumble, but some deep, hidden signal was telling me to be careful: that sharing secrets with the wrong person could be fatal.

What was going on in the woman's mind? When Inspector Hewitt came to question her, she had been all in a tizzy at being a suspect, before pretending it was all an act when left alone with Dogger and me. Her wild laughter at the memory of things she had seen meant something deeper—much deeper—than mistaken identity.

Still, the two of us had sworn to protect her. In one way or another, she could well be an accessory to murder. Unless she told us the whole truth, it was going to be no stroll in the sunshine.

I sidled in a carefree manner into the kitchen. Mrs. M was polishing the cooker.

"What-ho, Mistress Mullet," I said. "What do you know about shellfish poisoning?"

"Well, I've seen it once or twice," she said. "Up at Lady Rex-Wells's. Big place like that, you're bound to, aren't you? Seafood from Africa to Zanzibar. Fish knives and oyster forks, all sterlin' silver. 'Course, when there's a slipup like that, they 'ushes it up. Don't want it gettin' about. I mind the time we got a bad bit of cornered beef from Ireland. Botulism, the doctor said it was. Very nasty business."

"Tell me about the shellfish," I said, already guessing half the answer.

"Oh! That was 'orrid! Cook served up some butter clams that Professor Maybank—the famous polar explorer, you know—brought from Alaska. Twelve people throwin' up their garters! Two dead, includin' the professor. It was in the *Daily Mail* an' all."

"So, it would be fair to say you're well acquainted with shellfish poisoning?" I said, without pressing the point.

"Prob'ly as much as you are." Mrs. Mullet said, pouncing on my question like a cat. She was no fool.

"I hadn't seen it firsthand before Major Greyleigh," I said.

"Was it shellfish for certain? I thought as much. Vomit like a fire 'ose."

"Yes. I did a chemical analysis."

"I knew it! I knew it! I knew it!"

She took a deep breath, then looked me in the eye. "I've brought somethin' you wanted to see."

She rummaged in a sideboard and pulled out her purse. It was a flat straw Monday-go-to-market receptacle, good for carrying everything from a check to a chicken. She reached into the depths and dredged up a small sketchbook.

"I'm not very good yet, but Alf says I'll improve."

As she flipped the book open to the first page, I gasped. There, in pencil, flat on the floor in all his departed glory, lay Major Greyleigh. She had caught him to the last gruesome detail: the half-light in his dead eyes, the clean-shaven chin with three missed whiskers in the shadow of the jaw. His mouth was open, and a tiny Niagara of spittle hung from the lower corner of his mouth.

"He was not long dead, then," I said. Spit evaporates.

"No," she whispered. "I thought there might still be some life in 'im, but there was no breathin'."

She reached again into her purse and extracted a round compact made of Bakelite in imitation tortoise-shell.

"I 'eld it to 'is lips . . ." She simulated the action, stooping almost to her knees. "No mist on the mirror. No fog. I started to cry. Couldn't 'elp myself."

Even now Mrs. Mullet was quivering at the memory. I gave her time to recover by glancing quickly at the remaining sketches.

"There, there," I said, putting my hand on her shoulder. "Your drawings are quite extraordinary. You missed your true calling, Mrs. M. But why?"

"Why what?" she asked.

"Why did you sketch him? Weren't you afraid?"

"Afraid?" she said. "I 'aven't been afraid since I've been grown up. You gets over it."

"But why?" I persisted.

"Why did I draw 'im? Ahhhh." She let out a long sigh.

"Love," she said at last, "or what used to be love—what's left of it—'as roots as deep as them yew trees in the churchyard. You never knows what's goin' on down there. I knew I'd never 'ave another chance. Might not make much sense right now, but you'll understand in time."

"But I *do* understand," I said. "I understand perfectly. That's precisely how I feel."

I loved the feel of the word "precisely" in my mouth. It was like a swig of cider on the terrace on a hot summer's day. It made me feel somehow more adult; more wise; more in control of my scattershot world.

I threw my arms around her, and she hugged me back—then pulled away as if she had said too much.

"So you like 'em," she said. "My little portraits . . ."

"They're brilliant," I said.

For an instant I felt an utter fool. I had been grousing earlier about facing a case without a corpse and now, right here in our own kitchen, before my very eyes, was a notebook containing sketches of the scene, as beautiful as if they had been drawn by the hand of Leonardo da Vinci.

And then a horrid thought occurred. "Did you show these to Inspector Hewitt?"

"No. 'E never asked. And besides, 'e was almost accusin' me to my face of bein' a killer. If 'e'd got a gander at my drawin's, 'e'd 'ave known that I was at whatchacallit—the scene of the crime. That I 'ad the—what is it Mrs. Christie calls it?"

"Means, motive, and opportunity," I said. "You might have had all three."

"'Might have' don't cobble no cauliflowers. 'Might have' don't cut no rice. 'Might have' don't pluck no chickens."

"I see your point," I said, "but that isn't how the minds of Agatha Christie and Inspector Hewitt work."

"No," she said. "I don't know about 'im, but I've borrowed some of 'er books from the libary. Alf says they're all the same: *A shot rang out* . . . followed by three 'undred pages of village folk dancin' about in smocks."

"May I borrow this?" I asked, covering the notebook protectively with my hand.

"Keep it for now," she said, with what might have been a wink. "If I ever want it, I'll ask for it."

I was shoving the treasure into my pocket when I heard a most peculiar squeaking noise outside. My painfully acute hearing was able to detect certain sounds at an almost unbelievable distance, and this was one of them: an asymmetrical squeak like a baby bird with the wobbles.

"It's the vicar's car," I said. "What could he possibly want?"

The vicar's tired old Morris Oxford had not one but two defunct wheel bearings, which went in and out of synchronization at various speeds, all of them annoying.

"I 'ope it's not bad news," Mrs. Mullet said. "It sometimes is, with vicars."

The kitchen door swung open and in stalked Undine, followed by the vicar. She was in a state, and I knew it before she spoke. The vicar was wringing his hands.

"Ah! Flavia," he said. "Mrs. Mullet."

"What is it?" I asked. "Has something happened?"

"Well, no and yes," the vicar said. "There's been an incident, you see . . . at the confirmation class."

"More stink bombs?" I asked, trying to sound jovial.

"No, nothing like that," the vicar said. "It's just that Undine—I thought of having Cynthia bring her home, and then I thought, no, that's not fair to the child."

Whatever Undine had done, it must have been a corker. The vicar was accustomed to dealing with unruly children, and in his time had handled more than a few nasty breaches of Christian fellowship.

"Well, you see," he began, "we set aside a time to take the little ones from the vicarage into the church, to mingle with some of the older parishioners. The good ladies of the Altar Guild volunteer for this reception into the religious community, if you will. We sing a hymn, to establish a bond of music . . . a bond of, ah, Christian citizenship. It is a solemn moment in the new life of the candidate: a sharing of love and faith; a sharing of youth and age. A most solemn moment."

"Yes," I said.

"One of the ladies presides at the organ. We always have a children's hymn: simplicity and great reverence. Today the hymn was 'Fairest Lord Jesus.'"

Since I had sung it myself on several occasions, I remembered it well. I could still hear the perpetual greenery of the words echoing in my head:

Fair are the meadows, fairer still the woodlands . . .

"Our singing was suddenly interrupted," the vicar

said, "by a most unholy music, and I use that word advisedly. It may only be described as a god-awful twanging."

As he spoke, he fished in the pocket of his vest and extracted a peculiar metallic device, which he gripped between his thumb and forefinger. It dangled in our faces like a dead rat.

"I borrowed Carl's jaw harp," Undine said. "You should have heard it with the organ, Flavia! Simply smashing."

She clasped her hands beneath her chin in ecstasy.

I wiped my mouth, using the movement to shape my face into a disapproving look.

"Some of the older ladies were so upset," the vicar said, "I had no choice but to cancel the class."

"I'm sorry, Vicar," I said. "I'm sure Undine is sorry also. Aren't you, Undine?"

"Yup," she said. "With peas and cream and sugar on it."

Her eyes, as she spoke, were like those of a blue-eyed tiger, deep and feral. She terrified me.

"Well, then, I'd better be getting back," the vicar said. He caught my eye and gave me a look that was more shocking in what it didn't say than in what it did.

It was Mrs. Mullet who broke the spell.

"Run along to your room, miss," she said. "I'll bring you up a nice cup of tea with biscuits directly."

The vicar rubbed his hands together and with a tight smile made his exit. A few moments later we heard the old familiar squeak of his Morris's faulty bearings.

Undine had vanished from the room like smoke.

"It's us as needs the cup of tea," Mrs. Mullet said. "Young miss can cool 'er 'eels upstairs and brood upon 'er crimes."

I smiled and Mrs. Mullet smiled back; then I chuckled, and Mrs. Mullet chuckled with me, and before we knew it, we were both gripping the kitchen table and shaking with helpless laughter.

Then just as it began to subside, Mrs. Mullet said "crimes" again and set us off once more.

I had never in my life felt so close to another human being. It was a fierce and frightening new experience.

"I have to go upstairs," I said. "I'll take Undine her tea."

Mrs. Mullet shook her head. "I shall see to that," she said. "You run up and have a good squint at my drawings."

That was precisely what I was planning to do. This woman was uncanny. She seemed to possess all the powers of the witches in the Scottish play, minus the cackle.

She was formidable. Yes, that was the word I was after: "formidable."

·ELEVEN·

UPSTAIRS, IN MY LABORATORY, I placed Mrs. M's sketchbook on Uncle Tar's desk and picked up a magnifying glass. Again, I was astounded by the quality of the work. Like all the best artists, her sketches gave the impression of being tossed off casually when they were, in reality, anything but. They shared a dignity and lightness of touch with E. H. Shepard's ink drawings in *Winnie-the-Pooh*.

I looked, for instance, at the dead fingers of Major Greyleigh, the subtle angles of the fingers, not relaxed as you might expect in a corpse, but as ready to spring into action as the finger of a marksman on the trigger: the tight, tortured muscles of a poison victim, written as clearly in Mrs. Mullet's sketch as a newspaper headline.

She had caught the slightly threadbare nature of his

collar and the subtle shadowing of his skin as the horse-man of Death came galloping toward him.

I wet my thumb and turned the page, and there, in addition to the major's body, were the articles of kitchen furniture: the table, the chair, the sideboard, the little tin food safe. She had even captured the wet results, on the floor tiles, of the major's vomiting.

It was obvious that Mrs. Mullet had been there be-fore the industrious Mary Belter had cleaned the place up. Had anyone else, besides the police, been in the kitchen of Moonflower Cottage between her visit and mine?

So much to think about. So much to sort and sift. Sometimes I wished I had two skulls and two brains, so that I could think two things at once. As far as I can see, this is the greatest shortcoming in our human de-sign.

As I pored over the sketches, I noticed something I had missed before: a smudge on the floor beside the dead man's hand. Mrs. Mullet had shaded it in with the lightest touch of her pencil. It was rather like a waffle: the faintest hint of crossing lines.

Something clicked. It was a footprint!

Just thinking about having a second head had given me one. Whether it was second sight or what is called the subconscious, I do not know, but I gave praise and thanks anyway.

And it paid off! In another instant my newfound brain coughed up another message: The pattern was one I had seen before, and recently. But where?

With two brains my mind was teeming. Did Mrs. Mullet's pencil sketch prove that she had not mopped the floor of Moonflower Cottage? Would a person record a vital clue on paper and then obliterate the original? Or would they obliterate it anyway, realizing that no one would ever suspect them of doing such an illogical thing?

Sometimes, there are no answers. At other times there are too many.

The answer, of course, was always at hand. I would show the sketchbook to Dogger.

As light on my feet as Moira Shearer clinging on to a rope dangling from the Graf Zeppelin, I dashed down the stairs and out the front door. I didn't want to attract too much attention by cutting through the kitchen. But Dogger was not in the greenhouse, nor was he in the coach house. I dashed to the edge of the overgrown lawns we called the Visto: a couple of acres of weeds and crumbling statues that had once been an immaculate Georgian vista.

Dogger was nowhere in sight. Had he experienced one of his spells? Although he had been mercifully free of them for many months, they could recur at any time—and when they did, Dogger could in an instant become a shattered soul howling at the moon. The agony of captivity and torture during the war had broken him, and I sometimes wondered if he could ever be set right again. His Furies lay always in waiting.

Dogger had said more or less the same thing one horrid day when I found him huddled trembling in the potting shed. He had slowly regained his senses with my arms wrapped around him.

"My name is Humpty Dumpty. My rank is captain. My serial number is—" he had whispered, before slumping over in a bundle, and I had crooned him into a sleep that was to last for almost eighteen hours. Because I was reluctant to move him, I brought pillows and his old army blanket from the house and bundled him against the coolness of the night. In the morning I told everyone that he had been called away on business, which was more or less the truth. Afterward, he didn't remember a single moment of the episode.

Now, half in horror, I ran to the house and up the stairs to his room. I knocked but there was no answer. I tried the door, and it swung slowly open. I stepped inside and let out a sigh. The room was empty.

I was about to turn away when a scrap of paper caught my eye. Centered neatly on the bed was a handwritten note.

Miss Flavia—I have taken the liberty of borrowing the Rolls-Royce to visit a friend. Yours faithfully, Arthur Dogger.

Good old Dogger. Propriety oozing from every pore. Not a word too many or too few. He knew that I would check his bedroom first out of concern for his well-being. And he didn't want his note to be found by any-one other than me.

I have to admit an instant curiosity as to who the friend might be. The only one of Dogger's friends I had met was Claire Tetlock, that quietly shining creature who had known Dogger in another life: in the long ago, as they had explained it to me. Dogger would scarcely consult her about a murdered hangman, though. Or would he? I should have to wait and see.

I had concluded that Dogger was as much a mystery to himself as he was to me. His ordeal had left his mind sometimes dancing in starlight on the outer edges of the universe, and other times trodden face down in the mud. The fact was that these two states were like the two sides of a shilling: bound forever together to be flipped through all eternity until the Final Furnace.

"On the snoop again, Flavia?"

Undine again.

I spun round, partly embarrassed and partly because I hadn't heard her coming. Was I going deaf?

"I'm practicing walking around with bed socks on," Undine said. "All the better to eavesdrop. I'm also try-ing to find a way to suck up to you, so I'm going to help you find this Asterion you were looking for. Who is he, anyway?"

"He's a mythical creature who lives in a subterra-nean maze on the island of Crete. Go ask Daffy to look it up in the encyclopedia."

"I don't need to ask Daffy. I'm quite capable of look-ing it up myself."

"I know," I said, "but ask her anyway. She needs to feel wanted."

"You're trying to get rid of me, aren't you?" Undine said.

"Yes," I said. "Now go haunt Daffy. She has a soft spot for spooks."

"I can't," Undine said.

"Why not?"

"She's not speaking to me."

"Oh, really?" I said. "Why not?"

"Don't you remember what happened at Pentecost?"

"How could I ever forget it? You screamed 'Boo!' as we were singing 'Come Holy Ghost.' The vicar asked you to leave. You ought to be ashamed of yourself."

"Well, I'm not. I told them Daffy had put me up to it. I told them it was a joke, and that they had missed the point."

I sighed. "What kind of person are you, anyway?"

"I am a bright and intelligent girl. I have a kind heart and not too shabby a soul. I once told that to the archbishop of Canterbury. To his face."

I was instantly agog.

"You met the archbishop of Canterbury?"

Undine nodded. "At a garden party. Ibu introduced me to him as 'my little stigma.' "

I had an irresistible urge to hug her and heal her. What kind of monster had Lena de Luce been? What kind of monster would her child become?

"You're joking," I said instead. "Who would do a thing like that?"

"Ibu would. As soon as we got outside, she told me that Sir Arthur Shipley had pointed out that even the archbishop of Canterbury comprises fifty percent water."

Sir Arthur Shipley, I recalled, was the world's foremost authority on parasitic worms.

"I'll tell you what," I said. "Why don't you go gather some death cap mushrooms? I desperately need a few for an experiment."

I didn't, but it sounded genuine. Because I firmly believe that death caps do furnish a room, I like to keep a few of these bright red warty wonders scattered about in small vases as resting places for the eye. Undine would skip off merrily with thoughts of dark deeds stewing in her brain, and I would be left alone to get on with my investigation.

"They're the ones with the colorful caps. You'll find them growing under the three oaks just beyond the Visto.

"And after you've picked them," I told her, "don't put your fingers in your mouth. On second thought, take some gloves from the greenhouse, do you understand?"

"Yowza," she said, and she was gone. I heard the sound of her thundering feet fading away down the stairs. It reminded me of something, but I couldn't for the life of me think what.

I began to have second thoughts almost immediately. Who in their right mind would send a child to handle deadly poison? But then I thought: *Why not?* There comes a time in every girl's life when she must be trusted; a time at which she must, even in a small way, be set free. It's like riding a bicycle for the first time, and even more like later discovering you can let go of the handlebars. I had done so myself, hadn't I? Even though it had cost me a black eye and a trip up to London and a visit to that despised dentist's office in Farrington Street.

Gladys had fortunately come to rest without a scratch, despite ending up in a nearby bramble bush, so that the only real damage had been to my mouth and Father's pocketbook.

I touched my face and felt a smile forming. Undine would come through with flying colors, and I would not be dragged into the dock on a charge of manslaughter.

It's called trust, and it's often the hardest thing we are called upon to do in our lives.

"Don't lick your fingers!" I whispered.

I went to one of the east windows and looked out almost fondly. Undine was already just a small figure with a wicker basket striding determinedly toward the distant trees.

Her mention of Sir Arthur Shipley (how odd that she had remembered his name) reminded me that Sir Arthur had been not just vice-chancellor of the University of Cambridge, but also the author of several dozen publications on zoology. At least one of these, *Pearls and Parasites,* I remembered seeing in Uncle Tar's library. Despite the promising title, I had not found time to read it. If only I could find it now . . .

Uncle Tar's books were shelved by size, and then by

color and then alphabetically, which made a lot of sense to me. In my experience, the visual memory of a book is the one that first comes to mind, followed by the color, then by the title and/or the name of the author. Indexing is a juggling act: a gift possessed by very few. Or at least, so says my sister Daffy.

A dark book, as I recall, bound in rough, soiled linen the color of rancid olive oil. And here it was: *Pearls and Parasites*.

Sir Arthur got off to a good start on the very first page by quoting Sir Edward Arnold:

Know you, perchance, how that poor formless wretch—
The Oyster—gems his shallow moon-lit chalice?

And then almost immediately, before you've had time to digest that tasty morsel, he quotes the poet Thomas Moore:

Precious the tear as that rain from the sky
Which turns into pearls as it falls in the sea.

"Certain Eastern peoples," he begins, "believe that pearls are due to raindrops falling into the oyster shells which conveniently gape to receive them."

He goes on for a while before getting to the poisons, but even by skimming, I could see that Sir Arthur knew what he was talking about.

I was leafing through the book to see what the author had to say about poisoning by bivalve when I heard a distant scream. If it hadn't been for my extremely acute hearing, and for the fact that it was calling my name—"Flavia! Flavia! Flavia!"—I might have missed it entirely.

I rushed to the window and looked out across the Visto.

A wall of black roiling smoke was blowing toward the house. As if out of nowhere, an east wind had sprung up, driving the flames from the burning grass. I lifted the heavy window in its frame just long enough to shout "I'm coming! I'm coming!" then slammed it shut again. A brick wall and thick window glass were a good fire retardant; an open window was not.

I raced down the stairs, grabbing two brooms from the butler's pantry on the way. Out the kitchen door I went, flying like Pieter Bruegel's Mad Meg, leading her army of women on the way to pillage Hell. Across the Visto I went, through the acrid stench of the smoke, waving the brooms as if their faint breeze could drive back the flames.

By the time I got to Undine, her eyes, too, were red and streaming. She was trying to wipe them with her elbows.

"Take this," I shouted, shoving one of the brooms into her hands. With the other, I began to beat at the flames, as if cleaning the filthiest carpet in the world. Undine joined in and we swatted away at the burning grass like a pair of blacksmiths on a German town clock.

The flames were already halfway to the house and were getting ahead of us. If they reached the coach house, which still had old bales of hay stacked in the loft, we were lost. The bristles of both our brooms were black and burning, the wooden handles smoldering.

"Keep going!" I shouted to Undine. "This is fun!"

She shot me half a smile, not entirely convinced.

Now we were working in silence as the facts struck home. It was like a scene in a horror film. Two girls with two brooms working against utter disaster. No time to think.

Swat! Swat! Swat!

It is a remarkable fact that the human mind, when threatened, can generate hilarity, perhaps as an antidote to danger.

A little broom closet at the back of my mind had been flung open by the broom in my hands, and out sprang the words of Lewis Carroll. I shouted them to Undine:

"If seven (swat!) *maids with seven* (swat!) *mops*
"Swept it for half a year,
" 'Do you suppose,' the Walrus said,
" 'That they could get it clear?' "

And Undine shouted back:

" 'I doubt it,' said the Carpenter (swat!),
"And shed a bitter tear."

"'O Oysters, come and walk with us!'" I replied, coughing and almost in tears.

Here were the oysters again! Oysters, oysters, everywhere. What could it all mean?

It was at that moment that I saw Dogger come swarming onto the Visto, a stirrup pump in hand, with which he began spraying a red fire-retardant liquid onto the flames. He looked as if he knew precisely what he was doing: very businesslike, as if he had been putting out fires all his life.

As Undine made a few last whacks at the grass and we laid down our brooms, Dogger made quick work of the remaining flames. Soon there was nothing left but the three of us amid the rising smoke.

"Excellent work," Dogger said. "Quick thinking and perfect execution. Take a bow."

And the two of us, Undine and I, grasped our waists and bent, sweeping off imaginary hats to an invisible audience, much as Carl Pendracka had done at the damaged lych-gate. The only difference was that our bows were not a joke; they were deadly serious, and we stood basking for as long as we could in imagined applause.

"How did that get started?" I asked Undine. "Did you see anyone in the woods?"

"I heard a motor, but I couldn't see it. Poachers, possibly?"

Dogger had now led us to the far side of the Visto: to the very verge of the woods. This was where the burnt grass began, forming a long wavy line. Despite the recent rain, the wind and the barren exposure of the Visto had dried the grass to tinder.

But that wasn't all.

"Petrol," Dogger said. "You can smell it. We knew that anyway, didn't we? From the black smoke."

Actually, I hadn't, but I nodded agreeably. Dogger was right: Grass smoke is essentially gray.

"And," Undine chimed in, "fires start from a central point, not a long line. They taught us that during the war."

"You were barely born during the war," I said, but I said it nicely in honor of her recent firefighting service.

"It is fair to say," Dogger said, "that we learned a great deal during the late war, especially about incendiary devices."

"Who would do such a thing?" I asked before realizing with a start that I already knew the answer. And the question remained: How much did Dogger know of the big picture? Of the wheels within wheels?

"The answer might well lie in the woods," he said. "Shall we take a stroll?"

Our shoes blackened with ashes, we walked slowly toward the standing trees. This part of the Buckshaw estate had once been part of a royal hunting preserve but was now all that remained of an even earlier ancient forest. The few shady trails among the trees had been reduced to little more than footpaths. In the litter of leaves behind a fallen oak was a double line of zigzag tracks and the single mark of a boot sole.

"Rough diamond or oval shape, filled with pineapples," Dogger said. "Most distinctive."

I was too afraid to speak. I knew I had seen the prints of these boots before.

I even fancied I knew who was wearing them.

"We'd better get back," I said, looking round at the dark trunks of the trees and the blackened Visto beyond. A sudden wariness had arisen in my mind, and I began to tingle from being out in the open.

Dogger glanced up at the sky. "It's going to rain within the hour. The ground will be soaked. We shall keep an eye on the situation from the greenhouse."

It is surprising how much comfort can be created by sitting on a few potato sacks draped over an upturned pail. Above our heads, the rain streamed down the glass, bathing us in a weird and watery light.

It was like being let down into the ocean's deepest trench in Professor Piccard's bathyscaphe: down and down and away from all the cares of the world, coddled by water. It was no wonder that seeds flourished here. I had never felt so safe and insulated.

But how very odd, I thought, *that I should feel the greatest security in a house made of glass, and with two other people.* It was a puzzling development—and perhaps a troubling one. I pushed the thought aside.

Undine poured the tea for us. I had never noticed until now how beautiful she was. For an instant, her late mother was before us—not as she was in life, but as she might have been.

"Do you like my hair?" Undine asked, smoothing down her frizzled locks. Her face was streaked with soot, and although I suspect that mine was also, I didn't care. Appearance is nothing among friends and a runny nose is like gold in the bank.

"Isn't this lovely?" Undine said, glancing round at our cozy bubble.

Dogger and I both nodded and sipped at our tea.

"Do you happen to have any Peek Freans lying about?" she asked, innocently raising her eyebrows. Which told me instantly that she had been snooping about in the greenhouse when neither of us was there. Dogger did, in fact, keep a spare tin of the biscuits on a shelf among the flowerpots. "In case Her Majesty drops by," he had once told me.

And there was once a time when I had believed him. There were many tales of the Queen's late grandmother presenting herself unexpectedly at decayed estates, demanding to be fed and slashing away with her cane at any rogue ivy on the ancestral bricks. She had quietly breathed her last just a few months ago, and I wondered idly if there were any vines left on the gates of Saint Peter.

I was smiling at the thought when Undine said abruptly: "Do you suppose it was Asterion?"

I didn't want this conversation: not now, and perhaps not ever. I couldn't allow it to happen.

"In Greek mythology," Dogger said, "Asterion was the name of the Minotaur: the bull-headed man in the labyrinth in Knossos."

"Really?" Undine went goggle-eyed. Dogger's description had obviously impressed her far more than mine had.

"Some believe," Dogger went on, "—and I am perhaps inclined to agree with them—that the myth of the labyrinth was some dim perception of the coiled physical structure of their own brains. Perhaps they had studied the brains of their enemies, beaten out in battle."

I held my breath. Was Dogger intentionally steering the topic away from our present danger, or was he genuinely still in the dark about Father? The conversation had become a tightrope and I walked it gently, swaying from side to side, from storybook to the prospect of sudden, unexpected, and violent death. It had happened to Major Greyleigh and it could happen to us.

"Can you guess what he was fed, this Minotaur?" Dogger asked, looking directly at Undine.

"Sausages!" she said.

"No." Dogger smiled. "Every nine years he was sent a meal of human flesh. Fourteen boys and girls. Or was it nine boys and girls every fourteen years?"

God bless you, Dogger, I thought.

Undine squirmed with delight. This was the sort of mucilaginous information which attracts girls at a certain age and boys forever.

"Which part of the Minotaur was bull?" she asked.

"Just the head," Dogger replied. "The rest was human."

"Criminy!" she said. "Bull breath! It must have been awful for those boys and girls."

"Yes," Dogger said. "I believe it was."

"Bull breath!" she said again. "We could distill it and sell it as cologne. *Evening in Knossos*. We'd be rolling in the dough."

I sensed the ghostly presence of Carl Pendracka.

But as the conversation drifted away from cannibalism, I could see that she was becoming bored. She got up off her pail and drifted about the greenhouse, picking up various objects, putting them down again, and looking quickly around in search of something else.

She had begun fidgeting with a Victorian vase, one that Dogger always kept filled with fresh flowers for my mother's bedroom.

"Look!" she said suddenly. "The rain has stopped."

We had been so wrapped up in bulls and labyrinths, we hadn't noticed.

"I can go for the mushrooms now," she said. "They'll be growing like weeds after the rain."

"You'll get filthy," I said. "That charred grass will make an awful mess."

Undine laughed a laugh of cut glass. "I'm already a mess," she said, and it was true. I couldn't argue with that kind of logic. Her dress and her jumper were streaked with soot, her face like a music hall zany. Mrs. Mullet would sigh and reach for the Sunlight.

There seemed little danger of the arsonist still lurking in the woods. Dogger smiled, meaning "yes."

Undine skipped to the door, then stopped and looked back over her shoulder.

"Ibu simply adored death caps," she said, as if it had just occurred to her. "She called them her 'pimpled persuaders' and then she'd laugh."

My blood ran cold, and I wouldn't be surprised if Dogger's did, too.

"Happy hunting," I managed to say. "Don't forget your basket."

When she was gone, there was a long silence, but it was Dogger who spoke first. "She misses her mother," he said at last.

I could only nod. I missed *my* mother, too, but now was not the time to bring it up.

I was still wrapped in the warm glow of companionship, which was immediately replaced with a sudden sinking.

The time had come to tell the truth. The *whole* truth. I couldn't remember the last time I had done so. Like a defense counsel at the Old Bailey with his long white fingers tucked into his lapels, I was accustomed to doling out as many or as few of the facts as the situation required.

"Dogger," I said, "I have a confession to make. I haven't been entirely honest with you."

"Oh?" Dogger said, surprised.

Should I tell him and betray a confidence, or would we go forward into the future with an invisible wedge driven between us?

I took the plunge. "Mrs. Mullet confided in me that Major Greyleigh had courted her in their younger days. But please—Alf mustn't know. He's insanely jealous."

Dogger stared out for a moment through the clouded window, then looked me in the eye.

"Yes," he said. "I was aware of that."

"Did she confide in you, too?"

"Logic dictates that I mustn't say," Dogger said.

So here it was: another odd banana peel to be stepped

over. Another argument, pro and con, about secrets and virtuous friendships.

"Life's a bramble bush, isn't it, Dogger."

"Yes, Miss Flavia, it certainly is."

"There's something I'm dying to show you," I said in a sudden flush of companionship. "I'll run into the house and get it. Will you wait here?"

Dogger nodded, and again I was reminded of the great silence he could summon upon himself. He radiated calm, as if he were carved in stone. At this very moment, he reminded me of one of the great stone kings at Luxor, except that Dogger was sitting on a pail.

"I'll be right back," I said, and Dogger may have smiled.

Into the house I went, upstairs into my laboratory, where I snatched up Mrs. Mullet's sketches and dashed downstairs again. I saw no one and heard no one: The house might as well have been abandoned.

Dogger was sitting as I had left him. He apparently hadn't moved a muscle.

"Have a look at these," I said, thrusting the drawings into his hands.

He leafed through them slowly, maddeningly, turning back again to a previous sketch. "Major Greyleigh," he said. "I recognize him. Who drew these?"

So he didn't know.

"Mrs. Mullet," I said.

Dogger let out a long, low whistle. I made a mental note to ask him to teach me how to do that. It seemed to me a whistle of immense possibilities: a whistle with many useful functions, like a Boy Scout's jackknife.

"What do you think, Dogger?"

"I had no idea," he said. "No idea whatsoever."

"Nor did I," I told him.

"Our Mrs. Mullet is a woman of immense and often unsuspected talents," he said. "Not that we didn't know that—of course."

"Of course," I said.

"Have the police seen these?" he asked, shuffling again through the sketches, turning them upside down and then right side up again.

"No," I said. "At least, not as far as I know. Do you think we ought to hand them over?"

"Yes," Dogger said, and my heart sank. "But not until we have squeezed the juices out of them."

I leaped to my feet and pulled my pail closer to Dogger's.

"And out of Mrs. Mullet," I added.

·TWELVE·

THERE ARE MOMENTS YOU know you will remember
until the sun and all the stars burn out, and this was
one of them. Sometimes we don't appreciate, or even
realize at the time, our most cherished moments, so
that when we do, we do so with regret.

But this time was different. I knew in an instant that
the aura of our friendship, as I thought of it, had formed
itself already, and I hugged myself.

We leaned close together over Mrs. Mullet's sketches.

Dogger spotted the footprint at once. "Ah, yes," he
said. "U.S. Army issue. Type two. Oval diamond sole.
Thirteen studs on the heel rather than hobnails. As
were the prints in the wood."

"Well done!" I said. "You amaze me, Dogger."

"You must bear in mind," he said, "that I have a great
deal of experience with gentlemen's footwear."

234 · ALAN BRADLEY

I clapped my hands together in delight.

"You must also bear in mind that this particular pair of boots could have been worn by a magistrate, a pawnbroker, or, for all we know, a charlady."

"Or a Minotaur," I said. It just slipped out and I was immediately sorry.

"Or a Minotaur," Dogger echoed, his face giving nothing away.

Does he know? Does he know?

Surely, he could hear my thoughts leaking out through my ears—they were that loud.

"While the boots are certainly suggestive, they are not conclusive," Dogger said. "One remembers the horseshoes in Sherlock Holmes, made to look like the hooves of cows."

"Would anyone actually do that in real life?" I asked.

"Oh, yes," Dogger said. "Much more so than in fiction. Characters in fiction must remain believable. It is not so in real life."

He turned his attention back to Mrs. Mullet's sketches. "It is important to notice the very slight rigor of the jaw," he went on, "and Mrs. Mullet has captured it nicely. Her handling of the light is exemplary. Fifteen or twenty minutes earlier or later and she might have missed the delineation of muscle. We must congratulate her."

And with that, he closed the sketchbook.

"Is there anything more that we have missed?" I asked anxiously.

"There is *much* that we have missed." He smiled. "But I fear my duties to my employers must take priority."

I had come to think of Dogger as a member of my family, and the reminder that he was an employee was like a pail of cold water thrown into my face.

The fact that I was one of his employers made it even worse.

"It's all right, Dogger," I said. "I'll let you off."

"That's very kind of you, Miss Flavia," he said, "and I shall remember your offer. But one must always remember that no matter *who* the employer is, Duty holds the higher rank."

I bit my lower lip and let air out between my teeth.

Just what Father said, I thought. *Duty holds all the cards—next to God, who holds the fifth and all succeeding Aces.*

I needed to be alone.

"Of course," I said with a sunny smile, which cost me all I had. "I'll go make ready for Undine and the death cap mushrooms. I've been dying to try a new analysis that reacts with all three toxins."

Dogger touched his cap, which made me even sadder, and I tried not to run as I made my way to the house and my room.

I got no farther than the bottom of the stairs before I heard voices from the library. I deadened my footsteps by assuming a sneaking stance, and tiptoed my way to the library door.

I put my ear against the panel.

They were discussing the American author J. D. Salinger.

"*The Catcher in the Rye?*" Daffy was saying. "I've read better prose on a pickle bottle—*and* been provided in the end with something to chew on."

I had to agree with her. We'd been forced to read the book for the parish book club. It had been proposed by Fayne Weekley, a pimply young man with delusions about his own intelligence. "It's an unusually brilliant first novel," he had argued when the vicar wondered about its suitability. Daffy told me later that Fayne had stolen the quote from a newspaper review, but his earnestness and probably his pimples won the day, and we all wound up reading the meandering plod. I was hoping to be asked for my opinion, but I wasn't. If I had been, I'd have said that any book of more than two hundred and fifty pages without a single mention of chemistry or poisoning was a wicked waste of time.

On the other side of the library door, the other voice spoke. It was Carl Pendracka. I recognized him instantly by his accent.

"It's a boffo book," he said. "I read it on the boat coming over. It's prob'ly the best book I ever read."

"Have you read *Tristram Shandy?*" Daffy asked.

"No."

"I rest my case," she said.

I chose that moment to make my presence known, so, like all superior lurkers, I burst into the room as if I had just arrived.

"Tennis, anyone?" I bellowed in my best games-mistress voice.

Daffy and Carl leaped to their feet. I had truly startled, perhaps even frightened them.

"You stupid crack-wit!" Daffy shouted. "You fat-kidneyed chuck-head; you duck-haired mumblecrust!"

It was almost a pleasure to be insulted by Daffy. She knew words that, when thrown into them, were known to have curdled rivers.

"What do you mean by bursting in here?" she shouted, getting her second wind.

"It's my house," I said, and planted my hands on my hips for effect.

It was true: My mother had left Buckshaw to me in a complicated will that was simply awash in "whereas"es and "hereinafter"s. I knew that reminding her of this would hurt Daffy, and it did.

"You nasty little shite goblin," she said in a suddenly normal voice, and I could see that she was close to tears.

Without waiting a heartbeat, I rushed across the room and flung my arms around her., knowing that she hated it. I hated it, too. This was probably the only time since we were almost babies, when we had been made to hug by being forced together with a couple of pillows and a shooting stick by a photographer who was notable for his creative baby photos and his fees.

I also took into consideration the fact that Carl was watching. I pressed my face into her shoulder and counted to ten, then flung myself down onto the settee in a loose and carefree posture.

"You missed the fire," I said.

"No, I didn't," Daffy replied. "I saw the smoke blowing past the window. Thought it was Dogger burning grass."

"Did you come in your jeep?" I asked, swiveling toward Carl and watching his face intently.

"Yup," he said. "Always do. Always will. Uncle Sam's Taxis, Inc."

"Did you make a diversion round the Visto, along the edge of the woods?"

"Nope," Carl said. "Came straight from the gates to the front door. Jeep's still parked out there. Why?"

"Oh, no reason. I thought you might have taken the scenic route and thrown a cigarette butt in the grass."

"Thanks a lot," Carl said, crossing his arms and stretching his legs out to their full extent. It couldn't have been more perfect: I now had an unobstructed and close-up view of the soles of his boots. They were almost in my lap.

The pattern on his soles was what I expected it to be: thirteen studs on the heels and a sole with a pineapple pattern.

I looked away quickly. All I needed to do now was to get rid of Daffy. Boredom would do the trick.

"I was just teasing you, Carl. No hard feelings. Tell me again about the time Babe Ruth kissed you."

Even though I knew nothing much about baseball, I knew that Babe Ruth was roughly the equivalent of our Dr. W. G. Grace, the legendary—even godlike—cricket phenomenon.

"Well," Carl said, "I was just a baby when it happened. My old man took me with him on the train all the way from Cincinnati to New York City and Yankee Stadium because he couldn't afford a babysitter. He ran into a guy named Norman Boze that he'd met at the beach when they were just kids. Norman's dad had been a scout for the Yankees and he knew Babe Ruth personally. Pop was almost speechless for the first time in history when Norman invited him to come and sit in the dugout."

Daffy sighed. Carl was just getting into it.

"There's a tradition of getting someone famous to osculate your kid. It's supposed to bring good luck, like finding a four-leaf clover, only better. And to get someone as famous as Babe Ruth to do the honors—well . . .

"So, when Norman introduced Pop to the Babe, instead of sticking out his hand, he stuck out his baby: *me*! And do you know what? Babe Ruth planted a big wet one right in the middle of my forehead." Carl touched the spot with his forefinger and rubbed it in a circular motion, as if stirring a cauldron of memories.

"Want to touch it, Daffy?" he asked.

Daffy slammed her book shut and stood up.

"Not without surgical gloves," she said, and walked out of the room.

Carl looked after her, puzzled. He examined his forefinger and then jammed both hands into his trouser pockets and hunched his shoulders, like a boy in a schoolyard.

"It's okay, Carl," I said. "She's just testing her tether."

"You think so?" he asked, brightening.

I laid my finger alongside my nose and gave him a knowing look. I'd teach that hag Daffy to call me a fat-kidneyed chuck-head.

"Actually, I'm glad we're alone for a minute," I said. "I wanted to ask you another question."

"Fire away," he said.

"That sergeant—the one who drove me home. What's his name?"

"Could be anyone. Did he have a badge?"

"I think so," I said. "Blue and white. Air Police. An eagle and a cloud."

"That'll most likely be Sergeant Malone," Carl said. "We call him Poker, but not to his face, of course. His name's Preston. Preston Malone. He's a one, I'll tell you. Why do you ask?"

"Oh, no particular reason," I said, examining my fingernails—or what was left of them. "Does he actually talk?"

"Not much," Carl said. "He used to be a Marine, but he got posted to the Eighth on special assignment."

"Meaning what?" I asked.

"He's what we call a swabber," Carl said.

"And what does a swabber do?" I asked.

"He swabs."

I laughed dutifully but my mind was already shifting into top gear.

Here was Lewis Carroll again. Could a swabber be one of those seven maids with seven mops?

"Swabs *what*?" I asked.

Carl laughed nervously. "Whatever needs swabbing," he said. "You know . . ."

I thought I did, but I didn't want to say so.

"No," I said. "I don't know. Tell me."

"Well," Carl said, "wars are messy things, and there are always little details that need cleaning up afterward."

"Such as?" I asked.

Carl scratched his head. "Well," he said. "You've heard of the Nuremberg trials?"

"Vaguely," I said.

If only he knew! Was he saying that Sergeant Malone was an executioner—like Major Greyleigh? Could there possibly be a connection?

"They say he was at Nuremberg," Carl said.

"Then what's he doing as a driver at Leathcote?"

"Who knows?" Carl shrugged. "Maybe swabbing— maybe making sure things don't need swabbing. Who knows?"

I do, I wanted to say. *I'd like to know whose hands I have been in. I'd like to know whose power I have been under—and still may be.*

"Oh, well," I said. "As Mrs. Mullet puts it: 'It's all water under the fridge.'"

I hated to poke fun at Mrs. M but I needed desperately to lighten the situation.

Carl pulled his hands out of his pockets and rose from his chair. "Well, I'd better be moseyin' off," he said.

"All right," I told him. "Thanks for the chat."

"Tell Daffy," he said, "I'm sorry I bored her with my baseball story. Next time, I'll—"

"Never mind," I said. "I loved it. Do you think Babe Ruth's kiss changed your life?"

"You never know," Carl said. "That's the thing about luck: You never know. If you did, it wouldn't be luck: It would be mere foreknowledge."

I laughed out loud and clapped my hands together.

"What did they feed you in Cincinnati?" I asked.

"Toenails," he said.

Blast you, Undine, I thought. *Her baleful influence is everywhere.*

Where was she? She ought to have been back with the mushrooms ages ago.

The easiest way to find out was to head straight to her destination: the woods on the far side of the Visto. After a quick recce around the house, I went out the kitchen door and set out toward the east.

I was made immediately filthy by the ashes of the grass fire, which were still warm in places. Little tendrils of smoke arose here and there and within fifty feet my shoes were black with soot. I trudged on, keeping my eyes fixed on the woods beyond, alert for any signs of motion.

As I drew closer to the tree line, I fancied I heard a kind of faint mewing. Had a cat, or a kitten, been caught by the fire? I sent up a quick prayer begging that it not be so.

It wasn't myself that I feared for: I had stalked through today's grassfire without hesitation, even though it felt as if my feet were about to burst into flames. But now, at the thought of a helpless animal being injured, my blood ran cold.

Animals are so vulnerable when it comes to fire. I had been taken as a child to see the film *Bambi,* and the blazing forest had terrified me so much that I had to be removed, screaming, from the cinema.

Smoke still hovered above the Visto. The wind had died, and I noticed for the first time that the light was beginning to fade. I felt an almost overwhelming urge to call out to Undine, but some ancient wisdom told me not to draw attention to myself. Better to approach quietly whatever was making the noise, which, as I neared the edge of the wood, was slowly growing louder.

Caution told me to move slowly from tree to tree, peering carefully round each one before slipping to the next. I had now reached the spot where we had earlier seen the tire tracks.

It is amazing how quickly we revert to our primitive selves when we are alone among the trees. The senses are instantly shifted up into a higher gear, allowing us to smell the bark, the leaves, and the sap, as well as to hear the mushrooms growing and the sound of our own breath.

I had just steadied myself by placing my left hand on the trunk of an old oak and was about to peer around the trunk when my right shoulder was seized in an iron grip and a large hand clamped over my mouth.

"Don't make a sound," a voice hissed into my ear. "If you do, I'll slit your throat."

The feel of cold steel at my neck told me this was no idle threat.

"Now walk slowly," the voice said, pushing me toward the heart of the woods—and away from Buckshaw.

I did as I was told.

Why hadn't I told anyone where I was going? Would anyone even think of searching this lonely wood on the outer edge of our estate? What could I do to leave a trail?

I began by pressing the soles of my shoes deeper into the ground to make my footprints easier to track.

"Stop that," said my captor, uncomfortably close to my ear. Although I could feel his hot breath on my neck, I hadn't yet seen him.

On we went, through dead leaves and mold. I tried to step on fallen twigs to leave a trail of broken wood.

"Stop that," he said again, and again something cold and metallic touched the side of my throat.

Could I learn anything from the tone of his voice? It was worth a try.

"Where are you taking me?" I asked.

But he did not answer.

Here among the trees, a smoky mist was rising from the ground, creating a false darkness that had the sharp, sour smell of burnt grass.

I had now lost my bearings. We had twisted and turned, and I no longer knew in which direction lay the Visto and the house. Even if I were suddenly free, I wouldn't know which way to run.

My captor seized my elbow and jerked me roughly round the end of a fallen tree, and there before me, suddenly and unexpectedly, was a jeep.

And sitting in the back seat, her eyes as wide as saucers, was Undine. A broad leather belt wrapped round her head held a piece of khaki cloth across her mouth, and as soon as she saw me, she began making the pitiful mewling noise that I had heard, rising now in volume and strength. She was frightened out of her wits. She half leaped to her feet but fell back heavily into the seat, and I could see that her wrists were in handcuffs looped through the tubular metal of the jeep's front seat. As she turned, I saw that she had a gash above one eye. Blood was dripping from her brow.

She's the bait in their trap, I thought. *They knew I'd come to find her.*

"What have you done to her?" I shouted. "Let her loose. She's a child!"

Undine nodded furiously, her eyes suddenly red and full of tears.

A powerful hand seized my shoulder, dug into the flesh, and shook me as if he were an eagle and I a baby rabbit.

My head swam and I let out a tortured shriek.

"Shut up!" he said and shook me again.

This time I did as he ordered because shutting up gives you more time to think.

I let my eyes wander slowly on the scene, making a mental catalogue of which items might make a suitable weapon. In front of the jeep's radiator, Undine's basket of mushrooms had been dropped and spilled out onto the ground.

I had still not seen the face of my captor, and something told me I didn't need to—not just yet. More important were the surroundings.

I waited until I had taken in as much as I could possibly remember. It was like Kim's game in the Rudyard Kipling novel, where the boy was allowed to gaze at as many as fifteen jewels or odd objects on a tray and then, when they were covered with a sheet of paper, try to remember and name as many as he could.

I took in the nearby details of the wood: a sharp piece of broken branch that looked uncomfortably like a Roman spear; Undine's overturned wicker basket and spilled death cap mushrooms; an empty paper cigarette packet (Lucky Strikes); a couple of giant puffball mushrooms, most of which fall into the family *Lycoperdon*, or wolf farts—and for good reason.

Only then did I decide what to do.

I turned slowly round—no sudden moves—and found myself staring up into the face of the sergeant who had taken me to meet my father: the man who had driven me home to Buckshaw, Preston Malone.

"Hello, Poker," I said, trying not to let my voice sound surprised, even though I had been fully expecting to see someone else.

"It was you, wasn't it? You're one of the assassins for the Nide. Am I next on your list? Is that why you set the fire?"

I know I ought to have been white with rage, but I wasn't. I was filled with contempt.

"It's interesting that you chose poison to murder Major Greyleigh," I said. "It's a method usually used by women. Is that why you chose fire this time? Fire isn't a woman's way, Poker—it's a coward's."

I waited for my words to sting, but Malone said nothing. He met my gaze with the steely-eyed look of a man who kills for money. Or for pleasure. His breath was hot on my face. Blood sausages, I noted.

"But then you wanted Mrs. Mullet to be accused, didn't you? Very sly, Poker. Very clever."

He shook me like a terrier shakes a rat, and I gloried in it. My words were hitting home.

"She's hurt," I said, trying to break loose and pulling toward the jeep. Undine's brow was now a bloody mess, as most scalp wounds tend to be. *It's not as bad as it looks,* I kept telling myself. *Steady on.*

"Let me put something on that," I said, bending over to grasp one of the puffballs. "These will stop the bleeding. They're like the styptic pencils men use when they cut themselves shaving. They're also antiseptic."

This much was true and I didn't bother telling him the rest.

Malone said nothing, but I felt the blade in his hand move slightly away from my throat.

"No tricks," he said in a raspy voice.

"No, sir," I told him. "I just want to keep her from being permanently scarred. She's such a beautiful—"

Rule Number Nine: Strike while you're still speaking. It's unexpected.

I rammed the puffball into his eyes and collapsed it with a clap of my hands. A cloud of blue dust appeared as millions of spores exploded from their casing and into his eyes.

He screamed. And with good reason. The spores of the puffball not only are the most prolific in nature, but also consist of millions of tiny needles.

The pain would be excruciating.

He threw his hands up and clawed at his eyes, bellowing like a maddened bull.

And it was at that instant that I made my next move.

Daffy had once told me what to do if ever I were accosted by a man: "Kick him in the Casanovas, then run like blue blazes."

I have remarked elsewhere that I didn't know where the Casanovas were precisely located, so rather than take a chance, I delivered as powerful a kick as I could with the toe of my shoe to his right kneecap. Poker Malone let out the beginning of a bloodcurdling scream before collapsing vertically, like the dynamited chimney of an abandoned factory raining down at the hands of the demolition crew. Sensible shoes can be murder.

He writhed on the ground, clutching and clawing at his useless leg.

The man was down for the count, as they say in pugilistic circles, but there was no time to gloat. As distasteful as it was, I needed to rifle through his pockets for the key to the handcuffs. Luckily, it was in his right-hand trouser pocket, where I assumed it would be. He was so focused on his agony that he didn't even seem to notice.

I ran to the jeep, jammed the key into the darbies, and snapped them open. With blood still coursing down her forehead, Undine sprang free.

"Hold on," I told her. "This is going to sting."

I scooped up a second puffball and pushed it to her wound, giving it a good twist.

Undine didn't make a sound. She blinked and stood staring at me blankly.

There was a weak moan behind us. I spun round to see Malone lifting his head and gazing blearily around.

Without another thought I picked up Undine's basket of mushrooms, bent over, and shoved one into each of his nostrils.

Sergeant Malone's watery eyes swiveled and tried to focus on me.

"Those are death caps in your nose," I told him, fighting to keep my voice calm and cold. "They're the deadliest mushrooms known to science. Inhale the spores and they'll eat your lungs out from the inside. Better breathe through your mouth."

His watering eyes stared at me: an awful and unforgettable look of pure hatred.

He opened his mouth and tried to raise himself with one hand.

"Stay," I said. I turned and took a step toward the vehicle.

I looked back to see Undine kneeling almost tenderly beside Malone and thrusting a finger busily up one of his nostrils. I thought at first she was simply tamping the fleshy mushrooms into place, but realized quickly that she, like Holden Caulfield in *The Catcher in the Rye* said of his teacher, "was really digging the old thumb right in there."

Poker Malone was no longer moving a muscle.

"Let's go," I said. "Quick sticks."

I ran round and jumped into the driver's seat. Undine leaped in beside me with amazing energy. The machine started at the touch of the pedal, and I sent up a prayer of thanks to the gods of American automotive ingenuity.

"Hang on!" I shouted.

I let in the clutch with a jerk and twin showers of dirt shot out behind the rear wheels, as if a pair of unseen gravediggers were tossing soil with shovels up and out of an open grave.

Undine held her hand pressed tightly to her forehead; her eyes, although large and staring, seemed focused on something I could not see.

"We'll laugh about this when we're old ladies!" I shouted into the wind and above the roar of the jeep's engine. The woods rang with the roar. No wonder they called it the Go Devil. In all their thousands of years, the old forest at Buckshaw had never seen a sight as strange as me and Undine, bucketing at speed among the trees, jolting and tipping, teetering and almost overturning among the ruts and the deadwood.

If this scene was in a film, I thought later, *it would be accompanied by fiddles and banjos.*

"Yarooo!" I wanted to shout, but I didn't. I was too busy steering.

·THIRTEEN·

IT WAS LIKE DRIVING through a graveyard. The Visto was a minefield of overgrown flowerbeds and tumbledown statues, some of them half-sunk like submarines surfacing from the land of the dead. Hardened gods and goddesses, their skins green and gray with moss and fungi, reached out with dead hands as if to grab us as we passed.

Undine stared straight ahead with glassy eyes. Was she in shock, or had she fallen into a delayed coma from that bleeding bang on her head? I needed to get her to the house as quickly as possible. I would race to the telephone and ring Dr. Darby—or should I drive her to his office directly?

I needn't have worried. As we approached the house, I saw Dogger emerging from the greenhouse. The instant he spotted us, he dropped his watering can and began

252 · ALAN BRADLEY

running toward us. I slowed enough to let him leap aboard, into the rear seat. He leaned forward and let his fingers run around the base of Undine's skull. I noticed that he avoided touching the open wound. He reached round and lifted her eyelids, then twisted in the seat to remove his gardener's apron, which he draped around her shoulders and tied neatly behind her neck. Only then did he take her wrist between his thumb and forefingers.

"Front door, please, Miss Flavia," he said, and I turned the jeep along the east side of the house.

"There's a man in the wood," I said. "We've knocked him down, but—"

"Well done," Dogger said. "We shall leave him to Constable Linnet."

Constable Linnet was the village policeman: the terror of small boys who refused to eat their gristle.

Dogger leaped out even before we had come to a full stop and scooped Undine up into his arms. He stooped to open the door and carried her easily across the threshold. I followed as he went directly to the kitchen and stood beside the kitchen table.

"There's a lap robe under the sink," he said. It was true. Mrs. Mullet had taken possession of the ancient blanket to wrap herself beside the cooker whenever she felt one of her "icy turns" coming on.

"Better here than out in the territories," Dogger said, nodding toward the distant vastness of the house.

I found the lap robe and folded it into a makeshift mattress on the table. Dogger gently lifted Undine, who was curiously unresponsive, onto the tabletop.

"Upsy-daisy," he said. I could hardly believe my ears.

Then suddenly, as if by magic, I found myself applying the back of my wrist to her forehead and rubbing her wrists in circles with my thumbs. I didn't say "there, there," but I might as well have. Had this Florence Nightingale instinct been hiding in me all along?

"Now then, Miss Flavia," Dogger said, "I shall boil some water and you can use a hot compress to clean her wound."

I was taken by surprise. Most men—Inspector Hewitt included—would send the female to boil the water while they themselves stepped into the spotlight.

Not with Dogger. I almost fainted out of respect.

Dogger had already filled the kettle and was placing it on the Aga.

Undine lay staring up at the ceiling.

"How's your tea company coming along?" I asked her. "Any interesting investors yet?"

Undine's eyes rolled slowly down to meet mine. I could see them pulling into uneasy focus.

"Your tea company," I repeated. "Breakfast in bed for all. I shouldn't mind taking a flutter myself. Shall we say ten pounds? I understand the early investor gets the worm."

I saw the smile start at the corner of Undine's mouth. Through dry lips she said: "That man banged my head on the spare tire. My neck hurts."

"I expect it does," Dogger said. "Miss Flavia will call the police as the kettle comes to a boil."

The police! I had forgotten about them. Constable

254 · ALAN BRADLEY

Linnet had to be called immediately, before our assail-
ant in the wood could make his escape—if he hadn't
already.

Without a further word I dashed to the cupboard
under the stairs where, among the moldering piles of
newspapers, the telephone was kept.

I picked up the handset and clicked the cradle.

"Could you connect me, please, with Constable Linnet?" I said, trying to keep my voice matter-of-fact.

There was a haughty sniff from Miss Runciman, who
expected you to suck up to her before requesting a connection.

"Is there a problem?" she asked.

I pretended not to hear, and rubbed my hair against
the phone, as if I were adjusting the apparatus.

"Hello?" she said. I maintained radio silence until, at
last, I heard the telephone ringing at the constable's
residence. It was picked up immediately.

"Police. Bishop's Lacey. Constable Linnet speaking,"
he said.

"Flavia de Luce at Buckshaw," I said. "There's an armed
man in the east wood. His name is Preston Malone. He
attacked my cousin, Undine. We've knocked him down.
Would you arrest him, please?"

"I know the place," Constable Linnet said.

I couldn't help smiling. It had been said more than
once at Buckshaw that Father's pheasants had been
taken in the morning mists by a poacher who wore
stripes—and those not in the biblical sense.

"He has an injured leg. I don't know if he can walk."

"I shall look into it, miss, straightaway."

And with that, he rang off.

I had a sudden gnawing desire to gallop off across the Visto to the woods: to be in at the kill. What wouldn't I have given to see the darbies slapped on those hairy wrists? The brute had attacked my cousin Undine, and in a savage part of my mind, I thought he ought to swing for it.

But hold on, Flavia, I argued. *He didn't kill her, did he? He didn't go that far. But he might have, though. Who knows where he would have taken her or what he might have done if I hadn't shown up in the wood?*

The condemning to death and execution of a criminal is, I reasoned, the public revenge for a private crime. Private revenge is not permitted, which seems a pity.

If it was up to me, anyone who harmed a little girl would be strapped to a bull's-eye on the south lawn so that anyone who wanted to could take a shot with the archery sets provided free of charge.

I shivered at the thought of my own brutality. Surely we were more civilized than that. Surely the better part of our brains had evolved since the Stone Age?

What would I look like with my mask off? I wondered. Who was the real Flavia de Luce beneath the skin? And what did she think of me?

I pondered this as I came out of the cupboard and went back into the kitchen.

Undine was sitting up on the edge of the table. Dogger was taking the kettle off the hob.

"Lie down!" I said.

Undine looked as if I had slapped her face, but she obeyed. Back she went onto her elbows, then flat on her back on the table.

I was shaking but I didn't know why. Was I in shock as well?

Or was it that I didn't want to be cheated out of the chance to mop her bleeding brow with hot water?

Dogger had brought out an enamel basin into which he was emptying the kettle. With a table fork he lifted a sheet of gauze, dipped it into the water, then lifted it out and swung it lightly side to side in the air to cool.

He held it out to me, and I picked it off with my thumb and forefinger, pretending it didn't hurt. I folded the hot gauze into a pad and applied it to the gash on Undine's head.

"This might sting a little," I told her, as one always does. It's a custom that probably goes back beyond the Inquisition, when the torturers were preparing to cut out their victim's tongue.

I dabbed lightly with the pad at the clotting blood on Undine's brow.

"Owww!" she cried, jackknifing up into a half-sitting position.

I placed my hand on her shoulder and pressed her firmly down, then went on dabbing, alternately dipping the cloth and wringing it out, even though the hot water was burning my hands.

Dogger was looking on approvingly, and I didn't want to disappoint him.

This must have been what Florence Nightingale felt

like. I could hear, not far off, the boom of the artillery and the blaring of bugles. It was intoxicating.

"Nicely done," Dogger said as he stepped in beside me. He had produced from somewhere a sewing needle and a spool of black thread, from which he snapped off a length before dropping it, and the needle, into the basin of hot water.

From the pocket of his jacket, he produced a bar of orange carbolic soap, with which he proceeded to lather and scrub his hands.

"Careful, Dogger," I said. "That's hot."

"Yes," he said quietly, holding his hands vertically in front of him. "That's the point, isn't it?"

He fished the needle and thread from the water in the basin, and produced from another pocket a small silver flask, which he decanted onto a corner of his pocket handkerchief, then dabbed on Undine's wound.

She clutched at my hand and squeezed it to the point of pain. I gently loosened her fingers, but she gripped all the more tightly.

"This is hunt medicine," Dogger said. "Cherry brandy. The Master of the Hounds will be no end peeved."

We had never hunted at Buckshaw, as far as I knew, but we had neighbors who did, and it was considered boorish not to offer them a tipple in little silver cups when they arrived suddenly in our forecourt, all baying hounds and horns and lathered horses.

Undine managed a weak grin as Dogger began to stitch up her wound. I couldn't watch: The sight of needle going through skin made my stomach crawl. But when he was finished and I dared to glance, I saw that his needlework would have done a London seamstress proud.

"You've done this before," I said.

"One learns . . . over time," Dogger said quietly.

"Now then," he added, "for a proper dressing. Would you prefer to look heroic, or would you rather look piratical?" he asked.

"Like Boris Karloff in *The Mummy*," she said.

"So shall it be," he said, "if you will excuse me for a few moments."

He slipped quietly out the kitchen door, and I knew he was going to fetch the first aid kit from the Rolls: an extensive set of medical supplies from Harrods that rivaled a field hospital, with everything from slings to folding stretchers, and from iodine to morphine.

"Can you tell me what happened in the wood?" I asked.

Undine rolled her head slowly from side to side.

"My head," she said. "I think I blacked out. He had hold of my carotid artery—with his thumb, I think. He was pressing my head down. I thought I heard the angels singing."

"I doubt it," I said. "The angels don't perform for brats with baskets full of poison."

A beatific smile spread across her face. "I gave him a jolly good nose full, didn't I, Flavia?"

"You certainly did," I said. "He deserved it, the—"

Fortunately, the doorbell rang, and I didn't have to say the word that was on the very tip of my tongue.

"Don't move," I told Undine. "Pretend you're on a raft in the Pacific and the water is infested with sharks. I'll be back in a jiffy."

I was at the front door before the bell could ring a second time. I flung it open, perhaps too quickly, and there stood Constable Linnet.

"Oh!" I said. "You startled me. I wasn't expecting you."

The constable raised his bushy eyebrows. "You rang me, I believe?"

"Yes, I did," I said. "I was expecting you to go to the east wood and arrest the man who attacked my cousin."

"No man in the wood now," the constable said. "I've been and had a look. Footprints, yes, but no man."

"His name is Preston Malone," I said. "He's an American soldier—a sergeant. A military policeman. You'll find him at Leathcote."

"And how do you know this?" the constable asked me, narrowing his eyes at his own canny remark.

"I met him once or twice," I said. This was the truth, but only just barely.

"And why would he attack your, ah—?" He pulled out a black notebook and consulted it. "Cousin."

"I couldn't possibly say," I said. Which was also the truth.

"He was driving a jeep," I continued. "I expect you can take castings of the tire prints and the soles of his boots."

The constable pulled out a Biro and scratched himself between the eyes. "That would be the detective sergeants from HQ in Hinley," he said. "That would be their territory. I shall request their services."

"Is that all?" I asked. I could feel my color rising. "Perhaps you could call in Inspector Hewitt."

"Ah, Inspector Hewitt," he said, shifting his scratching from his nose to one of his ears. "He does mostly murders, I believe. Has anyone been murdered that I haven't been informed about as yet? Other than the late Major Greyleigh, that is?" His shoulders trembled at his own witticism.

"Not that I know of," I said. "But you might tell him to have his lads look up 'saxitoxin' in the *British Pharmacopeia,* or any of the better chemical dictionaries."

The constable produced a notebook, his Biro hovering.

"S-a-x-i-t-o-x-i-n," I said, with a helpful look on my face.

"I'd better come in and interview the little girl," Constable Linnet said. "I'll have to write a report."

I opened the door more fully. The constable wiped his feet on the doorstep, removed his helmet and tucked it under his arm, then stepped into the foyer.

"This way," I said. "She's in the kitchen."

Constable Linnet knew the way to the kitchen as well as I did. He had been coming to Buckshaw for the Christmas Yule dole for most of his life: probably since he was a boy.

Dogger had returned from the coach house and was wrapping the wound on Undine's head. He looked up and smiled politely at Constable Linnet but said nothing.

The constable produced his notebook and poised his Biro. "Now then, miss," he said, "tell me what's happened."

"I was gathering mushrooms and a man grabbed me and gagged me," Undine said. "There was blood. I don't remember anything else."

Wise child, I thought.

Constable Linnet looked disappointed. "Nothing else? You're quite sure?"

Undine shook her head in slow motion.

"Miss Flavia?" the constable asked.

"I went after Undine when she didn't return. She was already in the jeep, handcuffed, when I found her. I couldn't get her out. Malone attacked me. I kicked him in the knee. While he was down, I jumped in the jeep and drove it to Buckshaw."

The constable's eyebrows rose like hot air balloons. "You drove the jeep?" he asked.

"Yes, Constable."

"Had you ever driven a jeep before?"

"Yes, Constable. Quite recently. I helped a couple of servicemen with a jeep that had become stuck in the lych-gate at St. Tancred's."

He bit his lip. "Do you presently hold a driving license, miss?"

"No, not at the moment," I said. "But I'm planning to apply as soon as I'm old enough."

"I see," he said, and began to scribble what seemed like an endless note. He had to flip the page to finish it.

"I'm afraid I shall have to report that," he said when he had finished.

What was it, precisely, that he would report? Was it my driving of the jeep? Damage of church property by American servicemen?

I shrugged with my eyes. I didn't want to criticize Constable Linnet directly for the time he was wasting, but neither did I want him to diddle away the day.

"I expect you'll find Malone at Leathcote," I said. "He'll make his way back there sooner or later."

"It's not that easy, miss," the constable said, putting away his pad. "We have no jurisdiction at Leathcote. For all practical purposes, it's part of the United States of America. We shall have to go through the proper channels."

I could have spit bullets. Here was an agent of a foreign government abducting two British citizens on their own property while the law thinks about mentioning the matter to some far-off ambassador.

"Good luck," I said, as I turned on my heel and left the room. The human spirit can stand only so much.

I needed to think. I needed to be alone.

Leaving Undine with Dogger in the kitchen, I went to my laboratory, sat on the stool, and began to wash my glassware. It is comforting, when the whole world is spinning, to take refuge in the certainties of science: to touch the flasks of precisely calibrated measures, to touch the tools of certainty—a world in which a gram is a gram and a grain is a grain, now and forever and forever until the very end of time.

Then, to begin again at the beginning, one must iso-late that which is known, while putting aside the un-known things until they can be made to fall properly into place.

What did I know for certain? After a quarter of an hour, I realized that only one fact could be established definitely: I was in over my head.

This came as such a shock that I almost fell off the stool.

Although I was drowning in mysteries, I had never seen a thing so clearly. The whole business of Father, for instance, and that shadowy ministry—or whatever it was—they called the Nide. What was its function? What did they do?

I had already toyed with the idea that they were an assassination bureau: an Inquisition, whose members tracked down and punished certain sinners. My own mother had died on assignment in the East, her mission swept conveniently under the carpet, even after all these years.

And Father!

How could a father simply walk out of our lives like that—as if he had fallen under the spell of some strange woman? A woman called Duty. Did he really believe her to be more important than his own flesh and blood?

And how many people had he had killed? Was I next on the list?

Whom could I trust?

I went to Uncle Tarquin's massive desk, took out a piece of paper and pencil, and wrote out that question at the top of the page. After a quarter of an hour, and a great deal of thought, I had just one name: Dogger.

I put a match to the corner of the paper, then, almost in tears, watched it burn to ashes. I washed them down the sink.

I needed to make my next move, and I needed to make it quickly. With Father effectively beyond reach, only Aunt Felicity remained at the top of the dung heap.

With a flannel, I gave my face a good scrub with cold water. It would give my face color, and the look of youthful exuberance.

"Dogger," I said in a firm voice when I returned refreshed to the kitchen. "I need to run up to London tomorrow. Are you able to drive me, or shall I take the train?"

"I thought you might," Dogger said. "I shall have the Rolls fueled and ready before eight."

But when bedtime came, and I had tucked Undine tenderly into a nest of blankets and pillows (God help me!), I could not sleep. My mind had become a gigantic concrete mixer, churning endlessly away at tons of gray, sloppy speculation that only time could harden into fact.

I lay on my back for what seemed like hours, staring at the ceiling, imagining the water stains to be a map of some fantastic kingdom, like those in the endpapers of novels, with tiny trees for forests and wavy lines marking the divisions between lands and seas.

Where was I on the map? What monsters was I expected to fight?

Suddenly, it seemed as if the map were growing brighter, as if a rising sun were illuminating the land. I sat up as I realized the light was coming in from outside.

Moving quickly to the window, I saw that in the distance, beyond the Visto, the headlights of several vehicles were shimmering slowly through the trees.

Were they jeeps? Were they coming for me?

Malone was still at large. Constable Linnet was powerless.

Had the constable made good on his promise to ring police headquarters in Hinley and request that plaster casts be made of the tire tracks in the wood? Were these lights in the night Inspector Hewitt's men at work?

Or had Malone returned with his henchmen to finish his job of abduction? Were they creeping, even now, toward the house in the darkness? Ought I to wake Undine—and perhaps Dogger and Daffy?

My heart was racing like a trip-hammer when I lost consciousness.

When my eyes sprang open, daylight was streaming in through the window glass.

It was morning! I had been shocked into sleep. I was still alive! I had the urge to pinch myself, like Scrooge. I could have kissed the sunlight.

I laughed out loud. How can your brain terrorize you like that?

I dressed and dashed down the stairs. Daffy and Undine were already at the table, where Dogger was serving them breakfast.

"Mrs. Mullet's taken the day off," Undine said. "She's got the chingoolies. Dogger's making us cinnamon toast."

"Indeed I am," Dogger said, setting down on the table a silver-plated toast rack.

"The cinnamon's in the little dish. You may sprinkle your own. Some people take more than others. And your butter is in the center dish, Miss Undine."

We tucked in, the three of us, spreading and sprinkling like orphans in a nightmare workhouse.

It took a moment for Dogger's words to sink in.

"*Your* butter—"

Then all the world came suddenly crashing together just as it must have at the Creation.

Undine's mouth was open, her toast already at her teeth. I leaped to my feet and slapped her—hard—in the face. She let out a shriek and the toast went tumbling to the floor.

I swung round and with my other hand ripped Daffy's food from her fingers.

"*Your* butter!" I roared at Undine. "Where did you get it?"

The beast must have taken it from the dead man's kitchen.

Undine was cringing, still half-senseless from my slap, her hand held to her cheek, her face red and her eyes already leaking tears.

"Moonflower Cottage," she whined through her sobs. "It was in the major's icebox. American butter. I brought it to please you. You made me take an oath in the churchyard, remember? To be kinder and more gentle with each other. Because we were orphans, you said."

I felt an utter fool. How could the little idiot betray me like this?

"You stole it!" I said, to cover up.

Undine leaned across and, with no warning, punched me in the biceps. It hurt like holy Hannah but I tried not to show it.

"If I hadn't, they'd have wasted it, wouldn't they?" she said. "Butter's rationed, remember? I only meant it as a peace offering."

"How do you know it's American?" I demanded. I wasn't letting her off lightly. We had all of us nearly been poisoned on the spot.

"It says so on the label, doesn't it, Dogger?" Undine said.

"Indeed it does," Dogger said. "Please don't lick your fingers."

And with that he vanished into the pantry, only to emerge pulling on a pair of felt gloves he had once used to wear to polish the family silver.

He lifted the toast rack and its deadly cargo daintily and discreetly, as if removing the remains of a duck from a banqueting table. He placed it on the floor in the far corner of the room.

Only then did he vanish for an instant into the pantry and return with a greasy paper label.

"Marigold Butter," he said, holding it out for our examination. "And as Miss Undine has observed, produced in Chicago, Illinois."

"They must have given it to the major at Leathcote," I said. "He was there the night before he died. Mrs. Mullet said they sometimes gave him little gifts of rationed food. So there was never a murderer at Moonflower Cottage. Major Greyleigh brought the butter home himself.

"And Mrs. Mullet fried his mushrooms in it," I added.

"I believe you've hit upon it," Dogger said. "That would explain a great deal. And we must give Miss Undine much credit for retrieving the evidence."

Undine snuffled but broke into a happy smile.

My mind was exploding like those fireworks I had set off in St. Tancred's churchyard. I couldn't wait to get that butter and its wrapping paper into my laboratory to test for saxitoxin, though I knew already what I would find.

The rest would be up to the police.

And then there was Mrs. Mullet. I had been putting off asking her the whole truth about what she had seen at Moonflower Cottage, as well as what she had overheard at the Cluck and Grumble. There are things we are secretly afraid to know.

"We must eschew rash decisions," Dogger had once told me, "and the more rash, the more we must eschew."

"Look before you leap, you mean," I had said, and Dogger had smiled.

So, it was to be first things first.

"We're off to London," I said to Undine. "You keep an eye on things while we're away. If there's any trouble, call Constable Linnet. Understand?"

"Yowza!" Undine grinned.

Daffy hadn't lifted her eyes from her book: a new novel by Daphne du Maurier I hadn't seen before. By sucking up to the librarian at the Bishop's Lacey Free Library, Daffy was able to collar new publications before the riffraff were allowed to lay hands on them. Judging by the dustjacket of this one, it seemed to be another about a young woman in mortal danger.

Holy macaroons! I thought. *I could give old Daphne a tip or two!*

"I've packed a thermos and your breakfast," Dogger said. "We shall eat as we go."

"Righty-ho," I said, trying to look jolly.

Although I dreaded the day, I needed to get through it. Tackling Aunt Felicity was going to be no bag of sugarplums.

Dogger went ahead to the coach house, and as I stepped out into the garden, Mrs. Mullet came suddenly around the side of the house.

"I'm glad I caught you," she said. "I thought you'd be away before I could get 'ere."

"And I thought you had the chingoolies and were taking the day off."

"Well, I 'ad to get over 'em. I didn't sleep a wink last night."

"No wonder," I said. "You've been put under terrific pressure. I'm very sorry about that."

She caught my eye, then turned and spat in the grass. She actually *spat* in the grass!

"That's for your Inspector Whatsis," she said. "I don't give a fig for 'im or any of 'is gondoliers."

"Gondoliers?" I asked.

"You know well enough what I mean."

"I think I do," I said.

"Look 'ere, Miss Flavia, my trouble is I 'aven't told you the truth. Not all of it, anyway, and it's eatin' out my 'eart."

I put my arm around her shoulder. "That's all right, Mrs. M," I said. "All of us stumble now and then."

"The fact of it is—" She swallowed, and her eyes filled suddenly with tears. "Your father—Colonel de Luce, I mean—'e's—I don't know 'ow to tell you this, but—'e's still alive. I seen 'im with my own eyes."

"Yes," I said, "I know you did. I've seen him, too. But thank you for telling me."

So Father had been telling me the truth. He *had* gone to Moonflower Cottage. He *had* tried to prevent Major Greyleigh's killing. His was the jeep that had been seen in the lane; the jeep whose radio Mrs. Skinnett had heard in her earpiece.

Mrs. Mullet pulled a handkerchief from the bosom of her dress and dabbed her eyes, then blew her nose. "It's the 'ardest thing in life to tell a girl 'er dad is dead, but tellin' 'er 'e's still alive is even 'arder. My mouth wanted to keep it secret. I 'adn't the 'eart to tell you."

I put my arm around her shoulders.

"It's over now," I said, although I knew it wasn't. The Nide was still at work. The next move was up to me.

"Major Greyleigh told me 'e ran into your father at Leathcote. It was dark. 'E was walkin' in the rain. Thought 'e was seein' a ghost."

A chill ran down my spine. It was Mrs. Mullet whom the major had told about my father being one of the undead. It was this telling that had sealed his own death warrant. And perhaps had almost sealed hers.

"And who did you tell?" I asked, my blood turning rapidly to ice.

"No one," she said. "Not a soul. Not even you—until now." She drew an imaginary zipper across her lips. "No one," she repeated. "Not even Alf."

And I believed her.

"He's not a ghost," I said. "He's a military secret. I'm proud of you for having kept it. But now that you've told me, you must never, ever tell another soul. Promise me that."

She made the sign of crossing her heart.

"I know now 'e's not a ghost. I seen 'im with my own two eyes. Dressed in an American officer's uniform, 'e was. We ran into each other on the path to the back door. We both jogged to the same side, the way you do. Bread and butter. I smiled at 'im but I was wettin' my knickers, I don't mind tellin' you. I reckernized 'im in a flash. 'E pretended 'e didn't know me. As if 'e were somebody else, like."

"Just a minute," I said. "You've lost me. You left Major Greyleigh eating breakfast, then came to Buckshaw, fed us, and went back to the cottage to find him dead?"

"Yes," she said, casting down her eyes.

"And Father just leaving?"

"Yes," she said without raising her eyes.

She was dissembling. As an expert dissembler myself, I knew all the signs.

"Why?"

"Because I'd took somethin' and I needed to give it back."

"You might as well tell me," I said.

"It was just a box of little figurines—little dolls. I found them on the kitchen table. 'E must 'ave been lookin' at them just before 'e died. I didn't want the police to find 'em. Goodness knows what they'd 'ave thought."

"Hold on," I said. "That can't be right. Let me get this straight. You gave him breakfast and then left. But you didn't take the dolls until *after* you found him dead. It doesn't make sense. Did you, by any chance, go back to Moonflower Cottage more than once?"

"I might 'ave," she said, touching a finger to her temple. "I'm gettin' all muddled up in my 'ead, like."

I could see the red flush crawling slowly up and across her throat like scarlet fingers. *The fib bib,* the vicar's wife had once called it. She and her husband, she said, in their parish duties, had been told every lie in the library.

"Please, Mrs. M," I said. "I need to know if my father's in the clear. I'll never tell another soul. Did you go back to Moonflower Cottage more than once?"

"I suppose I did," she said, looking away.

"Why?" I persisted.

"Like I said, I needed to take something back."

"Something else? Besides the figures?"

Mrs. Mullet nodded, glancing quickly to the right and to the left. "A necklace," she whispered. "'E'd give it to me while I was cookin' the mushrooms. 'E pulled it out of 'is jacket pocket all of a sudden and 'eld it up for me to see, then 'ung it round my neck.

"'Take this, Meg, for old times' sake,' 'e said. A token of friendship, 'e called it. The beads was amber. They was the color of new rope.

"'Is 'ands was right there at my throat. At my throat! I couldn't breathe. I knew in the blink of an eye what it must have been like to meet the 'angman. I nearly fainted. I was taken in a tizzy. I 'ad to get out of there. Into the fresh air."

I reached out to touch her, but she shrank away, as if she were suddenly sanctified by the truth.

"And you came straight to Buckshaw," I said. "And after you gave us breakfast you—"

"Marched right straight back to the cottage," she said. "I could see where all this jewelry was leadin'. I made up my mind. It wasn't fair to Alf. I 'ad to give back the necklace and make it clear to Tommy that the past was past."

"And when you got back you found him dead."

Mrs. Mullet bit her lip and nodded as she reached into her purse. She slowly pulled out a string of beads, barely looking at them, but letting the major's gift dangle in a loose loop from her fingers. The amber globules oozed with inner color and glowed like liquid honey in the sunshine. She was right: The necklace *was* the shade of new rope. I didn't want to touch the thing.

"And *that* was when you took the box of little figures. When you took the necklace back. You didn't want the police to find them and get the wrong idea."

"That's right," she said. "I was pushin' the box into my purse, out of sight, when I run smack-dab into your father—Colonel de Luce, I mean. Fair shook me up, it did."

I could feel the tears welling up in my eyes. What on earth was happening? Just minutes ago, Mrs. Mullet had mentioned Father and I'd been as cool as ice, and now suddenly some unguarded part of me was melting.

Get hold of yourself, Flavia, I told myself. *It's just a reflex.*

I faked a sudden sneeze, pulled out my handkerchief, and wiped away the evidence.

"Oh, pardon me," I said. "The sun just came out from behind a cloud." And it had. "My trigeminal nerve overloaded. It's not just me: It happens with horses, too."

Mrs. Mullet didn't move a muscle. She didn't believe a word of it. I needed to tell the truth.

"Father was on a mission," I said. "Trying to save the major's life. But he was too late."

"I thought it must be something like that," she whispered.

"But how awful for you," I said. "You must have been simply sick."

"That's it," she said in a rush of words. "Sick. And then when I got 'ome with them little dolls I realized I 'ad to take *them* back, too—same as the necklace. 'Ide 'em away under the silverware."

I nodded reassurance and touched her on the wrist with two fingers.

"And you might as well know, there was one *more* thing I 'ad to do," she added, looking at me sideways. "I'd better tell you now an' get it over an' done with."

I took the beads from her hand and slipped them gently back into her purse.

"Please do," I said. "What else did you want to do?"

"I needed to kiss 'im," she said.

"Kiss him?" I blurted.

"Goodbye," she said. "On the cheek. I knew I should never ever see 'im again."

She raised her hand as if to cover her face.

"You see, I still 'ad feelin's for Tommy. Deep down. Can you understand that?"

Of course I could. Deep down feelings were strangling my brain. I could hardly be unaware of them.

"Perfectly," I said, floundering for the proper words. "It's called true and perfect love, and it lasts forever."

"Really?" she said.

"It's in the Bible," I told her, inventing madly on the spot. "Undimmed by time," I fabricated. "'That love which is true, that love which is perfect, endureth until the very end of days.' Zechariah. I've forgotten the chapter and verse."

She reached out and touched my hand lightly. "You'll keep it under your 'at, won't you? I'd die if it got out."

"Have you a pin in your purse?" I asked.

"I've always got one," she said. "I'd rather go out without my 'ands than without a pin."

She rummaged in her purse and came up with a stout silver safety pin. I took it from her, opened the clasp and jabbed it into the fleshy part of my index finger. A drop of bright scarlet blood sprang into sight.

"Now you," I said, handing her the pin. In an instant she had pierced her own forefinger and held it out toward me.

"Same color, look," she said.

"Secret sisters." I grinned.

Seizing her wrist, I touched my finger to hers. Our blood mingled. I could feel the warmth.

"Your secret's safe with me," I said. "I swear never to reveal that which you have told me upon pain of death."

I realized, even as the words left my mouth, that I would not be able to share the information with Inspector Hewitt. If he were to dig out Mrs. Mullet's girlhood love, he'd have to do it with his own shovel.

"It's like Alf, isn't it?" Mrs. Mullet said, smiling. "'E 'ad to sign the Official Secrets Act, and there's things 'e can't tell even me. 'E's full to button-burstin' of military secrets, Alf is. 'E keeps talkin' about them. Now I shall 'ave somethin' not to tell 'im."

She smiled at the thought. "Alf says those who've signed and break their word are taken out and 'anged. I used to think if it was me, it might've been Tommy Greyleigh 'oo did the honors, turnin' me off. Wouldn't that 'ave been a pretty 'ow-do-you-do? I'd of died of embarrassment. But when 'e actually touched my neck—"

She gave a violent shiver.

"It shall be forever between you and me," I said.

"We've pricked our fingers and sworn a blood oath, haven't we?"

She beamed and straightened her hat.

"There's just one thing I need to know," I said. "Didn't you think of calling the police? What with the major lying there dead?"

"I might 'ave," she said. "I didn't really think. I knew 'e was dead. Like I said, I've seen that kind of poisonin' before. No great rush for an ambulance. And then runnin' into your father. It was more than a body can stand. 'Alf of my 'eart wanted me to take to my 'eels. The other 'alf wanted me to sketch my old love that was lyin' there dead on the floor, as if it could some'ow preserve 'im. Call it odd if you like, but it was that second 'alf what won out. And then I just wanted to get away from the place."

"And where did you go?"

It was a question that had been eating at my mind for some time.

"Why, I come directly back 'ere, of course. To Buckshaw."

"And the mushrooms—what did you do with the rest of the mushrooms?"

"You lot 'ad 'em for breakfast," she said. "No use wastin' a good basket of Molly's buttons."

My throat tightened and I gulped. It was true: She had served us creamed mushrooms on toast on that fatal morning and all of us were still alive: proof positive—if any were needed—that Mrs. M's mushrooms had not killed Major Greyleigh.

"Then that means you're off the hook, Mrs. M. They can't have been poisonous if we all ate them."

I gave her a hug for reassurance.

"That's what I've been trying to tell you," she said, half hugging me back.

Poor dear maddening, mixed-up Mrs. Mullet. If only she had told the whole truth from the outset.

Conscience grabbed his pitchfork and pricked me in the liver.

Was I as guilty? I suppose I was.

Truth is like nitroglycerine. It must be handled with kid gloves.

But best not to get too worked up about it.

"We'll talk later, Mrs. M," I said. "Right now, Dogger and I are off to London."

"'Ave a good trip, dear," she said. "But before you go, I 'ave to tell you what I over'eard at the Cluck and Grumble. I won't feel right until I do."

"I think I can guess," I said. "They were talking about you, weren't they? That's why you begged off telling me at the church, isn't it? You pretended it was your anniversary. Another touch of the old Ophelia, eh?"

I said this with a slight chuckle, to keep her from being offended.

Her eyes widened. "It was me and Major Greyleigh they was talkin' about," she said. "Shockin', the things they said. I'm ashamed to even think about it."

"You don't have to," I said. "You and I are above that sort of thing, aren't we?"

She seized me by the wrist and squeezed, and all the

world was in her eyes. With her other hand, she reached out and touched the old brick wall of the kitchen garden. It must have been warm in the morning sunlight: An azure damselfly opened its new wings as if in astonishment.

Despite the pain, I put all my love into the biggest grin I could manage.

I kissed her.

The Rolls hummed along through a landscape of hedgerows and cottages with tipsy chimneys and old stone bridges where dogs were barking at ducks on village greens, until at last we were on the motorway to London: "That great cesspool," Sherlock Holmes had called it.

My stomach grew tighter with every mile.

"Aunt Felicity won't be expecting us," I said.

"No," Dogger said. "That can often be an advantage."

I knew what he meant. "Surprise is the sharpest arrow in the quiver," I said. I had read that somewhere but had forgotten it until now.

"Precisely," Dogger said.

I would take special note of Aunt Felicity's eye muscles and those around her mouth: those dead giveaways—at least according to detective Philip Odell, in the BBC wireless series.

"Forget the feet and fingers, Dick," he had told Dick Dakin, his assistant. "Keep your eyes on the old *orbicularis orbis* and the *extraoculars*."

I smiled at the thought.

By little and by little we made our way through the outlying towns, the houses growing larger and more tasteless by the mile, until at last, after a maze of identical streets, we drew up outside Aunt Felicity's flat in South Kensington, just round the corner from the Victoria and Albert Museum.

"I shall wait here," Dogger said. "If you're not back in ten minutes, I shall search for a place to park."

I made my way to the front door of the imposing white structure.

"Good morning," I said to an antiquated gentleman who was making his exit, holding the door open for him helpfully. He smiled, tipping his hat, and I slipped in as neatly as if I owned the place.

I took the stairs up to the first floor and ambled casually along the corridor. Aunt Felicity's was the corner flat at the end.

I took a deep breath and knocked on the door, then put my ear to the wooden panel.

There was not a sound. I knocked again, and again, and still there was no response.

With a sudden swish, a door behind me opened, and a woman with a purple dress and turban looked out.

"She's not at home, dear," she said. "May I help you?"

"I'm here to see my aunt Felicity," I said.

"She's not at home, dear," she repeated. "She's at the shop today."

"Of course," I said. "How foolish of me. Do you have the address?"

The woman narrowed her eyes and studied me.

"I'd have thought you'd know that," she said.

"I do, of course," I said. "At least I *did*. But I've only been there by motorcar and I'm a stranger when it comes to London."

"From the provinces, are you?"

I smiled a fetching smile. Could I forge a dimple?

"Well, I keep an eye on the place for your auntie when she's away—in case of deliveries and so forth. Anything important and I direct them to number four Ramillies Buildings, the Strand. Do you know where that is?"

"I'll remember it when I see it," I told her.

"You can't miss it," she said. "It's the ugly yellow brick just along from St. Clement Danes. Oughtn't to be allowed."

"Of course," I said. "I remember now. Oranges and lemons. Thank you, Miss . . ." I guessed.

"Ingleby," she said. "That's it. Tell her all's well at the Rookery."

I gave her my most genteel smile: the one without a ferocious show of teeth.

Dogger was waiting by the curb.

"Number four Ramillies Buildings, the Strand. Step on it!" I said, and Dogger had the grace to smile.

It wasn't far.

St. Clement Danes, when we got to it, was not the only bombed building in the Strand, but it was the most shocking: a gutted black hulk of a church with its tower still pointing helplessly to Heaven. I could not think of anything to say, and neither could Dogger. I turned my head as we passed, my senses pummeled at the sight, but Dogger kept his eyes on the road in a determined manner, as if not looking could will it whole again.

I could see the yellow facade of the Ramillies from half a block away.

"There it is," I said, pointing. Dogger slowed and pulled up at the curb in front.

The little shop at number four was rather the worse for wear, as if it had shared in the bomb damage and had simply given up. Set to one side of the window was a door whose black, peeling paint told its own story.

"Look," I said, "there's a card in the window. I'll jump out and have a look."

I hurried across the pavement, cupped my hands against the dark window, then turned and gave Dogger a shrug: a quick pantomime for "No one's in."

The card, when I bent to examine it, was no larger than a calling card, with a few words written in an old-fashioned copperplate in ink: *Felicity Yardley—Philately—Inquire Within.*

As if it had a life of its own, my hand reached out for the battered brass doorknob and gave it a gentle twist. To my amazement, the door swung open in silence.

I stepped in.

Just inside the door was a glass counter, and beneath it, cards of postage stamps. The walls on both sides, and most of the rear, were covered with shelves bearing row upon row of large, colored albums.

I shivered. It was almost a replica of Father's study

and stamp collection at Buckshaw: bright blizzards of gummed paper captured and mounted, as if they were so many exotic butterflies.

If the place had electric light laid on, it was nowhere to be seen. The room was awash in gloom. I felt as if I had been catapulted in time, shot back as if in one of Mr. Wells's novels, into the eighteenth century. Even the air was ancient, and it reeked with the smell of old paper, old ink, and the slight dry stink of covetousness.

As my eyes became accustomed to the gloom, I saw that there was a small inner room, in which a small, low-wattage bulb hung from the ceiling by a frayed cord.

I gave a light, respectful knock to the frame with my knuckles and stepped across the threshold. A dowdy woman in a tailored suit put down a large handheld magnifier.

"Ah, Flavia," she said. "I've been expecting you."

It was Aunt Felicity.

There were no hugs, no kisses, no smiles. She was, after all, a de Luce. There was only one possible response: I walked casually around the shop, peering at the spines of the stamp albums, running a finger over the glass countertop, and taking a seat at last in the rickety chair behind the counter.

She made her opening move. "Why have you come?" she asked.

"I believe you know that, Aunt Felicity," I said, surprised a little by my own boldness.

"Yes," she said. "I believe I do."

284 · ALAN BRADLEY

"You know, and have known all along, that my father is still alive."

It only stood to reason. With Father to all intents and purposes dead, this surprisingly frumpy old woman was again, possibly, the most senior living member of the Nide.

Aunt Felicity said nothing.

I said nothing.

It was to be the usual game, and only one of us would win.

"Well?" I said boldly. It was now or never.

"Flavia—" she said.

I'd given her the choice of saying yes or no, and she had taken neither. Like Father, she was going to hide behind the chains of Duty.

"It's all right, Aunt Felicity. You don't have to say anything. I've already seen my father and spoken with him."

She stared at me with that unnerving stillness, as she had obviously been trained to do. Cool as a cucumber in Antarctica.

"A man has been murdered in Bishop's Lacey," I said. "I suspect he was poisoned—or, rather, cunningly provided with poison, which he unsuspectingly ate himself—by an American serviceman, Preston Malone. I believe Malone might have been brought in by the Nide especially to do the job. And he's already been moved out, hasn't he, Aunt Felicity? Gone on to his next assignment, like a pawn in a game of chess."

Aunt Felicity remained a glowering iceberg.

"The crime of the murdered man, Major Greyleigh," I went on, "was not that he saw and recognized Father at the American airbase at Leathcote, but that he blabbed the news to someone else, jeopardizing this whole cruel charade of my father's death. That some-one else was Mrs. Mullet. But you already know all this, don't you, Aunt Felicity?"

"Flavia," Aunt Felicity said, "there are orders of duty and justice unknown even to the highest among us."

"The Invisible Masters, you mean."

"If you wish," she said. "But it is for the common good."

"The common good goes around killing innocent people and blaming it on their poor defenseless ser-vants, like Mrs. Mullet. Is that what you're saying?"

This was not nearly as elegant as I intended it to sound, but that's the way it came out. I was trying to be maddeningly rational.

Aunt Felicity picked up a magnifying glass and peered through it at a postage stamp she held up with a pair of tweezers. Even from where I sat, I could see that the specimen was a recent issue, with a value of no more than a shilling, even to some spotty schoolboy in a vil-lage collecting society.

"The Nide is more or less a society of assassins," I said, my voice rising. "How do you decide?"

"That is not my dominion," Aunt Felicity said.

"Assassin slaves!" I'm afraid I shouted. "You can't just go around killing people because some voice in a bottle says so. Don't lie about it."

"We are not permitted to lie," Aunt Felicity said, putting down the stamp and pretending to look at me through the magnifying glass. "Only to tint. Remember, even the shadows have shadows."

Only to tint?

That fitted me to a T!

She looked up at me with a cold eye. All my questions were answered.

In a millionth of a second, the way ahead was clear.

"Can't you spare even a scrap of your rotten heart for Undine?" I said in a clear, cold voice, my fists clenched like hand grenades. "Don't you care what you've done to her mind?

"Probably not. But let me tell you this, Aunt Felicity. If ever you harm a hair on Undine's head—or Mrs. Mullet's head—your balloon will be shot down in flames. I've left a full account of your doings in the hands of the highest authority. One wrong move by you—or Father—and pop goes the weasel! In fact, pop goes your whole stinking Nide."

I had done no such thing, of course, but I intended to. There are times when a good bluff is a better weapon than all the facts in the world.

Aunt Felicity said nothing. She sat staring like a reptile, her eyes locked on mine: fixing me with that cold, blue de Luce glare that is meant to freeze blood at twenty paces.

"I'm not afraid of you, Aunt Felicity," I said, my voice dripping with scorn. "I'm *ashamed* of you. And you ought to be ashamed of yourself. And the Nide, whoever they might be, ought to be ashamed of themselves. I want nothing to do with you again—ever!

"And—" I added, surprising even myself, "if you even *think* about threatening to take Undine away from us, I'll personally set white hellfire to the whole bloody lot of you."

And with that, I rose up from the chair with all the dignity I could muster, turned on my heel, walked out, and gave the door an almighty and bone-rattling slam.

As I strode across the pavement toward the Rolls, and Dogger stepped out to hold open the door, I realized fully, for the first time ever, who I am. I am a new person. I am the Phoenix reborn.

I am Flavia de Luce: a living and vital mushroom growing out of the dead wood of the de Luce family.

It is going to be quite a life.

· F O U R T E E N ·

SOMEONE ONCE SAID THAT each new day brings us the gift of a new pair of eyes. I don't know if that's true, but I felt it must be so.

After my confrontation with Aunt Felicity, I was no longer under anyone's thumb.

Rather than wait for Inspector Hewitt to summon me and pump me dry for information, I took the initiative by ringing up his headquarters at Hinley and leaving a message with the duty sergeant.

"Tell the inspector I shall be at home between two and two forty-five," I said, like some old duchess in furs and mothballs who never ventures out of her moldering country house.

Surprisingly, he came. His Vauxhall rolled up to the front door of Buckshaw at two on the dot. The doorbell rang, and Dogger answered it as we had arranged, after which he vanished at his own request.

I showed the inspector to the drawing room and took a seat with my back to the windows.

"Are you and Mrs. Hewitt keeping well?" I asked.

Niceties first, nastiness after.

"Yes," he said. "Now then, about this business at Moonflower Cottage."

"Oh, yes," I said pleasantly. "Perhaps you could refresh my memory?"

"Stop it, Flavia," he said.

"Very well, then," I replied. "I shall refresh yours. Major Greyleigh was murdered—on assignment, I might add—by one Preston Malone, an American serviceman based at Leathcote. His weapon was the poison saxitoxin, derived from shellfish. The blame was meant to be placed on Mrs. Mullet, who cooked the victim's mushrooms for breakfast. Since she had no motive, his death would be put down to accident."

Of course, Mrs. Mullet *did* have a connection to the victim: Major Greyleigh had courted her when they were both young. But without breaking my word and my blood oath, I could say no more. I could not tell Inspector Hewitt about Mrs. Mullet's abiding love for the dead man, nor could I tell him about the box of fetishes she had removed from, and then returned to, the scene of his murder.

I needed to change the subject.

"So you see, it was all in the butter, wasn't it?" I said

brightly. "The poison was in the butter from Leathcote.
Nothing to do with Mrs. Mullet, except that she unwit-
tingly used it to fry his mushrooms. If we'd been more
diligent . . ."

I left it hanging there. My intentional use of the word
"we" implied that the police were just as dense as I was
pretending to be.

"We'd have discovered that Major Greyleigh had
stopped buying butter in the village some time ago."

I saw the inspector's fingers tighten on his Biro. He
did not look up. I had told him something that he didn't
know. He might grill Mrs. Mullet for further details, but
she would give up no more than she wanted to.

I went on: "We've shown where the saxitoxin origi-
nated. My tests were conclusive. Mrs. Mullet has nothing to hide."

"And this Malone—" He pretended to consult his
notebook. "Preston Malone. Sergeant Malone. What
was his motive?"

It was time to put my cards on the table, and I did—
but I placed some of them face down out of necessity.

Was the inspector aware that my father was alive in
a burrow at Leathcote? He may well have been, but he
would never be allowed to mention it to me. I would
never be permitted to know the true facts about my own
parent. Blood may be thicker than water, but it's weak
tea indeed compared with the Official Secrets Act.

"I suspect Malone might have been hired by one of
Major Greyleigh's 'clients,'" I lied. "Someone he had
hanged. Or one of their families."

The words "might have been" were the slack in Houdini's knots: just enough rope to wriggle free, should it be necessary.

It was now my duty to direct official attention away from Leathcote, and my father's secret presence there.

There it was: duty again.

Aunt Felicity had been right. We were not allowed to lie, but we *were* allowed to tint. If you wish to be noted for truthfulness, you must always tell the truth—but not all of it. I remembered Daffy reading aloud to me a quote by Mark Twain: *Truth is the most precious thing we have. Economize it.*

"You ought to adopt that as your personal motto," she had said. "Have it printed on calling cards so that people are warned."

I must admit I've been a bit of a tinter since I was a toddler, so it came as easily to me as falling off a log.

"I'm sure you will find out Malone's motive, Inspector," I said, dead certain that he would not. The Nide and its members would remain invisible, perhaps forever. None but a few would ever know that Asterion, like some comic-paper villain, would remain as the oiler-of-the-gears in his subterranean cavern. No one would ever believe it.

The inspector would never breathe a word to me about Malone, or what would become of him. He didn't need to: Carl had already told me during an inconvenient and awkward visit just moments after our return from London.

"Just like Mordecai," he had said. "Vanished into

thin air. Cashiered, they say. But gosh, Flavia, what do you suppose he did? Just thinking about sleeping in the same barracks and driving around in the same jeep as that guy gives me the creeps."

I couldn't help noticing that Carl's eyes were all the while on Daffy.

"Me, too," I had said.

Now, back in the drawing room, face-to-face with Inspector Hewitt, I stood up and brushed off my skirt as if preparing for a public appearance.

"Will that be all, Inspector?" I asked. I couldn't believe my nerve.

"No," he said. "That will not be all," and my heart sank.

"There are a few more points. First of all, I'd like to thank you personally for handing in Major Greyleigh's box of figurines—and what remains of the butter."

"I knew you'd like to have them immediately—for chemical analysis, and so forth. Dogger got up before the crack of dawn to drive them over to your lads."

Had the inspector winced at the word? If he had, he recovered nicely.

"Removing objects from the scene of the crime is a serious offense, but I understand that, since it was done by a child, we may expect no further repercussions at this time. And your bringing to light of Mrs. Mullet's remarkable sketches has been of invaluable assistance. And finally, I have been asked by the chief constable to commend you and Mr. Dogger on your discovery and identification of the saxitoxin. Our chaps missed it completely. If it hadn't been for you—"

Mrs. Mullet's neck might be in a noose. He didn't need to say it.

"Sir Rodney Peck, our chief forensic analyst, is livid. I've never seen him like that. He's breathing sea-foam. I think it's safe to conclude that a couple of our chemical boffins will be playing accordion and banjo in Covent Garden tonight."

"Thank you for telling me," I said. "You didn't have to."

"No," Inspector Hewitt said, "but I wanted to. In fact, I insisted upon it."

"A commendation, you say, Inspector?"

"Yes, but not a visible one. Because of the circumstances, you understand, this must remain in confidence between you and those in authority."

"Something like the pope appointing his secret cardinals," I said, putting my hushing finger to my lips.

"Something like that," Inspector Hewitt said. "The important thing," he added, "is that you and Mr. Dogger know, and I know. Nothing else matters."

Could that possibly be true? Were the inspector and Dogger and I linked forever in the bonds of yet another official secret?

A smile started in my face, but I quickly stifled it.

I stuck out my hand, and by all that's holy, Inspector Hewitt took it and shook it.

Yaroooo! I shouted in my mind.

294 · ALAN BRADLEY

Although, if you'd seen my face, you'd have been forgiven for thinking that butter wouldn't melt in my mouth.

From somewhere in the house there drifted an extremely rude noise.

Sic transit gloria mundi, I thought. Daffy had taught me that:

So passes the glory of the world.

ACKNOWLEDGMENTS

ONE OF THE GREATEST pleasures in publishing a book is being given the opportunity to thank those whose assistance made it possible:

The stalwart Denise Bukowski, of the Bukowski Agency, who has been in this remarkable venture from the very beginning; Anne Speyer, my editor at Ballantine Bantam Dell, whose keen eye and boundless enthusiasm have made this voyage a treat; Amy Black, publisher of Doubleday Canada, for her wonderful support; Anna MacDiarmid, publishing manager of Doubleday Canada, for her helpful comments and enthusiasm; Sarah O'Hara, Orion Books, London, for her important suggestions; Loren Noveck, Penguin Random House, New York, for her sharp eye and luminous copyediting; Anusha Khan, editorial assistant, Ballantine Books, for keeping us all on the same page; my friend Amber Mylrea, for her always lively discussions and sparkling suggestions.

Bless you all!

© JEFF BASSETT

ALAN BRADLEY is the *New York Times* bestselling author of eleven Flavia de Luce mystery novels and the memoir *The Shoebox Bible*. His first Flavia novel, *The Sweetness at the Bottom of the Pie*, received the Crime Writers' Association Debut Dagger Award, the Dilys Award, the Arthur Ellis Award, the Agatha Award, the Macavity Award, and the Barry Award, and was nominated for the Anthony Award. His other Flavia de Luce works include the novels *The Weed That Strings the Hangman's Bag*, *A Red Herring Without Mustard*, *I Am Half-Sick of Shadows*, *Speaking from Among the Bones*, *The Dead in Their Vaulted Arches*, *As Chimney Sweepers Come to Dust*, *Thrice the Brinded Cat Hath Mew'd*, *The Grave's a Fine and Private Place*, and *The Golden Tresses of the Dead*, as well as the ebook short story "The Curious Case of the Copper Corpse." He lives and writes on an island in the middle of the Irish Sea.

alanbradleyauthor.com
Facebook.com/AlanBradleyAuthor

ABOUT THE TYPE

This book was set in Goudy Old Style, a typeface designed by Frederic William Goudy (1865–1947). Goudy began his career as a bookkeeper, but devoted the rest of his life to the pursuit of "recognized quality" in a printing type.

Goudy Old Style was produced in 1914 and was an instant bestseller for the foundry. It has generous curves and smooth, even color. It is regarded as one of Goudy's finest achievements.